MW00937333

O.R.

A Detective LaFleur Mystery

Steve Abbott

———

John Fountain

To Adrienne and Sandy,
who somehow put up with us

Murder in the murderer is no such ruinous thought as poets and romancers will have it; it does not unsettle him, or fright him from his ordinary notice of trifles: it is an act quite easy to be contemplated, but in its sequel, it turns out to be a horrible jangle and confounding all relations.

- Ralph Waldo Emerson

Foreword

Death is something all doctors and nurses deal with routinely. It most commonly visits our patients at the extremity of age or disease, or both. And we know it awaits us all. It is inevitable.

But it is intentional death that is unacceptable. The absolute inappropriateness of the thought of it has resulted in some of the senior nursing staff at our hospital coming to believe that "Angie's ghost" walks the halls of the fourth floor, where she died under unusual circumstances. I don't claim to know much about ghosts—or souls—yet the nurses maintain they have heard her, seen her.

Fairness in life is a condition little observed by doctors. We have all seen the drunken driver survive the crash that kills the young girl on her way to her babysitting job; the mother lost to ovarian cancer before her child graduates middle school; there are countless other examples. Paradoxically, this causes many of us to place the related concept of justice on a pedestal. Justice, we aver, we can depend on as a balance in our lives and in our practices.

If anyone, after reading this novel, thinks I am likely to swallow "Angie's" obituary without choking on it, he or she will be mistaken. Many of those who have learned this story along with me feel the same way.

So. Here is an attempt at some small measure of justice. Belated as it is.

In addition, proceeds from the sale of this novel will be directed to Oswego Hospital nursing endowment funds.
—Dr. John Fountain

A few years ago, I got a strange call from an old friend, John Fountain, now an anesthesiologist at a small hospital in Oswego, New York. Strange calls from John were nothing new, but this one had an intriguing aspect to it that previous calls had not. The call was to tell me the story of finding, inexplicably, a photocopy of a forty-year-old newspaper clipping attached to his anesthesia machine. This novel is the result.
—Steve Abbott

"Apparent Suicide," DA Says

Anesthesia Mask on Her Face, Nurse Found Dead in Hospital

A 21-year old nurse at Oswego Hospital was found dead on a couch in a nurse's rest area in the hospital operating suite Sunday morning a short while after she had invited two third floor nurses to join her for morning coffee.

The victim was identified by hospital officials as Angela "Angie" Frascati of 831 E. Fifth St., who was assigned to the fourth floor operating room section.

According to Police Chief Miles O'Conor, who was called by the hospital at 10:45 a.m. and informed of the death, Miss Frascati came on duty at around 7 a.m. Chief O'Conor said his investigation revealed she apparently went into the lounge ahead of the aides. He said Miss Martha Gale, the charge nurse on the floor, wanted to locate Miss Frascati and was told by the aides that she had gone to the rest area for coffee.

The police official said Miss Gale went to the lounge. When she arrived, he said, she found the door to the room locked and a radio playing inside. She knocked but could not get a response, he said. After failing to get a response a second time, Chief O'Conor said, the charge nurse left the area to obtain a key with which to open the door.

When she returned, at about 8:15 a.m., the chief said, Miss Gale opened the door to the lounge and found the victim sprawled on the couch with a mask from a portable anesthesia machine covering her face. According to the police official, a child's airway tube, generally used to depress the tongue, was protruding from her mouth.

Police were not called for over two hours after the discovery, they said.

A hospital official revealed to the Syracuse Times that the anesthesia machine, which had been placed in the hall outside the nurses' lounge, was turned on when the victim was found. A physician called to the scene by the charge nurse turned the machine off and removed the mask and airway from her mouth, it was reported.

Chief O'Conor said the charge nurse, upon finding the body of Miss Frascati, immediately called Dr. Paul Mahoney, who pronounced the victim dead. Her body was then removed to the hospital morgue where it remained until yesterday afternoon when an autopsy was performed. In a statement released this morning, the District Attorney said the death of Miss Frascati was "an apparent suicide."

Chief O'Conor said he went to the hospital yesterday afternoon to initiate an investigation into the death of Miss Frascati by questioning a number of persons on the hospital staff and those personnel with knowledge of the incident.

The police official said the victim did not leave a note, "as is sometimes done" in suicide cases. He said this afternoon he had not as yet received a report of the autopsy. He said his investigation revealed there were no marks on the body.

Miss Frascati was described by friends and associates at the hospital as a pleasant girl who enjoyed sports, especially fishing and bowling.

Miss Frascati was born in Oswego, and resided with her parents. She was a graduate of Oswego High School, and was a graduate of Crouse-Irving Hospital in Syracuse. She was an ardent sports-woman and a member of the Portside Tavern softball team. She was also an avid fisherman. She was a member of the National Council of Catholic Nurses. She was a communicant of St. Joseph's Catholic Church.

Surviving besides her parents are two brothers; a sister, nieces, nephews and several aunts and uncles.

Funeral services will be Thursday at the Abruzzo Funeral Home and St. Joseph's Catholic Church. Burial will be in St. Peter's Cemetery.

-- *September 6, 1964*

O.R.

Prologue: September, 1964

In retrospect, there is no denying that the Oswego Hospital weekend staff was singularly unprepared for the events of that Sunday morning. Understandably so, as it turned out.

It was the middle of the Labor Day weekend, and quieter than usual: no surgeries scheduled; no one in the I.C.U.; no patients waiting in the small main floor emergency room for stitches to be sewn, casts to be plastered, or stomachs to be pumped. The doctor on call, the head nurse, two junior nurses and a ward secretary were routinely preparing for an uneventful day. The only real activity was that of an industrious Catholic priest making his way from bed to bed, spreading regards and prayers, vying with the hospital for the donations of the captive ill. Church bells echoed softly through the hallways like lost souls.

Unknown to the staff, a young nurse was lying motionless on a couch in the fourth floor operating room lounge, arms neatly folded across her chest, an anesthesia mask strapped to her face. The portable anesthesia machine at her side whispered a soft susurrus, an eerie underpinning to the sacred music pouring from a table radio in the corner of the room. She was deeply cyanotic, her face and hands the same icy blue as her still open eyes.

Angel Baby

Angie Frascati stood on the pitcher's mound, trying to concentrate. Someone in the stands had turned up their new transistor radio, and the tinny sounds of early sixties Top 40 drifted out over the softball field. It sounded like the latest Bobby Darin hit. Probably WKBW in Buffalo, that seemed to be the station everyone was listening to this summer.

Angie adjusted her glasses, then took off her ball cap and swept a hand through her short, dark hair. She was having a hard time paying attention to what was going on. The chatter behind her didn't help. The constant batta batta batta coming from all sides droned in her head like an outboard motor. She would rather be fishing today. The cove up at Sandy Pond was calm and quiet this time of year.

She glanced over to the sidelines at Phil Cathcart, the stand-in coach. That was a mistake. Looking at Phil gave her chills, even in this heat. The only reason he was coaching at all was because their regular coach and sponsor, owner of the "Ted's Portside Tavern" that was stitched in big blue letters across the backs of their softball uniforms, had broken his ankle on the back stairs of the bar a few days ago. He claimed to have slipped while carrying a keg of beer downstairs, but Angie had heard a different story, coincidentally also involving a large quantity of beer. Not that she put much stock in small town rumors, or tried not to. She couldn't wait for Ted to get back to coaching; he had promised not to miss another game.

Phil was a pharmacist at Oswego Hospital, and was popular enough around town, she guessed, but a little stand-offish at times. He seemed to be trying too hard for some reason, always a little off balance, and a little too old to be hanging out with this crowd: junior nurses, secretaries just out of vocational school, one or two girls from the mill. It was like Phil was suspended in time, never making the kind of progress expected by his high school advisor or his commanders in the Army, or now by the hospital administrators. Angie's older brother, who had been in high school with Phil, said he was never the same after getting back from Korea. He had never really "moved on," as the counselors say. Well, she guessed she could understand that. But as a nurse at the same hospital, she was getting tired of having to deal with Phil's obnoxious attitude—he was constantly looking over her shoulder, God only knew why—and she dreaded every trip down to the pharmacy when he was there. He always seemed to be on edge, she thought. Now to have to put up with him on her time off, too, well it was too much. As if she didn't have enough to worry about—

"Hey, pitcher, did'ja fall asleep out there?" the batter yelled, swaying back and forth suggestively. "We came here to play. Afraid to pitch to me?" A few more players on the other team starting hooting.

Angie looked up with a start. Now the banter was coming from all sides, for her and against her. "Come on, Frascati, get with it!' This from Phil.

"Alright, already," she said under her breath. She straightened up, looked around at the bases, took a deep breath, adjusted her cap and glasses again, and then whipped a fast pitch towards the plate. The ball came right back at her, hard. She instinctively stuck her hand up in front of her face and the ball popped loudly into her glove.

"That's the way, Angie, baby!" Phil yelled from the sidelines.

She shot Phil a look in the stands, shaking her stinging hand back and forth. *And don't call me Angie Baby.* Sounds too much like that old song that he was always humming, *Angel Baby.* She was getting sick of it.

"Come on in, everybody, that was the third out. Come on, pay attention! Or no beer after the game." Phil thought the only reason anybody played softball was for the beer. "Angie, you're up first."

Angie trooped dutifully over to the bat rack—just a bench, really—and grabbed a bat. Even though she didn't really feel like being here today, as the most accomplished player on the team she still felt an obligation to do her best. She walked toward the plate swinging the bat listlessly in one hand.

"Go get 'em…" She cringed as she heard Phil call out, and looked back over her shoulder, knowing what was coming next, "…Angel Baby!" He was leering at her, just as she had known he would be. *What a creep.*

*

Angie was still distracted as she walked down along the river towards the Portside, late for the after-game ritual. They had lost, but only by one run. Angie didn't mind that. She had once tried to convince the other girls that losing was no big deal as long as you played as well as you could—why would you play otherwise?—and that the pure enjoyment of the game was the point, not necessarily winning. She really liked softball. Not as much as fishing, but that was a little different. But winning and losing worked the same way no matter what. *Doing* was the point, not whether or not some artificial goal had been reached, or that you caught a bigger fish than someone else, or that one side had been beaten down by the other. She cringed a little every time she heard one of those football cheers about killing the other team. She felt there was more to it than the old "it's not how you play the game" cliché, that it had to do with self-reliance and self-respect, not simply being "better." She enjoyed winning, of course. She just didn't think losing was something to worry about all that much. Try to convince any of these dopes that there was something, well, nobler about it—what was the point, really? She turned the corner on Water Street, pulled open the door to the Portside, and started to go in.

Even before she got to the cashier's booth, standing out in the entry next to the coat racks, she could hear Darlene off on one of her usual rants. "Did you hear Joey Reynolds on the radio the other night? He sang along with Lesley Gore on '*You Don't Own Me.*' It was hilarious. He's their best DJ."

She decided that she just wasn't up to this. No one had seen her yet, so she turned quickly and walked home.

16

Digging Up Some Dirt

The houseboat was tied up at the marina on Lake Ontario in view of the docks, some still in use in the declining port. Some of the larger shipping docks had been almost shut down, not getting any sustained use since the late seventies, leaving the marina with a lot of private fishing boats. Even these had seen a reduction in size and an increase in age: the eighties and nineties had been hard on the "Port City," as Oswego was sometimes called. The city had lost industries and businesses at an ever increasing rate over the decades. But Oswegonians are nothing if not resourceful, and the city continued to survive, even prosper moderately, by the time the century turned.

Just visible off the bow, the bright red roof of the small harbor lighthouse provided a touch of charm to partially offset the grey dampness of the harbor. In the distance, the dark bulk of the nuclear plant cooling tower sat not far from the lakeshore, out beyond the city. A thick steam cloud boiled up out of the tower, drifting towards Canada.

Ex-detective Alonzo Carlton "A.C." LaFleur looked over the poker table at his ex-partner, detective Amos Brown. There were four other players as well, all detectives or detective hopefuls, gathered at LaFleur's houseboat for their monthly game. LaFleur had been hosting the games on-and-off ever since his retirement a few years earlier. He had lived on the boat during every boating season, May through November, ever since his wife died. He had taken an early retirement, and six months later—well, he had not gone back to the force. So much for the golden years.

Brown was squirming in his chair, trying to decide whether or not to call LaFleur's three dollar check-raise. The other four had already folded. LaFleur was counting on a call. Brown was a regular player, and as close to a real friend as LaFleur had these days. He was close to retirement, but had stayed on the force much longer than LaFleur, putting his kids through college. LaFleur had only one daughter, and she had stubbornly paid her own way, mostly. Took after her old man, he liked to think.

Brown sat staring at the board: a flop of eight, nine, ten, with an ace at the turn and a two on the river. A possible straight, but a rainbow of suits, so no flush. No pair on the board. LaFleur knew he had him: he had started with a semi-marginal hand in the small blind, an unsuited queen/jack, and against the odds had flopped the nut straight. LaFleur had been betting carefully so as not to drive Brown out. He put him on aces, probably with a second pair; eights, tens, maybe. At worst they'd have to split the pot, but based on the way Brown had been betting, it was very unlikely he also held a queen/jack.

LaFleur had learned something in forty years of playing poker: no matter what the game, many players will call a bet even when they know they are beaten. Not only suspect that they are beaten, but know in their hearts that they cannot win. They even say it out loud; *I know you've got that queen*, they say, as they throw in their money. Of course, maybe you have the queen and maybe you don't, but that's the point. You have it often enough. Detective work was much the same, and LaFleur liked to think it made him a better poker player. And that playing poker made him a better detective. More times than he liked to recall he had seen the outrageous bluffs, the brazen denials of guilt, young punks betting their lives even when they knew they were beaten. Alexander Pope had gotten it right, he mused, but not in the sense originally intended: hope (or something like it) springs eternal in the human breast.

"Okay, A.C., I've got to see it," Brown said as he tossed in three more blue chips.

LaFleur grinned as he flipped over his jack, waited just long enough, then turned over the queen.

It took a few seconds for Brown to realize LaFleur really had the straight, and when he did he threw his cards face down in disgust. "Damn, I knew it!"

LaFleur pulled the unlit cigar out of his mouth—he'd light up later; poker night was the only time he allowed himself even this small vice, these days—and pointed it at Amos, punctuating his words with the Cuban. "Ever wonder about that, Amos? Why we insist on doing what we know we shouldn't do? The way you just called that bet, knowing you couldn't win?" He stuck the cigar back into the corner of his mouth and raked in the chips, stacking them up neatly alongside an already large pile. Amos had been more than usually generous tonight. "A study in human nature, that's what you are, Amos."

"Don't start getting all philosophical on us again."

"No, I'm serious, Amos. Think about it. That case you had a few weeks ago, what was her name?"

"That woman killed down on Water Street? Evangeline Escudo."

"Yeah. And the character you said you've got in custody. Johnny Rocco or Ricco something or other, name out of an Edward G. Robinson movie. He was her boyfriend?"

"Johnny Ricardo. Yeah, her boyfriend, or so he says. Who knows why he did it."

"Oh, he admits it, does he?"

"No, of course not, he says it was an accident, but—"

"But, nothing. That's what I'm talking about. No way in God's green earth did those two think that what they were doing was right. Not given what you've told me about it, anyway. Well, nothing ever changes. Always the same kind of weird stuff going on, even back in the sixties and seventies. Difference was then it didn't get on the six o' clock news. Maybe a toned-down account on the blotter page. That was when people still read newspapers, of course." He switched the cigar to the other side of his mouth. "Still, even after all this time, it never ceases to amaze me what people will try to get away with, even when they know better. And I believe that most of 'em *do* know the difference between right and wrong, they just don't think it matters all that much." Brown started to interrupt, but LaFleur waved him off with the now soggy cigar. "There's nothing complicated about it. Simple human nature. No one ever really expects to lose. And the higher the stakes, the more often they think they'll get away with it. And the

19

less guilt they feel." LaFleur held up a finger in mock pretentiousness, and quoted: "No man at last believes that he can be lost, nor that the crime in him is as black as in the felon." He looked around the table at the blank faces. "Emerson," he said. Blank stares. "Ralph Waldo Emerson? You've at least heard of—"

Amos's partner Dan, sitting at the other end of the table, interrupted. "C'mon, A.C., deal. I'm overdue." The others mumbled their general agreement.

LaFleur gathered up the cards and started shuffling, trying once more. "All I'm saying is that you don't need to know why he did it. The "why" seldom makes any sense. Whenever people get into any kind of extreme situation, logic short-circuits. Doesn't matter if they are responsible for getting themselves into it or not. Didn't matter to those two then, doesn't matter now. Like that last hand of yours, Amos."

The phone rang, cutting off whatever reply Brown might have had. LaFleur pushed his chair back, handing the deck to Amos. "Deal me out," he called back over his shoulder as he walked to the back bedroom to answer the phone there, rather than the one in the adjoining kitchen. Not that he had anything to hide these days, but the less that group knew about his private affairs, the better.

"LaFleur." No bright "hello" these days, he didn't see the use of making any telemarketer's life any easier. Not that he minded all that much, he tried to give them the benefit of the doubt; he supposed it was better than having no job and living off welfare. Or maybe he just hadn't dropped the habit of answering as if he were in the station house. He tried to focus on the call. Not a telemarketer, but still someone asking for something. But in this case, he decided after a brief conversation, it might be worthwhile for a change. He returned a few minutes later and sat back down at the table just as the deal was passing.

"Hot date, A.C.?" Brown asked.

"You know better than that," LaFleur answered in a low growl. "Now, like someone so politely suggested a few minutes ago— shut up and deal."

*

20

The next morning promised another cold, cloudy day, typical for this time of year, the weather mediating somewhere between the dog-sweat humidity of August and the impending onslaught of suffocating lake-effect snows. In the grassy area adjoining the hospital, a small audience sat in unevenly spaced rows of metal folding chairs in front of an open tent. A banner draped across the front of the tent rippled in the breeze, announcing the event in bold red lettering: "Bringing Healthcare into the 21st Century—*And Beyond.*" Other than the banner, it was a scene not unlike a backyard wedding, had it been summer and not early fall. Squat pumpkins and anorexic corn stalks decorated the corners of the tent, old married couples intent on one last fling.

Detective LaFleur stood watching the ground-breaking ceremony from the fourth floor office window of Dr. Michael Fuentes, head of anesthesiology at Oswego Hospital. It had been Dr. Fuentes who had called the night before, inviting LaFleur to visit him and his head nurse, Maggie Malone, at the hospital. Fuentes had been evasive with LaFleur on the phone, saying only that he was being urged by a staff member to contact him regarding a case LaFleur had been involved with at the hospital some years before. More than that, he wouldn't say.

LaFleur could just see past the fertilizer elevators at the harbor to the lighthouse. He couldn't see his houseboat. In the opposite direction, back towards the hospital, the Oswego River cut the town into neat halves. Oswego is not a city to put on airs, and when it tries, the results are mixed. Despite some recent river-front development—the old port authority building had been converted to an upscale Irish pub, for example, and the banks of the river were now bordered by wide, pleasant walkways and fishing docks—things move slowly in upstate New York. The money that left with the shipping trade and the shade cloth factories was slow to return. Up the hill stood row upon row of larger, more stately homes, built at the turn of the century while the city was still a major Lake Ontario shipping port and manufacturing city. Most of these homes, built by Kingsford Corn Starch moneyed management, local shipping magnates, fishing fleet owners, and Diamond Match executives, now stood in proud desperation— porticos drooping, columns sagging, paint peeling—the brutal winter weather, the economy, and a general sense of resignation all taking a toll.

LaFleur had been in the doctor's office for about fifteen minutes, and so far there had been only awkward introductions and some small talk concerning the ground-breaking; nothing concerning the reason for the invitation. A fuller explanation would have to wait for the now overdue appearance of head nurse Maggie Malone, Fuentes had apologized. In the meantime, he had explained that the hospital, built in 1910 and expanded in small stages over the intervening years, had had no major additions for nearly four decades—not since the early sixties, when a new surgical and office wing had been added. The latest round of improvements, being proudly trumpeted by the fundraising committee at the ceremony below, promised a new state-of-the-art O.R., an upgraded emergency room, and a PET scanner.

Fuentes was tall, with a close-cropped mop of dark curly hair, just starting to thin. He had a swimmer's physique and a brooding Latin/Sephardic look of the type that LaFleur suspected the nurses found irresistible. When he had first introduced himself, he had described himself as a "reverse boat-person." He explained that he had been at Oswego Hospital only about five years, having spent much of his medical career in the Dominican Republic. He had been born there, brought to the United States in the late seventies by his parents, who had relatives in Oswego who had emigrated earlier. After finishing medical school in the eighties he had done a residency in the D.R., then another in the U.S., before going back to the Dominican Republic for several years. He still kept up his connections in the D.R. and had just returned from a two month charity stint at one of his old hospitals, the "Iglesia Hospital de San Lázaro" in Santo Domingo. He described the contrast between conditions there and in Oswego as "dramatic." At Iglesia, he had told LaFleur earlier, about half of his patients were handcuffed to their beds. Not unlike some of the New York City hospitals LaFleur had been in, he mused.

Fuentes motioned toward the scene below, where the final ceremony was just getting underway on a small portable stage. "That's Dr. Franklin Montgomery at the podium. He's semi-retired, but still maintains a fairly regular schedule, considering his age. He must be over seventy. He's also the de facto administrator of the hospital, in spite of what the official administration claims. He's behind this whole expansion thing. He's pretty much behind most of what goes on here, actually. Has been for years. For better or worse."

LaFleur didn't comment on the note of disgust he detected in Fuentes' voice. Dr. Montgomery, impeccably dressed, (even ostentatiously, by upstate New York standards), stood at a portable dais adorned with green, white, and orange balloons. Tall and broad-shouldered, with fashionably long, grey hair swept back, Montgomery had long been a local celebrity. He even had a street named for him in the country club neighborhood over on the west side. To many of the women who served on the seemingly endless fund-raising, social event planning, and civic volunteer committees that he was invariably asked to co-chair, he was celebrated on a more personal level.

Montgomery was giving his speech as they looked down at the proceedings. His strong baritone voice was muffled both by the lake breeze and the office window, probably barely audible through the cheap amplification system even down below. From this height it sounded like the droning of bees, cold bees. As soon as he had finished the speech, Montgomery bowed and moved off to the side, then waved to the audience as he followed a small group of city councilmen and fund-raisers over to the area that had been designated for the ceremonial dig. After some confusion, he was led to a cordoned-off area next to a crane and handed a shovel. He looked uncomfortable holding the shovel, as if it were unfit for the delicate hands of a surgeon, but made a valiant attempt to turn over some dirt. He then handed the shovel to one of his lackeys. The ceremony over, people started wandering off in different directions. Montgomery continued looking around for a few minutes, occasionally giving a slight wave or an ingratiating nod to an important donor. As he turned to leave, he looked up at the old wing, seemingly looking straight into Fuentes's office window. In the first clear look LaFleur had of Montgomery's face, he had a small shock of recognition—not only the knowledge that he had seen Montgomery somewhere before, but also the uneasy feeling seeing himself in the mirror—the same swept back gray hair, lightly tinted glasses, and strong gaunt features. LaFleur thought he was better looking than Montgomery, so the self-comparison wasn't quite accurate. Montgomery looked a little flabbier, too.

Fuentes was saying something about the old wing, that it was soon to be demolished to make way for part of the new addition, and that he would be moving to a temporary office soon, when the door opened and the woman they had been waiting for walked in. She also looked vaguely familiar.

"Ah. Here's Maggie." Maggie was nearly as tall as Fuentes, but with an angularity that both disguised her size and was something at odds with the sunniness of her disposition. With reddish-blonde hair easing into gray, she looked younger than she should, considering that she had been at the hospital for over forty years. She was evidently nearly as much of an institution at the hospital as Dr. Montgomery, and had been head surgical nurse for nearly twenty of her years on staff. She must have had plenty of chances to move into an administrative position over the years, Fuentes had said, but adamantly stayed on as head nurse, at home with the level of authority and prestige it afforded. Big fish in a small pond syndrome would have been the easy diagnosis, but LaFleur was soon to learn that Maggie was more complicated than that. And administrative pay in hospitals was probably nothing to rave about anyway, he guessed. Maggie was not inclined to lord it over her staff, unlike Montgomery, who reportedly took every opportunity to remind everyone of his seniority. It was interesting that although it had been Maggie's idea to ask LaFleur to come to the hospital, she had insisted that Fuentes make the call.

"Hi, Michael," she said as she waltzed into the room, a handful of papers flogging her thigh. She turned and walked over to face LaFleur, still over at the window. "Hello, Mr. LaFleur," she said brightly as she reached out and shook his hand. "Maggie Malone. You probably don't remember that we've met, a long time ago; it was at a St. Joseph's charity function that the Father chaired. Oh, and I saw your wife at Mass regularly."

LaFleur's eyebrows inched up at that. "Ah, well, my attendance record wasn't great, even then, I admit. I knew your name sounded familiar, but I just couldn't come up with the connection."

24

"Well, there's also the…incident, I think you will remember it. Michael, have you shown Detective LaFleur the article yet?"

"Nope. Waiting on you." Fuentes walked over to his desk and picked up a single sheet of paper, and held it out towards LaFleur. It appeared to be a photocopy of a newspaper clipping. "This is what Maggie and I wanted to talk to you about, Detective."

LaFleur looked at it and waited expectantly for an explanation. Fuentes glanced over at Maggie, seemingly as uncomfortable as Montgomery had been with the shovel. Maggie nodded in encouragement.

"When I came in one morning last week, Wednesday, I think, no, Tuesday, I found this taped to my anesthesia machine," Fuentes continued. "I asked around that day, but no one admitted to putting it there, and then I got busy and it slipped my mind. And then it appeared again on Friday, taped to my machine again, the same way. I have been trying to find out where it came from ever since the first article appeared. Maggie thinks you may be able to help." He still had the article, holding it up a little higher now so that LaFleur could see it clearly. "Do you remember this?"

LaFleur tilted his head back, trying unsuccessfully to see the article clearly through the bifocal portion of his glasses. It was obviously a newspaper article which had been clipped out and arranged in two columns under the headline. The headline had been cut out separately and arranged above the clipping like words on a ransom note. He saw a handwritten date scrawled in blue ball point ink across the upper left corner: "September 6, 1964."

Fuentes turned the article back around and read the headline out loud before LaFleur could make out any more. "'*Apparent Suicide,' DA Says*." He then began to scan the rest of the article, almost talking to himself. "Angela Frascati, local girl, well-liked. Fishing, softball, bowling league…Came in to work early that morning…found in nurse's lounge at 8:15 a.m.…Police called later…"

LaFleur put up a hand to interrupt. "Nineteen sixty-*four*, was it?"

"That's right. Forty some-odd years ago."

LaFleur motioned to Fuentes, *give me the article*. Fuentes handed it to him. LaFleur read silently for a minute or so, and then looked up. "Well, I do remember it, but vaguely," he said. "I hadn't made detective at that time. Don't remember who would have been on the case." He turned to Maggie. "You say you don't know anything about it?"

"Well, sure, I know about it," Maggie replied. "I was there at the time, after all." She glanced away, sunny disposition fading fast.

"That's not what I meant. You say that you didn't put the article in the operating room?"

"No, I didn't."

"Do any of the other nurses know anything about it?"

"Well, they know the basic story."

"That's not what I mean. Do any of them know how the article got into the O.R.?"

"Not that I know of."

Fuentes interjected. "Maggie, tell the detective what you *do* know."

Maggie hesitated before continuing, then briefly described the history of the fourth floor nurse's lounge, a story known to many of the hospital staff. Converted years before into O. R. 3, the room was occasionally referred to by long-timers as "Angie's room." As one of only a handful left at the hospital that had also been on staff in 1964, Maggie was considered to have been the closest to Angie at the time. Fuentes interrupted to say that he had heard the story when he first came to the hospital, but had not given it much thought, until the article appeared on his machine.

Maggie apparently didn't have much more to say about it, so LaFleur held up the article and started to read out loud: "'A 22-year old nurse at Oswego Hospital was found dead on a couch in a nurse's rest area in the hospital operating suite Sunday morning a short while after she had invited two third floor nurses to join her for morning coffee.' Quite a sentence. I prefer more commas. Helps me pace myself." He continued, "'the victim was identified by hospital officials as...'"

"You don't have to read it to me," Maggie broke in. "I know what happened. I just told you I was there."

"Yes, you did say that, didn't you?" An uncomfortable silence hovered between them, just at eye level, a tension that wasn't there

26

just a minute earlier.

Maggie looked away again, then moved closer to LaFleur and gazed out the window. "You know, I don't think it really matters who brought the article in. But now that the subject has been raised, for who knows what reason, it seems like we have an obligation to do something about it."

"What do you mean?" LaFleur asked, not at all sure where this was leading.

"Oh, I don't know. Like not letting this wing be demolished without doing something to explain her death? It's...well, sacrilegious or something to just let it be torn down."

This was going somewhere, LaFleur thought, away from figuring out where the article had come from—which he had already suspected was not the real motive for asking him here—and onto the subject of the case itself. Still, she had piqued his interest. "Let me finish reading this." Maggie moved away and stood next to Fuentes as LaFleur quickly read the rest of the article. When he was finished, he looked up at them. "Is there still family in town?"

"No, no family that I know of," Maggie answered.

"So, what do you think can be done, after all this time?"

She had a pleading look in her eyes that had not been there moments before. She paused, obviously agonizing over what to say next. "Oh, I don't know. Maybe we...maybe *I*...didn't ask enough questions at the time. And I don't know what can be done. Nothing, I guess. It's just...well...it seems that..." Her voice trailed off.

"I'm sure you and everyone else did all they could. It must have been very difficult. Suicides are always traumatic, more than we all would like to admit. But as I remember it, the case was closed uncontested. I don't remember the details, as I said, I wasn't assigned to the case—but again, as I remember it," he stared at the ceiling for a moment before looking back at Maggie, "there was an autopsy the same day, and the D.A closed the case. Just like it says here."

Maggie hesitated a long moment before continuing, again as if uncertain about what to say. "Somebody here *knows* something."

This caught LaFleur a bit off guard. "Knows what, something

about why she committed suicide?"

"Um, yes. Something about how she died. About the suicide."

Fuentes reached over and took the article out of LaFleur's hand. "Who would know if you don't?" he asked Maggie. "What more is there to it?"

"I said I don't know." She looked over at LaFleur. "Detective, what do you think? Aren't there records you could get access to, people you could talk to get more information? I know it wouldn't be an official police investigation at this point. But you were on the force then, even if you weren't personally involved in the case. You said you remembered it, you must remember something about the investigation, surely. Isn't there any more you can tell us about it? Anything at all. Help us find out who brought the article in, if nothing else. That would tell us something. I'm sure the Father would appreciate your help as well."

LaFleur didn't answer right away. He was distracted, thinking back to those days, trying to dredge up anything coherent. He wondered again why Maggie had asked him here, and why he should let himself get involved in so obvious a wild goose chase. Cold cases are all the rage on television these days, he knew, but that didn't mean there is anything to them in real life ninety-nine point nine percent of the time. He would just be wasting time. But then again, it could be interesting. And what else did he have to do, outside of the occasional poker game? And he did think it was damn strange, the article appearing out of nowhere. He could at least try to find out why someone was bringing this up again, after all this time, just to ease her mind. Maggie certainly seemed determined to make this happen, in spite of Michael's reluctance.

He looked back at Maggie with a sudden look of determination. "What the hell. If you think I can help in some way, I'd be glad to look into it. I won't promise anything, you understand that."

Maggie beamed. "Yes, of course. Thank you. Very much." She turned to Fuentes. "Well?" she demanded.

Fuentes held up his hands in resignation. "I'll go along with it. But you know I don't like mysteries."

LaFleur glanced out the window at a motion that caught the corner of his eye. Down below, Dr. Montgomery had come back outside, and was wandering around over by the construction site. LaFleur folded the article and slipped it into an inside pocket. *No, I don't like mysteries much, either, if there isn't a chance of solving them.* Both Maggie and Fuentes walked him downstairs, Maggie thanking him all the way, Fuentes saying very little. LaFleur promised to call.

Standard Operating Procedures

The fourth floor nurses' lounge at Oswego Hospital had the familiar well-worn look of the typically overused and under-maintained hospital staff room. The kidney-shaped coffee table was the only gesture toward current style in the room, sporting wood-grained Formica, with a few recent *Life* magazines spread out on the table in a weird congruity: Marilyn Monroe and LBJ cheek-to-cheek, looking over the Warren Report. A battered industrial-style coffee machine sat on a dilapidated table along the back wall, with some worn stainless steel cream and sugar dispensers that had been appropriated from the cafeteria. A couple of vinyl chairs sat gloomily in the corner. An old couch lined the wall next to the door. A table radio murmured pop music from the corner.

It was after hours, around 8:15. Maggie had been waiting on Montgomery in the lounge. The procedure tonight was a little earlier than usual, 8:30. Maggie sat wearily in the corner, trying to decide if she had the energy to go downstairs to the machine for a pack of cigarettes. Her reddish-blonde hair was uncharacteristically tied back into a pony-tail, which she absent-mindedly kept flipping up over the top of her head with her hand. She usually wore it in a sort of modified "Sandra Dee,' long, carefully sculptured curls outlining her face in a heart-shaped frame.

Maggie had been up since 4 a.m, and had already assisted in three surgeries and a stillbirth, all this before noon, and hours to go. Unlike most little girls who grew up dressing their Ginny Vogue dolls in starched white nurse's outfits, caring for Betsy Wetsy, taking Raggedy Ann's temperature, never seeing a future of overflowing bedpans and tyrannical doctors, Maggie grew up without any idealized preconceptions to overcome when it came to nursing. Her mother had been a surgical nurse, first in the Navy Nurse Corps on hospital ship *U.S.S. Rescue* in 1945, then at Long Beach Naval Hospital after the war. Her father, a returning POW, met her mother on board the *Rescue*. Not long after Maggie was born he disappeared off the face of the earth.

Maggie had practically grown up at the hospital, while her mother worked the emergency room shift at night, a rarity at the time: a single professional mother making it on her own, and setting her own rules. She had insisted that the administrator allow Maggie come to the hospital with her during her night shift. Maggie often stayed in the emergency room, out of the way, watching everything. Sometimes a bed was made up for her in a side room, occasionally shared with an intern getting his forty-five minutes of sleep for the night. She was now just two years out of nursing school in Syracuse, making up for what she lacked in idealism with a hardheaded devotion to the practical.

Maggie decided cigarettes were too much trouble after all and went back out to the ward. Anyway, it was time to get to the O.R. and start setting up. As she left the lounge, she heard a sound in the stairway at the end of the hall, a door closing. Thinking it might be Montgomery, Maggie went over to the stairs to check. As she entered the stairwell, she could hear loud whispering going on at the third floor landing, one floor below, and instinctively paused. The whispering made it hard for her to recognize the voices at first, one female and one male, but even though she could not make out what was being said, after a moment she did recognize Angie's voice. So whose was the male voice?

Maggie moved a little closer to the stairs and shrank against the wall. At the edge of the landing, she carefully leaned over the railing and peeked around the corner. Looking down the stairwell she could see Angie and a doctor—but she still couldn't quite see who it was. One of the Mahoneys? Angie was shaking her head and drawing away from the doctor, who had his arms around her waist. As she backed away, he tried to pull her closer. Maggie thought she recognized him; yes, it was one of the Mahoneys. It was just too dim in the stairwell to tell for sure which one. One of them had a wife and a new baby, she knew, and she stiffened slightly as this thought flashed through her mind. Down below, Angie did the same, pulling away from the doctor.

She heard Angie, speaking more loudly now, "No!" Then they both began talking urgently, whispers hissing up the stairwell. Maggie didn't dare lean any farther over the railing.

There was silence for a moment or two. Was Angie crying? Maggie saw them shuffle around a little on the stairway, as if jockeying for position, for what, Maggie couldn't tell. Angie stepped up the stairs, backing away from him. "I've got to go," she said. "I left my paycheck in my—in our—locker, mine and Maggie's locker. I have to cash my check at the alley tonight; otherwise I won't have bowling money."

"Why are you sharing a locker with Maggie?" he asked.

"Oh, you know, the burglaries," she answered. "Mine got all banged up and the door won't close anymore. Wish I could get it fixed." Her voice sounded flattened, drained.

There was another short silence while the doctor apparently tried to decide if this needed a response. "Want me to come back up with you?" he eventually asked.

"No. Just go."

Angie's footsteps grew louder coming up the stairs. Maggie ducked out of the stairwell and slipped quietly back into the lounge. The door closed behind her just in time, and she heard Angie go past the lounge towards the locker room. After a few minutes, when Angie had not come back past the lounge, Maggie assumed she had gone out the other way, and walked across the hall to the O.R., wondering about what she had just overheard.

Montgomery would be here any minute and was not going to be happy if things were not ready to go when he arrived.

*

It was just after 9:00 p.m. when the O.R. door opened and Angie walked in. Maggie looked up in surprise. It had been over half an hour since she had seen Angie on her way to her locker; she thought she had heard her say she was going bowling. Angie looked even more surprised to see Maggie and Montgomery there in surgical masks and gowns, with a woman on the operating table, draped and unconscious, legs up in stirrups, an IV dripping into the butterfly on the back of her hand.

"Oh, Maggie, Dr. Montgomery. I didn't know anyone was here." Angie had already started backing out of the door but a sharp question from Montgomery stopped her.

"Angie. What are you doing here?"

"I stayed a little late tonight, and then I, uh, realized I left my paycheck in my—in our—locker. I was just on my way out when I noticed the lights were on in the O.R.; Maggie, I didn't know there was anything scheduled."

Maggie wasn't sure what to say to this. The schedules were made by the charge nurse, Martha Gale, with specific regard to leveling out responsibilities. It was not surprising that Angie was taken aback at seeing her here. This procedure was not on Martha's schedule. "It's all right, Angie, uh, we're just..." Her voice trailed off as Dr. Montgomery spoke up, not looking at Angie, but glaring at Maggie over his mask.

"Yes, well, we have a last minute case here, Angie" said Montgomery gravely. "But nothing you need to worry about."

The woman groaned. Maggie turned and looked down at her in concern as the woman's eyelids started to flutter.

Angie had also noticed. "Hey, where's the anesthesiologist?" she said suddenly. "Couldn't you get anybody tonight?"

Maggie watched silently as Montgomery narrowed his eyes, and imagined the grim look under the mask. "We have everything under control, thank you, Angie. Just a simple D&C. Some of these women who can't afford to pay for the procedure, you know, and sometimes we can just take care of things quickly for them. No need for an elaborate setup. We do this sort of thing quite routinely, actually." He turned back to the woman on the table as a dismissal.

"Oh. Well. Then I guess if you don't need anything..."

"No. Nothing, really."

Angie backed a bit farther out the door, still hesitant. "Maggie, I'm sorry, I really didn't notice anything on the schedule for tonight."

Maggie cringed as Montgomery turned in her direction, though he was still speaking to Angie. "I said it's completely under control. Isn't that right, nurse?"

"Yes, Angie," said Maggie. "Sorry I didn't mention it, it's really nothing." Maggie watched uneasily as Angie turned to go.

"Well, okay, bye then."

"Bye, Angie."

"Goodnight, Angie," Montgomery intoned.

As Angie retreated down the hallway, footsteps echoing hollowly, Maggie backed up a step or two as Montgomery again turned on her with vehemence. "I thought I told you to lock that door."

"Well, I didn't. Anyway, what's the difference? Everyone's got a key and could come in any time they wanted to. And besides, I thought you said this was just standard procedure. Why worry about locking the O.R. door?"

"I just don't want any unnecessary interruptions."

"Well, it's not like we're doing something that's a big secret, is it?"

"No, Maggie, of course not," Montgomery insisted. "I just prefer not to publicize the fact that I am taking cases the O.B.'s have obviously turned away for some reason. It's as simple as that."

Maggie frowned. This wasn't sounding much like a "standard procedure" anymore. The interruption by Angie and the simple questions she had asked suddenly seemed to take on more importance. "Maybe I should go ahead and do a regular patient registration when we're done here," she said, "so there are no questions later. Just to keep everything in order."

Montgomery's head jerked up at this. "No! Do just as I told you, book this as a walk-in, a simple D&C, inevitable or missed abortion. There is no need to retain the pathology. No other paperwork. I thought you understood that."

"Yes, Doctor," Maggie replied icily, followed by silence. In fact, they didn't exchange more than a few words the entire rest of the night, not even when he left her apartment the next morning at dawn.

On the Waterfront

LaFleur stood at the galley sink filling a plastic water jug. He counted out the time as the jug filled—one, two three…nineteen, twenty—a practice he had caught himself in more and more often as he went through the small routines of the day. A habit he hoped was not becoming obsessive. At least he wasn't counting out loud yet. He wasn't used to living alone, even after all this time. He had been a widower since 1999, with only a couple of cats to keep him company, but now even they were gone; his daughter had taken them when he started living on the boat. He spent his winters in Orlando, living in the condo bought with his wife's life insurance payout. While he was down there he ran a *Three Men in a Boat* ride for kids at a small water park, as much for the distraction as for the extra money. The houseboat was pulled out of the marina into its dry slip every winter. He figured he had plenty of time to work through whatever came of the nurse's "investigation" before he left for Florida.

LaFleur had reread the article again that morning, just skimming it quickly, hoping for something to jump out at him, some key point that would act as a starting point. He had been meaning to sit down and go through it carefully for the past two days, but had been distracted by a series of doctor appointments; routine, but it had taken an inordinate amount of time. In spite of a vigorous nature and overall good health, he was still saddled with what he thought was a bucket load of medication, two or three different pills a day—blood pressure, cholesterol—he couldn't keep track of them. He was glad that he had a GP he could trust, even if he was a bit of a pill-pusher. The meds, along with his daily walks along the river, seemed to keep him fit. He was walking more now, too. His car—a nice, old Pontiac Grand Am—was parked behind a friend's warehouse a few bocks from the marina, but he rarely drove it just around town anymore.

Michael had called that morning and asked LaFleur to lunch to talk about the "case." He wasn't sure he liked thinking about it in those terms. He hadn't talked to Michael or Maggie since the meeting at the hospital on ground-breaking day; he didn't really have anything to say yet. He found himself lying awake at night more than once, thinking about it, trying to remember everything he could about it, but by the time he woke up in the morning, it was still just annoyingly half-remembered. He had always prided himself on having a good memory. That and the fact that he had always seen himself as more than just another hack on the force, had actually taken pride and an interest in his work, not like some of the chief's cronies, made this memory lapse even more troubling. He was going to have to talk to Amos about it; maybe he knew something about it, or could at least help him track down whatever information might still be available.

He was still trying to ignore the self doubts as he went out to water the flowers. Up the back steps, eight. Out to the boxes up by the bow, ten. The geraniums were in their last stages, nights not quite cold enough to affect them yet—he admired their hardiness—but he knew that the first hard frost must be close at hand. Maggie's insistence that there must still be something new to learn about the case was another little fringe of doubt circling around him like a swarm of gnats. Not gnats, flies. "Pavlov's Flies," he thought. Now where did that come from? Something he had been reading about in *Science News*, or had seen on the Discovery Channel, fruit fly memory mutants that researchers in Cold Spring Harbor were using to study long term memory genes. That was it. For some reason this thought suddenly made him feel better about the prospect of getting involved in this seemingly futile enterprise, and he started to look forward to the meeting. This could be an opportunity to restore some small sense of accomplishment in his life, get him out of the rut he felt himself slipping into, a little deeper day by day.

He glanced at his watch (his retirement gift—how conventional could you get? but still, a fine watch); he had about half an hour to get to the hospital; the walk would do him good, help work up an appetite. He slipped on a light jacket, sat down and pulled on his loafers, locked the door on his way out, and counted the steps up the ramp to the dock, the fruit flies of memory fluttering around in his head.

*

LaFleur was waiting for Michael at the cafeteria door, reading the list of daily specials. Michael came around the corner, and without a hello waved at the white board menu in dismissal. "The only thing I like about this cafeteria is that it's normally off limits to the public," he said, motioning to LaFleur to follow him in. "Honestly, there's nothing worse than dealing with a complicated medical situation, and a usually more complicated family dynamic, and then twenty minutes later find yourself sitting at a table next to the family asking 'how's the goulash.'"

Michael walked across the room to the sandwich bar. "I usually make myself a sandwich. Quicker than waiting for the staff to do it, and you get it the way you want. All the fixings are here. Bread there. I like the light rye. The turkey is real, not chopped, pressed, formed imitation turkey breast."

"Looks great," LaFleur said. "I'm a turkey man myself."

They assembled a couple of sandwiches and found a table near the windows. They had just set their trays down and started on the sandwiches when LaFleur noticed Maggie heading over to their table. She called out to them from a couple of tables away.

"Michael. Detective LaFleur. Mind if I join you?"

Michael glanced at LaFleur, raising his eyebrows as if asking permission. LaFleur shrugged a casual *why not?* and answered for him, "No, not at all, Maggie. Come on over."

Maggie sat down, picked up her fork, and started shoving peas around on her plate. "I don't know why I got the special today. I hate peas. I should have known there would be peas; it seems to be the only vegetable Hannah has ever heard of. Frozen peas. This is her attempt at *Chicken Primavera*. The chicken is recognizable, but the basic concept of Primavera still hasn't sunk in, I guess. Her last job must have been at an elementary school."

They all ate in silence for a few minutes, until Michael put down his half-eaten sandwich and started searching his pockets for something. After a few seconds, he found what he was looking for and pulled it out. It was a copy of the article. "Detective, I didn't have a chance to tell you about this yet," he said as he unfolded it and laid it down in the center of the table. "It happened again. This was taped to the anesthesia machine in the O.R. when I came in this morning. This is the third time. Someone is getting a little pushy."

Maggie sat looking down at her plate. An uncomfortable silence settled over the table.

LaFleur was getting impatient. He turned to Maggie. "What do you know about it?" he asked her brusquely.

"I told you already, I don't know who is doing this," she snapped. "That's one of the things we want you to find out, after all."

"Touché." Now it was LaFleur's turn to look uncomfortable.

Michael leaned forward, as if he had suddenly decided it was time to get LaFleur really engaged in this, no matter who was leaving the articles in the O.R. "I still think in a suicide of this type there would have been a note," he said pointedly." LaFleur nodded but didn't comment. "Or maybe it's just the fact that the D.A. felt it necessary to make a special point in the article about there being no note. And the business of the autopsy. It says that an autopsy was done, but the D.A. or whoever was doing the investigation didn't have the results at the time, and still it's declared an 'apparent suicide?'" He picked up the article again and started reading. "Yeah, here. The police chief says, 'this afternoon he had not as yet received a report of the autopsy.' But here, right before that, it says that after she was found, 'Her body was then removed to the hospital morgue where it remained until yesterday afternoon when an autopsy was performed." So, the body was moved even before the police were called, and then they don't even get the results of the autopsy? I don't know; the whole timeline here just seems odd."

LaFleur reached over and took the copy out of Michael's hand. "Oh, I don't know. There could be a hundred explanations," he said as he skimmed over it, at the same time looking for anything he might have overlooked. "Maybe they got a verbal report, or maybe the reporter misunderstood something. And you have to remember that things weren't done as formally in those days. We were always getting left in the dark. And how do we know we've got the whole story here? Small town newspaper, a cub reporter, maybe, assigned to back page obits; how carefully do you think they researched the story, or thought they had any reason to?"

"Well, I still think it's damned strange." He looked over at Maggie, who was studiously arranging on her plate what was left of her lunch. "Or maybe I'm speaking out of turn here, sorry."

"No, that's ok," Maggie said. "Detective, I have been trying to convince Michael to take this more seriously. I'm glad to hear you are finally taking a real interest, Michael," she continued, turning to face him. "Someone must think there is something more to this, right? Why else would they be bringing in this article? The questions you just raised are exactly why I asked the detective here to help us figure this thing out." She paused and stuffed a bite of chicken in her mouth.

LaFleur was now both more and less sure about what was going on here; more sure that Maggie was driving this, and less sure of whatever motive she might have. Before he could say anything, Maggie turned and pointed her fork at him.

"And now he's also convinced that there is something very odd about what happened," she said. "You are the perfect person to try to find out more about this, Detective. You will have access to information that we don't have." LaFleur grimaced at Maggie's optimistic tone; the doubts he had been having just a few seconds before, the twinges over his faulty memory, came back in a rush. Before he could respond, she continued, "And you have the experience to sort through all the ambiguities."

LaFleur stared at the article as if waiting for a message in invisible ink to suddenly appear that explained it all. "All right, all right. I promised I'd look into it, so I'll ask around, see if I can find out anything new about the suicide. I know some people at the D.A.'s office, and down in records at City Hall. But I'm telling you again, Maggie, I don't think there's going to be much to find out. And I'll tell you another thing: if you expect me to take this seriously, I'm starting with you. You've got to know more about this than you've been letting on. Deal?"

"Deal." She paused. "This chicken is terrible."

LaFleur turned to Fuentes. "And you, Dr. Fuentes. Why you?" Fuentes gave him a quizzical look. "Why were you the one singled out to get the article?" LaFleur clarified. "Someone is going to a lot of trouble here. Why not give it to Maggie," he asked, looking at her now, "someone who knows something about it, someone who was there?" Maggie frowned, but didn't comment.

"How should I know that?" Fuentes said. "If we find out who's behind it, then maybe I can answer you."

"Okay, fair enough. Let's make that our second priority, then. In the meantime, neither one of you leave town." He got back two of the blankest stares he had ever seen.

"It's a joke, damn it."

Late Nights in the O.R.

The late nights D&Cs continued, once or twice a week, but without any further incidents in the O.R. Montgomery insisted that Maggie assist in every case; he told her he couldn't rely on the other nurses to maintain the level of discretion he felt was appropriate for these cases.

It was slowly becoming apparent to Maggie that regardless of his skill as a surgeon and his reputation at the hospital, Dr. Franklin Montgomery was not one to let moral ambiguity get in the way of his personal welfare. She had, in fact, heard him put it in exactly those terms when bending junior doctors and nurses to his will: "Never allow moral ambiguity to interfere with the medical decision-making process." This had come out in the early days of their relationship, but for some reason Maggie had not realized the implications, or rather had not let herself think too clearly about it. Moral ambiguity was, after all, more than inherent in his infidelity to his wife, and in Maggie's implicit agreement with it. It was hard to pin down exactly when she had first become infatuated, as she looked back on it, but there was no doubt that he had done nothing to discourage her impression that her romantic feelings for him were going to be reciprocated. The only real encouragement she needed were the little hints he had given that his high-society, distant, and supposedly ailing wife was addicted to Miltown, asleep by 8:00 p.m. many nights, after barely making it through dinner. As a result it was hardly what could be called an "active" marriage anymore, he maintained.

Along with a disregard for moral ambiguity—that is, a disregard for the complications moral ambiguity would bring to certain situations—was the willingness to profit from this disregard. It was one of the traits he unabashedly admired in himself and which he had traced to his time at a VA hospital at the end of the Korean War. Maggie was getting a little tired of the repeated rationalizations, which she heard every time Montgomery began to feel any hint of guilt. The "doctors' draft act" enacted at the start of the war, as he had never tired of explaining, had unintentionally provided many younger physicians and residents a way to both avoid actual military experience and an easy path to a career in public health. But what he had expected to be a fast track to the National Institutes of Health had gotten derailed somewhere along the bureaucratic line, and it was a VA clinic in New Jersey, not the halls of the NIH Clinical Center, where he ended up doing his war-time service. The subsequent delay in setting up a practice had made Montgomery impatient, and he made no apologies for taking an unorthodox approach in order to make up the difference.

Montgomery's visits to Maggie's apartment continued, but the edgy excitement of an affair with a handsome—and powerful—young doctor was starting to turn into just plain edginess. He was apparently beginning to doubt the advisability of continuing to use Maggie in his late night enterprise; for her part she was becoming more and more uncomfortable with the constant emphasis on secrecy. The hours before dawn the night before had been one long harangue from Montgomery. He had started out by telling her that there would be no more need for her assistance in his after-hours procedures, then withdrew that, insisting that she continue. Maggie responded by pressing him on what was really going on. She might be slow, she said, but she wasn't dumb. She wanted the truth. And even though she wasn't the most devout of Catholics, a lifetime of indoctrination in the Church's inflexible attitudes towards birth control—in spite of the current controversy surrounding John Rock and a possible relaxation of the doctrine—made her increasingly uneasy. And so he had finally admitted that he couldn't do without her—that she was crucial to the success of the operation, in fact. He played on her sense of medical obligation as much as on her loyalty to him. He was eloquent, determined, and quite convincing.

These were desperate women who came to him of their own free will, he said. He provided a service, nothing more, but a critically needed service. These were not fly-by-night, irresponsible floozies, but "casualties of domestic circumstance." Most were married. Many were Catholic—nominally, perhaps, but even so. None were underage; he made damn sure of that. If the OB/GYNs were too timid or risk-averse or tradition-bound to deal with the situation, well, then, he was more than willing and able to take on the responsibility. These women needed the kind of competent medical care he could provide, rather than putting themselves at risk in substandard facilities, or worse. Otherwise, husbands, children, marriages all suffered, and for what? Piety? A misguided sense of social propriety? Maggie was not sure. Montgomery began to rail at her. He had seen it go bad often enough in this Catholic straight-jacketed town, he said. Why don't you quit that Catholic church you go to and start coming to St. Jude's? Episcopalians kept things in perspective. Sensible religion, the Episcopal Church. Pragmatic from the beginning. Like Presbyterians but with more money. Nothing wrong with that. Keep things in perspective, that was the only way. What was that organization, "Planned Parenthood?" Another sensible idea. They were gaining ground, even in New York. She had never heard him carry on in quite this way.

By telling her—not directly, but in so many words—who these women were and why they were coming to him, rather than their own doctors, he had managed to assuage most of her doubts. Montgomery had contacts with several local lawyers who referred patients to him for a clean and quick abortion, some of whom had saved his ass in minor surgical lawsuits over the years. He had long since lost interest in whether any—or rather, how many— were for personal relationships. It was a small town, and in some cases it didn't pay to be all that curious; he had to balance the possible advantage of having something over on someone with the danger of adversely affecting his ongoing relationships. The referrals always came with the stipulation of an additional fee, to be paid directly to Montgomery, another reason to protect his sources. The majority of his patients came from outside of Oswego—from Syracuse or Utica or Albany—so there was little chance that they would be recognized, or ever seen again. It was a high end but unlucky clientele—or lucky, depending on your point of view. If by providing a needed service he was able to benefit financially somewhat in the process, well, why not? He was the one risking his reputation, his standing in the community, his chances for advancement, his career. He saved these women something much more important than money in the long run, and they knew it.

The patients reported to the O.R. without paperwork, typical for a small town hospital. But they were supplied with wrist bracelets and a hospital admittance number. Montgomery had told Maggie to use this ID number for the O.R. case book. What he didn't tell her is that he supplied the bracelets himself, outside of the normal hospital admission process. He had explained to her that he completed the charts himself, after she had gone home, and that the standard hospital charges were generated from the charts at a later date. That he did nothing of the sort was something Maggie would not find out until much later, along with the fact that it was a cash business and the hospital knew nothing about it—pure profit and no taxes. And as for the actual surgical results—well, the specimens were just sucked away with the daily rubbish.

Nobody but Montgomery, Maggie and the patient knew what had happened, he claimed. Not quite true, since he was relying on Phil for the Demerol and any other drugs he needed, but that was easily glossed over, and the general laxity surrounding the drug inventory made it even easier. Since Maggie wanted to believe that it was all above board somehow, Montgomery had only to give her a little something to build on. He told her that most of these women "couldn't afford to pay a thing," and how he hated to think that was the reason they were forced to come to him. Would she rather they resort to something much less safe? So many were being performed in doctor's offices, for Christ's sake, in less than sterile conditions, with little or no real anesthesia, and no immediate access to emergency medical care in case of complications, which were not all that uncommon. It had happened once to Montgomery, before Maggie had started assisting, and he had managed to both save the woman's life and still cover up the real reason behind it, not coincidentally having an "in" with a not uninterested lawyer. So—if he could help these women, who so often believed they had no other options, or had only very poor options—why shouldn't he do it, even if it meant working the system a bit, wasn't that better for everyone? In the end, she was willing to go along with it, motivated less by her feelings for him than by what she saw as a noble calling to serve—in spite of the ambiguities. The going to hell part she somehow managed to not think about much at all.

Second Hand Information

"Deal," said Amos.

LaFleur looked up in surprise. The big white dealer button sat in front of him, pushed from his right by Amos Brown. He took the deck of cards Amos was holding out to him and set them down on the table. "I need some information, Amos."

Brown riffled a small stack of chips on the felt. It wasn't a true card table, just an old felt blanket draped over a small dining table, but it was better than playing on a hard surface. "What do you need?"

"I need to get at some old records. Or at least find out if any records are still around. An old case from the sixties."

"Hey, what about the 'no shop talk' rule?" This came from one of the younger officers seated at the table, playing on probation tonight. If he didn't make a fool of himself—or of LaFleur—he would be invited back as a regular.

"I made the rules, I can break them," said LaFleur. This was acknowledged by the officer with a quick nod and a studied look in the other direction. No sense in aggravating the host, he was probably thinking to himself. Besides, he surely knew LaFleur's reputation.

Amos continued riffling chips absentmindedly while he talked. "Sixties? I don't think we have anything that old. Least not at the station. Probably only go back to the eighties, at most."

"Would there be something in storage?"

"Hell, I don't know. I can try to find out. What are you looking for?"

"Something related to a suicide at the hospital. Fall of '64."

Amos put on what he imagined to be his thoughtful look.

LaFleur recognized it for what it was and didn't expect much, so was more than a little surprised at what Amos came back with.

"The nurse. Yeah, I know about that."

The officer on probation broke in again. "Are we on a break or something?"

"Listen, kid," LaFleur started loudly, then paused and turned to others at the table, who had been talking amongst themselves, ignoring Amos and LaFleur. "Sorry, guys, yeah, let's take a break. Ten minutes, okay?" He waved them all out of the room as he stood up, stretching, his thoughts drifting to the bad beat from an hour ago—kings against jacks. The kings got cracked and LaFleur had lost a bundle. His least favorite hand, kings. They seemed so invincible. He turned toward Amos and forced his train of thought back to the nurse.

"So you know what was going on over there?" he asked. "With the nurse?"

"Sure. You were on it, too, weren't you?"

"That was a damn long time ago. I was still a rookie cop, and don't know much about it," he said, hating the admission.

"I remember it since it was one of my first cases as a detective," Amos said. "Made an impression. And besides, my sister used to be a nurse over there. We heard a lot of stories at family dinners. Hospitals are strange places, let me tell you. There was this guy she told me about once, he didn't have any—"

Before he could launch himself into one of the long, broken ramblings he was famous for, LaFleur cut him off. "Yeah, I'm sure it was strange as hell. But what can you tell me about this…um, this other business?

"Other business? You mean the burglaries? The pharmacist?"

"No, damn it, the nurse…" LaFleur interrupted himself. "Wait a minute. What burglaries? What pharmacist?"

They were still talking twenty minutes later. "So are we breaking up the game early, or what?" someone had called out from the kitchen. LaFleur waved as before, this time holding up a notebook and adding a meaningful glare to the gesture. Amos went into the kitchen and told them to cash themselves out, then went back out to the table to continue the conversation. Neither man noticed the others leave.

*

"So, you don't know about that?" Amos asked. LaFleur shook his head. "We were investigating a string of burglaries at the hospital," Amos continued. "Nothing much at first, some locker break-ins. Minor personal stuff, we weren't too concerned, figured it was an internal problem they would be better off taking care of themselves, maybe they just wanted us to try to scare someone. Then we were told of some missing narcotics; Demerol, in particular, quite a bit of it. Anything else, maybe we wouldn't have paid much attention. And there was some other stuff; I don't remember exactly what it was. Anyway, there turned out to be some odd discrepancies in the pharmacy records. Before we were able to narrow it down, though, the pharmacist involved died during an operation. Right there at the hospital. My sister told me all about it. Something weird was always happening in that place. There was another case she told me about, this woman came in for something routine, some kind of simple operation, gall bladder or something, and during surgery she woke up and tried to—"

"Does this have anything to do with the pharmacist? Or the nurse?"

"Well, no, not really, but—"

"Can we get back to that? I'm old and want to hear the rest of the story before my time comes."

Amos grinned. "Sure, A.C. So anyway, we never were able to pin anything down, no suspects, and the other burglaries stopped right after that."

"Which, the drugs or the lockers?"

"Both. We figured maybe someone was trying to confuse the issue, draw attention away from the pharmacy deal with the other stuff, since no one could really give us anything else. Or maybe it was just a coincidence. Nothing came of it, anyway, and with the pharmacist dead, it got dropped not long after."

"Nothing suspicious about the pharmacist's death?"

"Not that we saw. It was a fluke accident or allergic reaction or something. The surgeon provided a statement, confirmed by both the other doctor involved—the anesthesiologist—and by the nurse. Neither one had much to say about it, though, now that I think

48

about it. Left it up to the surgeon to provide all the details. Anyway, we followed up with the hospital on the burglaries for a couple of weeks, but they told us the problems had been resolved and to drop it. So whether the pharmacist was involved or not became a moot point, and there was nothing more we could do."

"You'll look for those records, too, on the pharmacist?" LaFleur asked.

"Sure, I'll look," Amos said, "but I doubt if there's anything still around."

"Thanks. Next question: how soon after the pharmacist's death did the nurse commit suicide?"

Amos nodded. "Yeah, I was getting to that. Like I said, everything about the pharmacist checked out, and with no way to follow up on the drug thing, we forgot about it. A few weeks later, we get the call about the nurse. I didn't make the connection at first."

"Connection?"

"Yeah. The nurse who committed suicide was the same scrub nurse who had been assisting when the pharmacist died."

Taking Care of Business

When Montgomery came in to the hospital the next morning, the first thing he did was to stop by the pharmacy and tell Phil Cathcart to meet him in an empty office. In the twenty minutes he sat at an empty desk waiting for Phil to show up, he went over again what he needed to do. He realized he had been…incautious. Inattentive. No harm done, yet, but he needed to get things back under control, and quickly.

Cathcart came in the open office door, slouched across the unlit room and into a chair in the corner.

"So how much Demerol are you skimming?" Montgomery asked, as soon as Phil sat down. If Montgomery was ever to let a glower cross his usually composed features, this was the time. Phil mumbled something incoherent.

"How much?" the doctor repeated from behind the desk.

"What do you care?" Phil said, coherent, but sullen.

"It's my ass that's on the line, that's 'what I care,'" Montgomery replied. "I don't need an addict on my payroll."

"I'm not an addict," Phil said, unconvincingly. Sullenness personified now, he scratched his arm aimlessly. "Anyway, no one even knows anything is missing."

"God damn it, Phil. I overheard Angie Frascati asking Gale why there is never much Demerol on hand. She said she had to go to another floor the other night to find some."

"You know we just keep the stuff lying around. No one is keeping track of it. She doesn't know anything."

"Probably not, but I can't have her, or anyone else, getting any ideas."

"Don't worry about it."

"All right, I've had enough of this," Montgomery said. "From now on, do what you're paid to do and nothing more."

Cathcart seemed to be genuinely offended by this. "Okay, I'll keep the floors stocked up, if that's what you want, and I'll still do what I want, too," he said. Then he went further. "And, I want more money."

Montgomery had not really been prepared for this, but after reflecting on it a second or two, he realized this was about all that could be expected from someone like Cathcart. *He is really getting to be a liability.*

"No," Montgomery said, flatly.

Cathcart shifted in the chair, jumpy and distracted. "What do you mean, no? You don't have a choice. Give me what I want or I'll go to the cops."

"You don't have anything to take to the cops."

"You sign for the stuff."

"You're the one who creates the invoices, you're the one who handles the deliveries. I can deny everything. I could even turn over the invoices as evidence *against* you; who's to say I knew you were stealing the pharmacy blind? Which one of us do you think they'll believe?"

Cathcart stood up, taking a belligerent pose. "Maybe that doesn't matter, now that I think about it, if certain other things became public," he said cryptically. "Maybe I wouldn't even need the cops. I can go to the administrator, let him know exactly where some of that Demerol is going." He let that hang a minute. "Nothing to say?" he jibed.

Montgomery was nearly caught off guard by this last threat, but was quick to realize what it meant. "Let's not get carried away," Montgomery temporized. "Maybe if we just lay off a while. Then we can make some new arrangements."

Phil seemed to consider this. "How long?"

"Damn it, Phil, I don't know. Not long. Just let me take care of some things."

Phil sat back down, somewhat mollified. "Okay. I don't want any trouble. I just think it's time that we made some adjustments."

"I said we could talk about it, just not right now, okay?" Montgomery said again. He didn't get an answer. "So," he prompted, "you agree to put things on hold for awhile."

"As long as you agree that things are going to change. Don't cross me."

"Just keep things quiet for now, everything back to normal, until I can take care of it?"

"Okay."

"We're square, then? Everything back to normal?" Montgomery repeated.

"Yeah, okay, I said."

Nothing was said for a minute or two while they silently appraised one another's commitment to the truce.

"So, are we done?" Phil finally asked.

Montgomery nodded. "Go ahead, get back to work."

Phil stood up and started out the door. As he left, he called out over his shoulder, "Just don't cross me."

As Cathcart walked out, Montgomery absently noticed that he looked awfully pale, and appeared to be favoring his right side.

On his way out into the hall Phil practically ran into Angie. Neither one said a word. Phil slumped on down the hall, glaring at her over his shoulder. Angie turned and went the other way, desperately hoping he would assume she was just passing by and had not been standing there the whole time. Whatever Phil had against her, thinking she had been eavesdropping sure wouldn't help. Even if she had been standing there for more than the few seconds she was actually there—she had hesitated outside the office when she heard the voices—she certainly could not have repeated anything she had heard. She tried to surreptitiously look in at the door of the office as she passed by. She could not tell for sure who was there; it was too dark, and she was afraid to stop. But she was pretty sure she had recognized the other voice. She didn't stop when she heard the sound of the door closing, echoing in the hall behind her. But she felt the eyes on her back.

*

The next morning Montgomery stopped by the pharmacy to talk to Cathcart on his way to the office. Something is obviously bothering him, Montgomery thought, and after seeing him shuffling to the parking lot on his way out the night before, he thought he knew what it was.

Phil was stocking. Montgomery leaned on the counter and watched him for a minute without saying anything. As Phil reached out to place some boxes on an upper shelf—Demerol, as it happened—he suddenly gasped and almost doubled over, grasping at his side.

"Phil, are you all right?" Montgomery asked.

Phil turned and looked closely at Montgomery as if trying to reconcile the angry conversation from the day before with the new benevolent tone. He turned back to the shelf, putting one last box in place. "Sure, I suppose so," he said, without much enthusiasm. Then he glanced back at the doctor. "Well, last couple of days, I've been really tired. And I have a pain in my side. Won't go away." He frowned. "I've been trying to get all this stuff stocked—before someone complains about the Demerol again," he said, pointedly. "What, you think it could be serious?"

"Could very well be," Montgomery replied. "Stop by my office later this morning—say about ten—and I'll take a look at you." Montgomery walked away.

"Thanks," Phil called out to his back.

*

"You've got appendicitis." It was late afternoon, and Phil was sitting in Montgomery's office. "The blood tests confirmed it." Montgomery tried to look compassionate.

"Shit." Phil balled his fists and smacked them down onto Montgomery's desk. "What...so, what does that mean? An operation, right?"

"Yes," Montgomery replied. "But it's nothing to worry about. Appendectomies are very common. Routine."

"Yeah, well. I don't know. Isn't there something else you can do? Antibiotics?"

"No, not really. This is not something you want to mess around with, Phil. It could be dangerous, fatal, even, if it's not taken care of right away. It is a very simple procedure."

"I don't want an operation."

"I just told you…"

"My brother in Albany died during a hernia operation. Last year."

Montgomery was surprised by this. That really was a very simple procedure, even simpler than an appendectomy. "That is extremely unusual, Phil."

"Yeah, well, that's what they said, too. It was supposed to be nothing. But they said he went into some sort of shock, with a really high fever, during the operation."

"I still don't—wait a minute. Can you describe exactly what happened? Did they give you any details?"

"All I know is that they said it came on very suddenly and that there was nothing they could do. They said it was caused by the anesthesia. They told me I might be susceptible to the same thing."

Anesthesia related? "Malignant hyperthermia? Is that what they told you it was?"

"Yeah, that's it. They said it was some new thing, and that if I ever had to have an operation, I had better not go under full anesthesia, not if I could help it. So what can I do instead?"

Montgomery didn't answer right away.

"Montgomery?"

"Sorry. Listen, I'm sure you've got nothing to worry about. Let me check a couple of things and I'll talk to you later this afternoon, all right?"

"Sure, I guess so." He leaned forward in his chair, as if to stand up, then paused, wincing. "You'll let me know right away? This afternoon?"

"Yes, Phil. Like I said, I just want to double check with the anesthesiologist, and I'll get back to you. I'll go over everything. All the details of the operation, exactly what we need to do to make sure it is taken care of properly. Trust me, there's really nothing to worry about. But right now, you really need to be in a hospital bed."

After Phil had been admitted, Montgomery stopped by his hospital room. He had scheduled the procedure for that night, explaining to Phil that it was dangerous to wait any longer; there was a risk of a burst appendix. He also reassured him that whatever had happened to his brother was a one-in-a-million fluke, and that it was perfectly safe for him to be anesthetized.

Nothing to worry about.

*

Dr. Montgomery called Angie over to the nurses' station, where he was standing with a medical chart in his hand. "Angie!" he said, in the way he always said it, as if she had nothing better to do than jump at his command. She turned away from the room she was about to enter and walked slowly back to the station. It was almost six; and she was just going off shift. *Now what?*

"Angie," he said, "I have an unexpected staffing problem. I have a procedure in about an hour, and the scrub nurse who I scheduled is not available, she had to leave early for some reason or other. Typical. Well, anyway, I've checked with Nurse Gale, and you are the only surgical nurse here. I'm going to have to ask you to assist." His tone shifted, almost apologetic, but she knew it was simply intended to make her more compliant. "I know you're shift is about to end, but don't worry, it won't take too long. We should be out of here by eight, nine, at the latest."

It was apparently another one of Montgomery's "unscheduled" operations. How he got away with it she didn't understand. First it was Maggie and whatever was always going on after hours, and now this; some sort of under-the-table arrangement, she was sure.

She was still wondering what was going on when Phil was brought in to the O.R. Montgomery explained to her that this was something he had promised to do for Phil, and that although it was being done outside of normal billing procedures, it was fully sanctioned according to the by-laws of the hospital. Angie suspected that the phrase "thou dost protest too much," ill-remembered from a high school English class, probably applied here, but she kept her mouth shut.

Angie stood to one side listening as Dr. Montgomery finished prepping Phil for the surgery. Phil was already groggy. "Nothing to worry about, Phil," Montgomery was saying. "As I've told you, an appendectomy is a very simple procedure. Dr. Mahoney should be in here any minute and we can get started. Just remember what I told you earlier."

This was the first Angie had heard that Paul would be doing the anesthesia, which made her anxious. She had worked with him before. That's how they had come to know one another; it was a small hospital, and not many surgical nurses to go around. Or anesthesiologists, for that matter. But she hadn't really seen him since the episode on the stairs a few nights earlier and was starting to feel uncomfortable around him. Uncomfortable with the whole thing. She suddenly realized that Paul had come in and was talking to Montgomery.

"Paul, thanks for coming in," Montgomery said. "Sorry to rush you. I already went over everything with Phil concerning the anesthesia—I've heard you do it often enough—the consent form is in my office. He was a little anxious, so I gave him 100mg of Demerol about twenty minutes ago," Montgomery explained. "So, nothing to worry about." If Mahoney was concerned about any of this, he didn't say anything. He just nodded and moved over to the anesthesia setup.

Montgomery moved over to the table. "Paul, let's get him under. Angie, you help monitor him."

Skating

It was about six o'clock when LaFleur walked into the 1850 House restaurant on Bridge Street, shaking the rain from his coat. He hung it on a hook in the hallway as he made his way back to the bar.

"I've got your table ready, A.C.," someone called to LaFleur from across the dining room.

"Thanks, Joe," LaFleur called back. "I'll wait back here. Friends should show up any time." He had been coming here for twenty years or more. It had been built originally as a boarding house, part of the expansion of the town during the decades following the building of the Erie and Oswego Canals. LaFleur wasn't exactly sure how much of the original 1850-era building was still intact, it had been remodeled so many times. The local Historical Society probably knew. They did a good job of keeping up with that sort of thing.

The restaurant's current owner, Joe, an Oswego native, had taken over management from his father a few years earlier. He had turned what had been just an old restaurant into one of the town's more eccentric hangouts: part restaurant, part museum, and part antique shop—everything in the building except the tables and chairs was for sale—those too, probably, if you made the right offer.

Joe got to the bar just as LaFleur sat down next to a small bronze sculpture. "Here you go. Shot of Famous Grouse and a half a glass of spring water." He saw LaFleur gazing at the statue. "Haven't changed your mind, have you?" he asked.

LaFleur gestured towards the figure, scotch now in hand. "So what's the price this week?" LaFleur had wanted the statue for years, but he hadn't yet convinced himself that he could afford it. Joe's price was reasonable enough, he supposed, considering the history of the piece (assuming Joe's story could be trusted). One of an original set of four statues, long ago separated from it mates, it had adorned one of the main corner posts of an ancient bridge in Amsterdam (or Bruges, or maybe Budapest). It was called "Winter," according to Joe. It was the figure of a skater posed midway in a languid sort of pirouette, arms closely wrapped around slender shoulders, lower extremities melting seamlessly into ice skates. Just what he liked about it he had a hard time explaining. There was an androgynous ambiguity about it that he had not yet defined. He liked to imagine what it must have looked like in its first life, sitting at one corner of an old arched bridge somewhere in Europe, river ice below, lit by glittering winter light, the embodiment of an elemental strength: grace in adversity. Spring, Summer, and Fall would have perched nearby.

"Price? Same as last week," Joe answered. "Anyway, you know it's a good deal. Where else you gonna get one?"

"Yeah, I know. Maybe one of these days you'll talk me into it."

LaFleur heard bells jingling as the front door opened; he looked up to see Maggie Malone and Dr. Fuentes come in, brushing the rain from their coats. He got up with his Scotch and went out to meet them. They immediately got stalled in the usual pleasantries that seem to start every social meeting among new acquaintances, and mumbled replies: yeah, the traffic, glad it didn't amount to much in Oswego, not like Syracuse; no, he had walked, it wasn't too far since they got the walkways on the west side done; you found a parking place close by? Yes, it was cold for this time of year, wasn't it.

Joe came over and rescued him. "I've got you in the Doctor's Corner," he said, taking Maggie's and Michael's coats while he herded them over to their table. Being close to the hospital, quite a few doctors patronized the place, and Joe had filled the bay next to that particular table with an esoteric assortment of items that he imagined all doctors would be interested in—small wooden cases filled with antique medical instruments, a velvet lined case of scale weights, and a large brass microscope he claimed had come out of

Louis Pasteur's laboratory.

As they sat down, LaFleur couldn't help noticing that Maggie looked a lot different out of uniform. She was wearing a slightly low-cut dress, suggestive but not brazen, just right for her age and build, LaFleur thought. He noticed that she had also changed her hair in some subtle way that he couldn't quite pin down. He realized how automatically he had regarded her at the hospital as simply a "nurse," with no thought as to what she might be like outside of that narrow definition. As he thought about it he realized he had done the same with Dr. Fuentes. He never thought much of doctors, or nurses, outside of their professional roles, and like most people, seldom had the chance to socialize in that circle. He wondered briefly if he had always been seen as just a "cop," no other identity, and then realized that his social network had always been pretty restricted, maybe even more so than medical professionals. Well, if for no other reason, working with them on the case would expand his social horizons a bit. Could even be fun. As he watched Maggie across the table he felt an unexpected flush of more than just casual interest. *Watch out, A.C.*

LaFleur was drawn back to the world as Joe came over and opened a bottle of red wine with his usual flourish. He let LaFleur approve (it was a good Australian Shiraz, an extravagance for LaFleur, but Michael was paying), then poured each of them a glass. Michael picked up his goblet, held it up to the light and rolled the wine around, watching it cascade in thick little rivers down the curved sides of the glass. "Nice legs," he commented.

"Hell, son, you're going to drink it, not dance with it," growled LaFleur.

LaFleur was relieved that both Maggie's and Michael's laughs were genuine. They had all started to relax, but even so LaFleur was not too surprised when Maggie started right in on him.

"So you've had some time to think about it since we last talked; what happened that day, Detective LaFleur? What was going on with that investigation?"

"Call me A.C., please." LaFleur hesitated, and chose his words carefully; relaxed or not, he wasn't too sure he liked losing the high ground. He would have preferred to have met with them in a more "businesslike" atmosphere, but Michael had convinced him that Maggie would be more forthcoming away from the hospital. "I've done some asking around, and gone back over what I remember of the case. It's not much, and I haven't reached any conclusions. All I can tell you is that the chief of police and the D.A. closed the case immediately, the next day, just like it says in the article. The coroner's office had to call the chief in from home Sunday morning. Of course, at 11 a.m. he probably already had a good start on a six-pack, even on a Sunday, so maybe he didn't much care." LaFleur paused. "The chief at that time...well, we didn't get along. Anyway...none of us ever saw the scene. As far as I know, no one outside the hospital even went into the lounge until late in the day. Apparently everything had been sanitized before we were even called. I do recall that the autopsy was done that afternoon, again just like the article says. The chief handled all the interviews."

"Do you know who called the police that morning?" Maggie asked. "I don't."

"No, I don't know," LaFleur said. He thought that over for a second, trying to remember what Amos had told him, and decided he had answered too quickly. "No, wait, I think it might have been a doctor—oh, hell, I guess I don't know, either," he said, interrupting himself. "I need to locate the records."

"Did you get involved in suicide cases very often?" Maggie asked, changing the subject.

"Well, yes, often enough, I suppose; if there are unusual circumstances you always want to rule out homicide as soon as possible. Though there's almost always a pretty good indication of suicide; you know, evidence of problems at home, psychological indicators of one kind or another, even if they are only identified after the event. And the method is usually pretty straightforward. Gunshot, razor blade in the bath. O.D. is the most common. Hanging is not as common as most people believe, though it does happen. I don't remember ever hearing of anything quite as unusual as this incident. But still, even in this case, there must not have been anything *really* odd..." LaFleur paused, looking a little nonplussed. "What I mean," he continued awkwardly, "is that there was never any indication that there was anything...well, anything...kinky about it."

Maggie's eyes widened at this. "What do you mean, *kinky?*"

"Because of the nature of the suicide," LaFleur said, "'self-administered anesthesia,' I guess you would call it, there would have been questions regarding, um, certain sexual practices—damn, I wish I hadn't brought this up."

Michael spoke up before Maggie could comment. "Autoerotic asphyxiation?"

LaFleur nodded. "That would be the technical term, yeah."

"What *are* you two talking about?" asked Maggie.

Michael explained. "It's usually done by strangulation or some other sort of suffocation, almost to the point of passing out; it's supposed to enhance the climax. It basically brings on hypoxia, which just means partial oxygen deprivation. Asphyxia can create what is sometimes called 'euphoric hypoxia,' a semi-hallucinogenic state. Not to mention the obvious masochistic elements. In this case it would have been oxygen deprivation with the added effect of the anesthetic."

LaFleur turned to Maggie apologetically. "I really didn't mean to bring this up, at least not now. Not very pleasant."

"No, no, it's fine," Maggie replied. "I am a nurse; I have seen and heard all kinds of things in my time, believe me. Though this particular, uh, activity, I was not aware of. Thankfully, I would add." She turned to Michael. "How come *you* know so much about it?"

"It comes up in the literature occasionally, that's all. Hard to forget once you learn about it."

"Well, Angie would *never* have been involved in anything like that," Maggie said flatly.

"So was it a part of the investigation?" Michael asked LaFleur.

"No, not really," LaFleur said. "For one thing, there wasn't time. I just meant to say that, in general, given an unusual method of suicide, it should have been standard for there to be some consideration given to anything else out of the ordinary. But I don't remember hearing about anything like that coming out of this case. The method was unusual, no doubt about that. But as far as I know that was the extent of it." He paused. "Sorry to keep saying 'as far as I know,'" he continued, "but until I've had a chance to look into the records, do some more interviews, and look into some of the details more carefully, everything will have to be 'as far as I know' for awhile. So, nothing kinky. As far as I know." He looked over his shoulder as Joe walked up with the menus. "Joe, your timing is perfect." He took a menu.

LaFleur flipped open the menu and started looking through it with an intense interest brought on by considerable relief. Michael and Maggie opened their own menus as Joe refilled everyone's wine glass.

"Be back in a few minutes to take your order," Joe said, as he raised the empty bottle questioningly. LaFleur nodded his order for another. He'd negotiate the bill with Michael later.

LaFleur's attention to the menu wandered as he sat there regretting how things had started. They were getting way off track. He had not intended to introduce speculation over any possibly unsavory aspects of the death, not until and unless they were warranted. He needed a better foundation. The business about the autoeroticism was a distraction that had now been given much more significance than it deserved. Then again, maybe it was better that it was out of the way early, and now he could focus on determining the real motives behind her suicide.

Joe had returned and began taking their orders. LaFleur hadn't decided and deferred to the others, but they had not decided either. Joe said they could take their time and started to walk away, then stopped and turned back to LaFleur.

"While you're thinking it over…I couldn't help overhearing, A.C., are you talking about a case, something happen at the hospital? I didn't see anything in the paper."

LaFleur sighed as Joe waited expectantly for a reply, wondering again what he was getting himself into. How to explain in thirty seconds that he had agreed to take on a forty year old cold case on nothing more than the appearance—ok, the mysterious appearance—of an old newspaper article, with no evidence, little hope of any new evidence, no eyewitnesses, and maybe a fifty-fifty chance of finding any records. He looked up at Joe and forced a smile.

"Well, Joe, it wouldn't have been in the news lately. Dr. Fuentes and Ms. Malone have asked me to look into something that happened at the hospital more than forty years ago, when I was first on the force. Nothing much to say yet, but I'll tell you all about it if anything comes of it."

"Sure, sure," said Joe, waving his hands in apology. "Sorry to butt in."

"It's all right, Joe. Don't get me wrong, there just isn't much to talk about at the moment."

To LaFleur's minor dismay, Maggie chose to speak up at this point. "A nurse died at the hospital, Joe. Maybe you remember it; she allegedly committed suicide in the hospital lounge. In 1964. Angie Frascati?"

"1964? Yeah, I think I do remember something like that. And I remember the Frascatis. They lived down on East Fourth. Fifth, maybe. It was some sort of weird thing, wasn't it?"

"She was found hooked up to an anesthesia machine."

"Yeah, that's what I mean. Weird."

"I thought you might remember something about it," Maggie continued. "You seem to know something about everything and everyone in town."

"Well, not everything. And that was when, 1964? Long time ago. You're an anesthetist, aren't you, Dr. Fuentes?"

"Anesthesiologist, yes."

"Is there a difference?"

Michael opened his mouth to answer, then just shook his head slightly without saying anything.

LaFleur was getting impatient. He had always hoped to keep this simple and not drag everyone in Oswego into it. Now that Joe was in on it, it would be harder to finish it up quietly. He gave Maggie a hard look. "Can we please go into this some other time? Maybe once we know more?"

Maggie nodded in agreement. "Yes, of course. You're right."

"Sorry, Joe," he said, looking back over his shoulder. "How about we get together later this week? Then you can tell me whatever you remember about it. I do agree with Maggie, you might be able to help. Just not right now."

"Sure. Just let me know, anytime." Joe held up his pad and pencil. "Okay, who wants what?"

A few minutes later, with dinners ordered and the prospect of a few uninterrupted minutes ahead, LaFleur took the opportunity to get back to what he had started earlier, trying to get Maggie's side on all this. He pulled a small notebook and a pen out of the inner pocket of his sports coat, along with a copy of the article, which he unfolded and laid out carefully next to his bread plate.

"Before we get completely off in the weeds again, Maggie, I made a few notes today. I'd like to get your side of the story, and maybe you can answer a few questions I came up with. You are one of the few people still around who have at least some firsthand knowledge of what was going on. If we can pinpoint the actions of those involved, build a picture of how things played out that morning, who she saw, what she talked about—and not just that morning, but the days, maybe even weeks before—that should give us some insight into why she did it. And I'll want to get some more background on Angie and her family, of course."

"Of course, Detective."

"A.C., please."

"Of course, uh, A.C." She said this extremely self-consciously, LaFleur saw, but it was a start.

"Okay. We already said we don't know who first called the police. I'll ask the others at the hospital if they remember. I want to get a basic time line established, along with exactly how she was found, and who found her. Dr. Fuentes—"

"If you're A.C., then I'm Michael."

"Sorry. Michael, at some point, don't know if we can get to it tonight, I'll want a crash course in anesthesiology. I know less than nothing about it, which means that what I do know about it is wrong. You know the old joke, doc says 'count backwards from ten'—patient says 't—.'"

Michael smiled. "Yep, heard it, once or twice. I'll be glad to tell you whatever I can about the anesthesia they were using at the time. I've already checked some references."

"Fine, later for that." He was starting to get back into the old groove. He had forgotten how much he had enjoyed certain parts of the job. Of course, he didn't miss the drudgery of petty crime, the prostitution, the bar fights, the car thefts; the long nights and longer mornings staking out would-be drug lords, only to see them on the streets weeks or even days later; the dirty (and as it turned out, dangerous) liaison with the FBI and EPA during a toxic waste scandal of the seventies. He certainly didn't miss the agonizing and all too often unrewarding rape investigations, his least favorite but always highest priority, despite the usual official lack of interest. But this was something different, more like the way the best cases played out back in the day—no textbooks, no sociologists, no police academy hot shots tiptoeing the party line; just a chance to work the leads, however thin, to worry the case down to the edges until you puzzled it out, maybe even a chance do some good, again. A noble cause.

"Where was I going to start?" He glanced down at the article, realized he couldn't read it, and rummaged around in his pockets for his reading glasses. "Okay. I can see again. I'm just going to start in as if I don't know anything at all about this—not that far from the truth—and go from there. Um, let's start here, I guess. Then work backwards a bit. Sometimes that opens up paths you hadn't realized were there. Or closes paths you don't need to waste time on, that can be even more valuable." He glanced up and saw that they were still with him. "Here's how it lays out in the newspaper." He started to read the first paragraph: "'A 22-year old nurse at Oswego Hospital was found dead on a couch in a nurse's rest area in the hospital operating suite Sunday morning a short while after she had invited two third floor nurses to join her for morning coffee.' First, who were the nurses, they still around?"

"That would have been LaNette Halloran and another nurse, Judy...something...Judy Jenkins. LaNette wasn't a nurse, she was a ward secretary. She still is a ward secretary, in fact. Well, she has other duties now too; she's sort of Montgomery's 'executive secretary.' I haven't heard anything about Judy for years; I doubt that she is still around."

"All right," LaFleur said. "I'll want to talk to LaNette. Can you arrange something?"

"She won't talk to you," Maggie said. "I already asked. When I brought it up she almost started crying. She really doesn't want to talk about it. Or maybe Montgomery told her not to talk to you, I don't know."

"Well, maybe we can work around that later. What about the head nurse, um, Martha Gale? Any chance she's still around?"

Maggie shook her head. "No, she left Oswego years ago, for

California, to a sister's or something like that. I don't think anyone ever heard from her again."

"No one said this was going to be easy, I guess," LaFleur said, resignedly. "We'll just have to work with what we've got. So, anyway, this meeting for coffee, was that a common thing, an everyday thing, or just an occasional meeting?"

"It was a regular thing. They always met at about the same time," Maggie said.

"You were one of the regulars?"

"An occasional. Angie and the others were the regulars. I wasn't there that morning to meet with them."

"You weren't there? But I thought you said—"

"We had traded shifts that day. I forget why now. By the time I got there she had already been moved."

LaFleur did not try to hide his frown at this as he made a notation in his notebook. He would have to get into this, he knew, but now did not feel like the right time. "Well," he continued evenly, "back to the timeline. You know, when I first read through this, it didn't strike me, but thinking back to the conversation we had the other day at lunch, I agree that there are some unanswered questions here. So, Angie comes in to work that Sunday morning. She invites two friends at the hospital to meet her in the lounge for coffee." He paused to see if there was any disagreement. Maggie did not say anything, so he continued.

"Then it goes on: 'According to Police Chief Miles O'Conor, who was called by the hospital at 10:45 a.m. and informed of the death, Miss Frascati came on duty at 7:00 a.m. Shortly after reporting to her post, the police official said, she met two nurses' aides and invited them to the lounge for coffee' and that 'she apparently went into the lounge ahead of the aides.' Pretty straightforward, so far.

"Then, it says here, she was found 'a short while' after inviting the two to coffee. But it also says, 'Miss Martha Gale, the charge nurse on the floor, wanted to locate Miss Frascati and was told by the aides that she had gone to the rest area for coffee.' It doesn't say here what time she asked them, but a few lines later, *here*,"— he tapped the page with a forefinger—"it says that Gale found Angie at 8:15. So I am confused." He flipped open the notebook and ran his finger down a page with a neatly written series of times listed down one side, followed by brief notations. He turned to Maggie and continued, warming up now, new insights swarming into his head as he talked.

"Angie had talked to her friends 'shortly after reporting to her post,' and was found 'shortly after' she had invited them to coffee; but Gale doesn't even start looking for Angie until *at least* 8:00. That's not 'shortly after' Angie invited them, it's an hour later. And that's when the aides say she had gone to the lounge for coffee, ahead of them. So, is this just sloppy reporting, or is there a real discrepancy in the timing of the invitation and Gale going to the lounge? Did anyone else see Angie that morning? What am I missing here?"

Maggie's silence and the perplexed look hanging on her face did nothing to boost LaFleur's confidence that he was going to learn anything here; but before he said anything, he regained his patience, took a sip of wine, and sat back in his chair. Maggie leaned forward. Before she could say anything, Joe walked up to the table.

"Who had the Chicken Primavera?"

Something was Happening

Something was happening. Phil opened his eyes. He closed his eyes.

"Paul, how's he looking?"
"Looks good."
"Okay, here we go."

Phil opened his eyes. There was definitely something going on here. What was it? He tried to think. He remembered that he was going to have surgery. He was having surgery. Was he supposed to be awake now? He didn't think so. There was a lot of pain. He had been told there wouldn't be any pain, that he wouldn't even know what was going on. Phil closed his eyes.

"Angie, clamp. Damn it, Angie, pay attention."

Phil opened his eyes. Yes, he was definitely in pain and he didn't think that he was supposed to be awake at the moment. Someone bent over him and adjusted something that was attached to his face. He felt a little better. He closed his eyes.

"Angie, what are you doing? Get out of the way."

Phil opened his eyes. The pain was still there, but he felt more awake now. Someone was doing something over to his left. No, his right. They kept moving around. He wasn't sure what was happening. Someone did something to his arm. Phil closed his eyes.

"No, I told you, Paul, I interviewed him; there's nothing to worry about."

Phil opened his eyes. He was definitely awake. He didn't feel too bad, except for the pain. He was definitely awake. He didn't think he was supposed to be awake. He was not supposed to feel anything until he woke up. But he was awake now. Why was he awake? He tried to look over to the left. Someone was doing something again. It was hard to breath. He saw someone bending over him. It was hard to breathe. He heard voices. It almost made sense. It was getting harder to breathe, but he was awake. Was he supposed to be awake? Phil closed his eyes.

"Paul, I don't like the looks of this. Isn't he showing signs of insufficient anesthesia?"

He tried to open his eyes. He could not move. It was as if his body was turning to concrete, muscles stiffening, constricting his chest. He felt heavy and hot.

"No! Just the opposite. Look at him, he's burning up with fever, his breathing is ragged. We've got to bring him out, now! This looks like M.H."

"We cannot bring him out. I've got to finish in here."

"God damn it, Montgomery, if it's hyperthermia he's going to die! He didn't say anything to you about a history of problems with anesthesia?"

It was hard to breathe. He felt his muscles clamping up all over his body. He was hot. He was having trouble breathing. His heart was racing. Something was wrong.

"He might have mentioned something about a brother. I didn't think it was relevant."

"Not relevant! Don't you read the *Lancet* that gets delivered to your office every month? How could you think it was *not relevant!*"

"Apparently you should have done your job and interviewed him yourself. It's ultimately your responsibility."

Mahoney moved back to the head of the operating table. "We've got to bring him out!"

"Don't touch those settings."

"God damn it!"

The light got brighter, then darker. Phil's last thought, had he still been conscious enough to realize it, would have been surprise at feeling his heart stop.

Not Exactly

LaFleur laid his knife and fork across the sides of his plate and picked up the notebook and flipped back to an early page.

"I have four people listed here," he began, "who were mentioned in the article as being directly involved in the discovery: one and two, the nurses—not mentioned by name, but you've identified them as Judy and LaNette; number three, the head nurse, Martha Gale; and number four, the doctor that Gale called to the room, a Paul M. Mahoney. One other person you've said was there, but not mentioned in the newspaper, that's Dr. Montgomery. When did he get there, do you know?"

"Gale called him right away, I'm sure. At least that's what she told me at the time."

"Called him at home?"

"Yes, I guess so. I don't really know."

LaFleur made a note next to Montgomery's name, *called by Gale? check this w/ Montgomery*. "All right. Back to this Dr. Paul Mahoney, he still around, can I talk with him?"

"Oh, yes, he and his brother, Paul, are both still there."

"His brother, Paul? Both? You mean Paul Mahoney has a brother also named Paul Mahoney and they are doctors at the same hospital?

"Yes, that's right," Maggie said.

"Isn't that confusing?"

Michael spoke up at this. "Not when you know them, no. There is no confusing those two. It's only when they're paged or you have to make clear for some reason who you are talking about that their full names are used. Paul Mathew and Paul Michael. Good Catholic boys, as you might imagine."

"Okay, so there are two Dr. Paul M. Mahoneys. I can live with that. So which one of them did Gale call to the lounge?"

Maggie paused to finish a bite of chicken. "Paul Michael," she said, swallowing. "He had the on-call that weekend."

"Then our timeline starts like this." LaFleur turned to a blank page. Referring to the article, he started creating a rough sketch of events by writing names and actions, creating a timeline as he talked. "Seven a.m., Angie comes into work; she meets her friends on her way in and makes a coffee date for eight-thirty or so. Later on, Nurse Gale starts looking for Angie, and she's told by the aides—Judy and LaNette—that maybe she's in the lounge waiting for them. So then she goes to the lounge. Simple so far, right?" He held out his notebook for Maggie to see:

7:00—Angie arrvs
8:00—Gale – where's Ang?

Maggie nodded. "Sounds right so far."

LaFleur went on. "Gale finds the lounge locked, and goes to get a key—is that unusual, by the way, she wouldn't have a key?"

"Well, the lounge was never locked, no one ever carried a key for it," Maggie said.

"If it was never locked, then at this point there was a pretty strong indication that something was wrong. She didn't say anything to anyone?"

"Maybe not. You have to understand, none of us had what I would call a good relationship with Martha. She was competent, thorough, and efficient, but not at all likeable. So she would not have gone out of her way to express any concern to any of us even if she suspected there was something wrong."

"Is there some reason to believe that Gale had a problem with Angie?"

"There had been some friction between Martha and Angie. Between all of us, but Angie especially. That may have had something to do with why Martha was looking for her."

"Meaning...?"

Maggie looked over at Michael as if waiting for him to step in with some explanation. It was obvious to LaFleur that Michael had no more idea of what she was talking about than he did. Maggie continued with what LaFleur mentally catalogued as a terminal lack of enthusiasm.

"There had been some…problems with certain pharm records. Martha had been instructed by Dr. Montgomery to restrict access to the narcotics and to put a new med tracking system into effect. Angie had complained about shortages of Demerol on the floors. And she was getting blamed, unfairly, for the problem."

"That brings us to the burglaries. And the pharmacist." LaFleur put down his fork.

"You know about that?" Maggie asked in surprise. Michael looked over at her expectantly. It had not been LaFleur's intention to surprise anyone; he had assumed *she* would be the one telling *him* about it. But since she hadn't yet…

"I have some information about it, yes," he answered. "Whether or not it's related to Angie and whatever else was going on in her life, you'll have to tell me. I only have this second hand and haven't had a chance to check it out in the records, so can't be sure of the timing. But there was an investigation going on at the hospital at the time of the death. I was not assigned to it, but I know something about it. Which you obviously also know about and have so far neglected to tell me. Among other things."

Maggie, still slightly stricken, started trying to make excuses, but LaFleur cut her off.

"I know you would have gotten around to it, I'm not saying that you wouldn't. I should have started right out with this. But we got there anyway, and now maybe with a better reason to look for some connection."

"Maggie, what are you two talking about?" Michael asked.

"It's complicated, Michael."

"Come on, what are you keeping from us?"

"I'm not trying to keep anything from anyone."

LaFleur nodded. "That's fine, that's fine. Just start by telling me what you know about the burglaries and we can take it from there. Was Angie involved?"

"Are you sure we have to go into this right now?"

He hesitated. This was obviously important, or she wouldn't be sidestepping like this. But he also didn't want to try to drag something out of her that she was not ready to give up, and he had the feeling that she didn't finesse easily. He had seen this kind of thing too many times not to recognize that it was time to change his strategy. Time for a check. He could always raise the bet later. The subject had been broached, even if not in the way he would have liked, and he knew he could come back to it. And he was still hoping to get some basic background on Angie. He didn't know a thing about her other than the tiny scraps of bio in the newspaper article. She had been a bowler, that's about all he knew, and a fisherman. Well, didn't everybody bowl in 1964? And didn't everybody in Oswego fish? So what? *Now what the hell was I thinking about? My methodology is all shot to hell.*

"All right," LaFleur said, "if you don't think it's the right time, we won't go into it now. Probably not important." He could tell that Michael didn't agree by the way he poured himself some more wine and glared at Maggie. LaFleur just smiled and tapped out a rhythm on the notebook with his pen, a few bars of "Sing, Sing, Sing"—Krupa at Carnegie Hall. "Where were we?"

"Martha went to get the key," said Maggie helpfully.

"Right." LaFleur tapped on the page. "At eight-fifteen, Nurse Gale returns to the lounge, alone, and opens the door." He stopped to make a note. [*Gale finds Ang.*]. "What then?"

"She called for Dr. Mahoney."

"Mahoney went up first, before anyone else saw her?"

"I guess so."

LaFleur stopped there and summed up the course of events. "So they—the nurses—had talked to Angie when she came in, and they were probably just about to go up to meet her when the head nurse starting asking for her. No one had any reason to think that anything out of the ordinary was going on, none of the nurses, anyway, until Martha Gale goes to look for her and finds the door locked. She goes back down, gets a key, goes back up; calls for help. We can ignore the 'short while' and 'shortly after' comments in the article and move on, since there is no real problem with the time line we've established up to this point."

He sat back. "Okay. Now we can move on to what happened when she was found, now that we've established that there were no mysterious time lapses, no real indication that morning that anything was wrong."

Maggie looked contrite. "Well, not exactly."

LaFleur always hated the moment when things started to unravel. It never failed in cases like this, where there were no clear motives, no clear path to enlightenment. If there was any one thing he had continually agonized over in his years on the force, and had never, ever gotten used to, it was this point in the questioning—he even had invented a name for it—the *not exactly* point. The point when the answers dwindled away into a fog of "not really" and "sort of" and "I guess so." Everyone who worked with him had heard him rant about it. And now Maggie had done it, even using his term. This was too soon for a not exactly point. He had just confirmed, he thought, that any uncertainty over the timing of events was strictly a matter of imprecise wording in the article. But now, not exactly? He was almost afraid to ask. He asked anyway.

"What does 'not exactly' mean?" He stopped himself from going on to explain the concept of the not exactly point to Maggie.

"We didn't know it at the time. But Dr. Mahoney had been to the lounge earlier that morning. He didn't tell us until later that day."

"He was at the lounge? What time? What did he see?" LaFleur was almost irritated by this.

"He said he didn't see anything," Maggie said. "He went by the lounge sometime before eight, he said, and noticed that the door was locked. That's all."

"That is not a 'not exactly' kind of answer," LaFleur said. "How did he know the door was locked, he tried it? He didn't look in? Are there windows in the door?"

"There might have been a small window in the door,' she guessed. "It's been replaced since then. There is a little window, up high in the wall, in a narrow hallway that runs along next to the lounge, well, the O.R., now. I can show it to you. Anyway, all he said is that it looked dark in the lounge, so there was either a window in the door or he just noticed it was dark in the hall window. And that there was loud religious music playing. He thought that was sort of odd and was kind of embarrassed about not saying anything about it earlier, I think, though how could he have known, right?"

LaFleur drained his wine glass and set it down on the table.

"You said he was there before eight? How much before?"

Maggie didn't know when Mahoney had passed by the lounge for sure, but after thinking it over guessed sometime around seven-thirty or so. LaFleur made a notation on the timeline. [*Mahoney at lounge – check this*]. Not all that long after Angie had reportedly seen her friends. A half an hour or maybe even less after she had talked to them, in fact, and the darkened lounge was already locked with the radio on. No explanation for why Angie had gone to the lounge so early, ahead of her friends. Still, he reminded himself, there was nothing here that could not be explained by what he had suggested earlier; it was just a tragic event, under unusual circumstances, and imaginary complications that were just that, imaginary. He started wondering if maybe this was not a real "not exactly point" after all.

Michael had been quiet throughout most of the meal, LaFleur realized, so he turned to him to ask what he thought. Did he think it was odd that Mahoney had not said anything to anyone earlier; was he concerned about the timing of Mahoney's walk by the lounge?

LaFleur turned the timeline around for Michael and asked, "Look right to you?"

7:00—Angie arrvs
7:30?—Mahoney at lounge – check this
8:00—Gale – where's Ang?
8:15—Gale finds Ang.

"Not exactly," Michael replied, whether intentionally playing on the earlier conversation or not, LaFleur couldn't tell. "Actually, I'm more concerned with what is not there yet, the more than two hours between the time she was found and the time the police were called. What was going on all that time?"

*

By this time dessert had arrived. LaFleur was as least as curious as Michael about what had happened in those two-plus hours. It had even come up at the lunch meeting earlier. It was impossible to miss it; the reporter had made it as obvious as possible in a one sentence paragraph in the middle of the article: *"Police were not called for over two hours after the discovery."* And he knew that not only had the police not been called right away, the whole investigation had been less than comprehensive.

But he was really not prepared to go into all that at the moment, especially given Maggie's recalcitrant mood. He wondered briefly if there was still anyone at the paper he could talk to—was it worth the effort to try to track down who had written the article? They had made a special point about the failure to call the police; why? And the related reference to Chief O'Conor arriving at the hospital late that afternoon *"to initiate the investigation."* He remembered that the very quick resolution of the case had been directly due to pressure from hospital administration. LaFleur was reminded again that he really needed to see some records, and how difficult that was likely to be.

These were all details that may or may not have any real bearing on whatever had driven Angie to suicide. He was experienced enough to know that everything they had covered earlier was not wasted—you never knew where a particular topic would lead—but he was more interested in Angie at the moment than in what had happened afterwards.

He decided he would rather put Michael's question off for the time being. "That's a very good question, Michael, but since it's getting late, let's not try to tackle that right now. In fact, I think we've probably done about all we can for the evening. Maggie started to protest, but he continued. "We still have plenty to talk about, I know. For next time. Maggie, in particular I want to know more about Angie; who her friends were, your relationship with her, Angie's relationship with Martha Gale, any problems with Montgomery, how she got along with the other nurses, anything else you can tell me about what was going on at the hospital before that day." He stopped for a breath. "We don't have to do it tonight, but I want to do it soon. The more I know about what went on, the more likely it is that I'll be able to find out who's behind the article."

They agreed, and he invited them both to continue the discussion the next day. Michael begged off; LaFleur hoped he hadn't offended him by sidestepping the two-hour mystery.

Maggie, probably feeling like she was left with no choice, agreed to meet with him as soon as she got off her shift late the next evening. LaFleur suggested off-handedly (he hoped) that they meet at his houseboat. He was inordinately pleased when she agreed, and even imagined he had concealed his delight successfully.

On the Ice

Empty promises were piling up like dead leaves on the sidewalk; Maggie swept them away angrily with her feet as she walked to the hospital to meet Angie.

There had been no after-hours sessions the past couple of weeks. Not in the O.R., and definitely not in her apartment. She didn't know who to despise more, Montgomery, his hypochondriac wife, or herself. She was starting to feel like—like what, she didn't know. She was getting twisted. Montgomery was putting her off again with stories of his wife's supposedly advancing illness. Up to now he had convinced Maggie to just be patient, that yes, he was serious, that he wanted nothing more than for things to eventually work out. *Damn it.* Life was not supposed to be like a Doris Day movie. Now this ridiculous illness of his wife's, again; very ill, so he said, and besides, she can make things very difficult for us. You just have to wait. She was past the "give it a little more time" stage. She thought again of the meeting with Montgomery earlier that afternoon. *That bastard.* What did he think he was trying to pull?

Maggie did not like to work nights, but welcomed any chance to get out from under Montgomery's thumb, so she agreed to trade shifts with one of the other nurses in order to work swing with Angie for a few days. Angie had pleaded with her to make the switch, saying she was still upset by Phil's death in the O.R. and needed someone there at night that she could trust. Angie had asked her to meet in the lounge before their shift started, but hadn't said what it was she wanted.

Without thinking, Maggie took her usual way into the hospital, through Emergency and up the back stairs past Montgomery's office. Montgomery was still there, stuffing paperwork into his briefcase, apparently about ready to leave. Maggie had already decided it was time for a confrontation. Now she unexpectedly found Montgomery alone, when things were quiet. She decided to take advantage of the opportunity. She walked in to the office and sat down across from Montgomery, who looked up, poorly hiding his annoyance at the interruption.

"Maggie."

"Doctor."

The silence that followed was like a badly rehearsed moment in a community stage production, each waiting mistakenly for the other's cue. Montgomery looked back down at the papers on his desk. Maggie tied her shoelace. They both looked back up at the same time.

Maggie broke the standoff. "All right. I've waited too long to do this. I don't care how sick your wife is, or isn't, it makes no difference to me. We're through."

Montgomery closed the folder he was holding, turned and filed it in the credenza beside his desk, never taking his eyes off Maggie.

"You don't say," he said, his tone even more acerbic than usual.

Maggie blinked, then continued, *sotto voce*, as if letting him in on a secret. "And another thing. No more late night procedures."

Montgomery just smiled and steepled his fingers in the way Maggie had seen too often. She exploded.

"You think I'm kidding? I'm not going to stand by and let this continue. I've let it go on too long already." No tears, that would ruin it. I'm no good at this, she thought; base-to-base thinking, like Angie, that's what she was good at, but now she felt like she was on an ice floe that was breaking up beneath her, drifting away alone, not even a polar bear in sight. She had to take control. "I've got evidence, and I'll use it."

Montgomery ignored the bluff. This was all so beneath him, he communicated silently, disdain evident in every measured breath, every movement. "You don't have a single thing you can use against me. Not a thing."

"You don't think so?" she said, standing up and glaring down at Montgomery now. "Maybe the D.A. would be interested in hearing what I have to say," she went on, surprising herself with this unplanned threat.

Montgomery still didn't flinch. "You're willing to give up your career for this? I can survive it, you know. Maybe not easily, and it's not a path I would choose gladly, but I *can* survive it. You think I haven't foreseen this eventuality? As I've told you all along, these women are merely symptoms of a broader social ill; I am providing a cure—not to mention possibly saving their lives."

Jesus, does he ever drop the façade?

"There would be short term consequences, certainly," he continued amicably. "There always are in situations like this—but that's all it will be for me, short term. You, on the other hand, have very few options. You have nothing to gain, really, and everything to lose. Are you willing to take that chance?"

Maggie felt the ice shift again. She grabbed at the edge of the desk as if to regain her footing, and without thinking made a desperate strategic lunge. "I have records. I have been keeping records of all the women who have come to see you. And I have a witness."

Maggie thought she saw Montgomery's resolve crack for the first time. He may have even turned a bit pale. Were his hands shaking ever so slightly? Had she called down his bluff?

Montgomery looked down at his desk and began shuffling though papers in an obvious dismissal. Maggie looked down at him for what seemed like a long time before turning away.

*

Maggie left the office and began to make her way up to the lounge. She barely heard the office door close as Montgomery went down the long hallway in the other direction, his deliberate footsteps hollowly mocking her own uncertain shuffle. What had he said, not a path to choose gladly? No, not exactly. She suddenly felt as if she was not herself, somehow, that she—the "real" Maggie—was watching all this take place from a point a few feet above her head, and a little to the right. Looking down on this strangely familiar nurse climbing the stairs. Wondering what she was going to do next.

When she got to the lounge, it was empty. Angie was late, thankfully; she would have some time to compose herself. She sat down, picked up an old magazine and started flipping pages, her alternate self still watching from above. It was a *Life* magazine, something about JFK. She allowed herself to become distracted. She had never really liked him all that much. Too East Coast for an upstate girl. But still, it was hard to resist the drama of it all. She even started to feel a little remorseful for not being more moved by the already famous picture of little John John, his tiny salute to the flag draped caisson as it passed by. *Who the hell did he think he was, anyway?* Her fingers were shaking as she tossed the magazine back onto the table. She sat there alone in the darkened room for several minutes, going back over what had just happened downstairs, rehearsing what to tell Angie; how to get her to go along with this evidence bluff she now had to follow through on somehow. Her usual methodological approach had suddenly and completely deserted her, she thought again. She drifted back to Angie's request to meet her here tonight; she had sounded desperate. Maybe something about the pharmacy, she thought, but after Phil's death, that whole thing seemed to have been dropped. Montgomery had not mentioned it in staff, Martha was apparently still paying little or no attention to supplies, and Angie had not said anything to her about it recently.

Maggie thought back to the time Angie had seen her and Montgomery after hours in the O.R. Oh, God, what if that's what she wanted to talk about? Had she seen them on other occasions? Wait. Maybe I can get Angie on my side. If Angie could be persuaded to come at Montgomery with accusations of her own, she thought, with Maggie orchestrating, maybe they could put a stop to it all. But how could they keep themselves in the clear? She could still deny she knew what he was doing; maintain she had been coerced into assisting with the operations all along; she hadn't really known, not until now. My word against his. Still, she needed to have some evidence, get someone to back her up. If we can put Montgomery on the defensive, I can get out of this mess. Maggie dimly realized she was thinking desperately now. Damn him.

The door banged open and Angie came in and immediately started pacing around. Maggie waited. Angie just kept pacing.

Maggie regretted it as soon as she said it, but had worked herself into a state of paranoia by this time: "I don't know what you think has been going on in the O.R. with me and Dr. Montgomery, but believe me, I don't like it either."

Angie was incredulous. "What are you talking about? You have some problem working with Dr. Montgomery?"

Maggie sat back. She had been sure that Angie was going to accuse her of assisting with the...procedures—she still couldn't bring herself to say it, even to herself. She'd had no time to come up with a plan, some way to approach Angie, to enlist her help in forcing Montgomery's hand. Now, not only was Angie not accusing her of anything, it sounded like she didn't really know what had been going on. She started again. "There's more to it than that, Angie. A lot more. I need your help."

Angie glared at her. "My help? You want to ask me for *my* help? Maggie, I need you to help *me*. I'm scared and I don't know who else to go to. You're the only person on earth that I can talk to...well, outside of confession, I mean. And I was even afraid in confession. I don't know what Father must have thought, I practically broke down sitting there in the confessional." She started pacing again; stopped, looked at Maggie. "I've been spending a lot of time in confession lately," she said forlornly.

Maggie stood up and steered Angie to the couch, trying to calm her down. "C'mon, sit down." Angie dropped onto the couch next to her, then leaned over and picked up the *Life* magazine Maggie had been looking at earlier and started flipping through it blindly. Maggie reached over and took it from her.

"So...what is it then?"

Had Maggie stopped to think about it for even a moment, she might have realized what was coming next. But she had so recently and regularly not stopped to think about so many other things she had been doing that there just wasn't room enough to stop and think about this thing too.

"I've been having an affair," Angie said. "And I—"

Maggie, who really should not have been surprised by the admission, did not mean to scream out quite like she did. "Angie,

83

how could you? God, Angie. How could you?"

By the look on Angie's face, Maggie could see that this was not the reaction she had hoped for, anticipated, rehearsed. A less dramatic person would have reacted differently. Wait. Maybe she was not thinking about this in the right way. If Angie was having an affair, maybe she would be more sympathetic to Maggie's own problems.

"Oh, Maggie." Angie started sobbing now, but trying to suppress it, sucking in breath. Then she stopped just as suddenly as she had started, and continued in a rush.

"I don't know how it happened. I am trying to break it off, I did break it off, but—" That was all she could get out before she started crying again. Maggie pulled her towards her and leaned her head on her shoulder until she quieted down again.

"It's all right, Angie. It's all right."

After a minute or so, Angie lifted her head, calm again.

"So, who is it?" Maggie asked softly.

"Well, Paul Mahoney, of course. I thought you probably knew."

"Well, there has been some talk," Maggie said. "You know how it is around here. And I saw you having a disagreement on the stairs with someone not long ago. I thought it might have been Paul. But I wasn't totally sure and didn't want to embarrass you, or me, if I was wrong. The rumor mill has been going pretty strong lately, but that means it is also more unreliable than usual." At this thought, she had a sudden doubt. "But which Paul Mahoney? Not...?"

"God, Maggie, who do you think. Paul Michael. Who have we been talking about all this time?"

Maggie was not usually this slow. She was just so distracted by this thing with Montgomery. "But he's married," she said lamely.

"Which is why it is called an affair, I believe," Angie said, clearly irritated by Maggie's evident lack of understanding.

Maggie took a few seconds and calmed herself. She asked the next logical question. "Are you...sleeping together?"

Angie flushed bright red. "No. We never...well, not any more. It was about a week ago, the...the last time I saw him, I mean."

She looked at Maggie earnestly. "But I swear, not since then, I told him I just couldn't go on any longer and I broke it off. Maggie, I never meant, I mean...I just thought that he, that he and I..." A rain of tears was threatening to break out again, a lake-effect emotional storm closing in fast. "Oh, Maggie, I feel so horrible. And now I don't know what's going to happen." She spoke more calmly now, each word falling like a drop of hot wax, flowing at first, then turning cold and hard. "It keeps getting worse. Paul thinks Montgomery is going to blame him for what happened to Phil. It's making him crazy. He's frantic about it sometimes. God, Maggie, now he's practically blaming me, for everything. Almost threatening. I don't know what is going to happen next." Angie had finally run down. She sat back, listless and worn.

Maggie held up her hands. *What does Phil Cathcart have to do with this?*

"In the first place," Maggie finally replied, not knowing where else to start, "I thought it was an accident. What happened to Phil, I mean. That was just an accident. No, it wasn't even an accident; it was some sort of allergic reaction or something like that. You told me yourself. Dr. Montgomery explained it to everyone. It was just bad luck that Paul was the anesthesiologist."

"You weren't there," said Angie, moving to the other end of the couch, straightening her uniform, crossing and uncrossing her legs. "You were not there. Paul tried to turn off the anesthesia..." She stopped and rubbed her eyes, left her hands covering her face as she went on. Maggie could hardly hear what she was saying, and leaned closer. "Oh, Maggie, I don't know. I wasn't even supposed to be in there that night." She dropped her hands and turned her head away. "When Phil started to have problems, Paul tried to tell Montgomery what was wrong, he wanted to wake Phil up—well, he was sort of half waking up anyway, for some reason—but Montgomery stopped him. Phil was having some sort of tachycardia episode, he started breathing faster and faster, tach...tach..." She faltered, groping for the word.

"Tachypnea?" Maggie offered.

"Yes. Dr. Montgomery acted like he knew exactly what was wrong." Angie's voice became more animated as she described the scene in more detail, her hands acting out various parts of the action. "He told Paul the anesthesia was too low, that he recognized the symptoms, even if Paul didn't, as if Paul didn't know what he was doing. You know how Montgomery gets. Paul tried to argue, but Montgomery kept after him, insisting that Paul raise the level of anesthetic. Phil kept getting worse and worse. His eyes were open; it looked like he was trying to turn his head. I think maybe he really was coming out of the anesthesia prematurely. He was flushed, sweating, feverish, his muscles were twitching, then stiffening up. It was frightening. Then Dr. Montgomery ordered Paul to stop what he was doing. Paul even tried to tell Montgomery that he thought it was malignant hyperthermia—I looked it up—but Montgomery told him to get out of the way. Then he took over, saying he would handle it, that he—"

"Paul took over?"

"No, Dr. Montgomery! But he wouldn't let him do anything."

"Who wouldn't let him, do what?"

"Paul."

"Paul wouldn't let Montgomery do anything?"

"No, he wouldn't let Paul turn it off, and he said that he was responsible."

"Who was responsible?"

"Paul."

Maggie was starting to lose patience. "Third base."

"What?"

"Damn it, Angie, this is starting to sound like an Abbott and Costello routine."

Angie turned away. Then she stood up, picked up her coat and walked out of the lounge. Maggie blew out an exasperated breath. "Wait a minute," she called out after her.

Angie hesitated for half a second but didn't stop or look back. Maggie had no choice but to follow her—all the way downstairs to the first floor hallway, catching up to her just past the darkened offices at the other end of the hospital. Maggie reached out and put her hand on Angie's shoulder before she could get out the door. Angie stopped, still not looking back. Maggie could feel the tension in her shoulder.

"All right. All right. Just give me a minute here, okay?"

Maggie kept her voice modulated and warm, the way she would with a frightened patient. "Let me get this straight. You think Dr. Montgomery did something that caused Phil's death; or didn't do something, or some combination of the two; and he would not let Dr. Mahoney assist. Is that right?"

Angie's shoulders slumped under Maggie's still outstretched hand. A good sign? "Well, I don't know. Dr. Montgomery pushed us both away, telling Paul not to bring him out, that he was the only one who could do anything, and if we wanted Phil to live we'd better stand back and let him do his job. You know how he gets," she repeated.

"Oh, Ang. How do you know he wasn't right?"

"You weren't there, "Angie repeated. "You didn't see how he was acting."

"Are you sure you weren't just imagining things? It must have been very confusing, everything happening at once—"

"Maggie. It's not my first time in an O.R., you know."

Maggie considered this for a moment. "Paul was right there the whole time?"

"Yes, of course," Angie said, annoyed. "Well, no," she amended, "he went out for a couple of minutes to get something, but he was there practically the whole time. It was all happening so fast, Montgomery was yelling for us to get back, everything was going wrong. Paul tried to figure out if there was something wrong with the anesthesia…then Phil just died…" She trailed off.

Maggie pursed her lips. "Well, you haven't convinced me there's anything wrong yet. Why on earth would Dr. Montgomery…" She paused, unsure of what it was she was really asking. "You're not making any sense."

Angie continued to look down at the floor, still with her back turned, and remained silent for what seemed to Maggie a long time. Maggie waited patiently for the actual thirty seconds or so that Angie stood there, not speaking. She finally interrupted whatever soliloquy was running through Angie's fevered brain.

"Well?"

"Okay," Angie said. "You're right. It was probably just what he said it was," she said, still looking down. "Malignant hyperthermia. There's only one article on it in the library at

Crouse, it's something they just discovered, in Australia or somewhere like that." She started to turn, then interrupted herself and stopped, as if she could not bear the thought of looking at another person, then finally turned to face Maggie. Her lips were drawn, but she appeared composed now. "I'm sorry. Let's go back upstairs."

Maggie involuntarily breathed what she immediately recognized as a sigh of relief. So that's not just a cliché, she thought. There really is a specific physiological reaction to a sudden reduction in stress.

Maggie followed Angie back up the stairs, who had somehow taken charge of the situation, leaving Maggie wondering how she was going to get Angie's cooperation—now that she had told Montgomery she had a witness—or if she should even try.

*

Back in the lounge, Maggie and Angie sat together on the couch. For a long time neither one of them had the courage to speak. It was Maggie who finally broke the self-imposed moratorium.

"Me, too, Angie." She forced it out. Angie gave her a blank look. "Me and Montgomery."

It took a few seconds, but now the look on Angie's face told Maggie she had gotten it.

"You and Dr. Montgomery, Maggie? Really?"

"Yes, Angie, really."

"How long? Are you still...?" Angie asked, repeating Maggie's earlier questions back to her.

"It's been going on for several months," Maggie replied slowly, gauging her words carefully. "And no, we are not still seeing one another. I'm breaking it off. I saw him about an hour ago. We had...words. I said some things. I was on my way here to tell you."

"Tell me what?"

"That I have evidence against him," Maggie said, with a note of desperation in her voice. "Evidence that would be embarrassing, to put it mildly, evidence of certain late night...procedures." If only she could just say it. "He threatened me in return, of course, but it's a bluff, a stone cold bluff. He's got nothing, Angie, nothing, and I have everything against him."

It was obvious that Angie was not sure what to think of this. For her own part, Maggie felt like she was walking yet another thin line. A line that was growing thinner by the hour. Maggie could see consternation clouding Angie's face.

Maggie crossed her legs and began again, trying to get back to where she had started. "Angie, I thought maybe you could help me."

Obviously, Angie still wasn't sure what Maggie was insinuating. She had never been good at insinuation, Maggie realized.

"Maggie, what are you trying to say?" Angie said, nearly pleading.

"God, Angie, don't you get it? Here I am, assisting Frank with these unauthorized operations, week after week, and at the same time, for God's sake, sleeping with him, with the fantastic idea that he is going to leave his wife—his perpetually sick wife—for me, when all the time, he had no thought at all of ever leaving her, stringing me along just to keep that after hours business going, and so…I just thought that maybe you could help me put a stop to it. All of it."

Angie let go of Maggie's hand. "Help you what? And what about me? I'm the one who needs help, Maggie. I think Montgomery thinks I know something. He keeps asking me questions, they hadn't even gotten Phil out of the room yet, and already he was asking me things like, did I understand what had happened, did I know there was nothing he could have done, make sure you don't say anything stupid at the inquest, on and on, he knew I would have to answer questions, and already he was pressuring me. And even more later, asking what I saw, exactly. And with Paul, every time it comes up, it's frightening. *Damn* it, Maggie." She ran out of breath.

They sat quietly for awhile as Angie calmed down again. Then Maggie told her more about the after hours procedures in the O.R., the sessions that Angie had seen but had either willfully or innocently misunderstood, or ignored, or what does she think, exactly? She told Angie that Montgomery was not reporting anything to the hospital, that she suspected there was more to it than what Montgomery had been telling her, and that she wanted the procedures stopped. She repeated Montgomery's rationalizations, and why she was becoming unwilling to continue going along with it, her doubts and her regrets. Angie interrupted once with her own question about what Maggie thought Montgomery had done in the O.R that night with Phil. That hadn't been authorized by the hospital either, had it?

Maggie thought she had finally gotten across to Angie what had been going on. And came to believe that maybe Angie was more progressive than she had thought. The knowledge that Maggie had been assisting Montgomery in unauthorized procedures—as Maggie continued to insist to call them—did not, as Maggie had expected, shock Angie back into the stone age, but rather drew from her some measure of sympathy. Sympathy not just for Maggie and for her clearly untenable situation; but even some measure of sympathy for the women to whom Montgomery had administered the procedures. Sympathy tempered by some anger, a confused and muddled sympathy, but sympathy nonetheless. And there was little enough sympathy to go around, they agreed. Maggie felt Angie must have known more than she let on. Even so, she did not try to talk her into backing up the threat she had made to Montgomery, to use Angie as her "witness."

They finally managed to come to terms with their respective problems. Angie resolved to stand up to Paul, whether over the affair or about Phil's death, and the same for Montgomery and the pressure he was putting on her. For her part, Maggie resolved to contact the District Attorney the next day.

There was to be no compromise, they each determined. No turning back.

*

The District Attorney was in a particularly good mood. He had been returned to office a few weeks earlier by a landslide—at least that is how he liked to think about it (he had actually run unopposed, as usual)—and his satisfaction at retaining office had not quite worn off. Like many of his counterparts across upstate New York, his position was for the most part maintained by generous donations from influential community members—family and friends, many of them attorneys—donations that could not be called bribes, certainly, not even attempts at buying influence. No, these donations were more like expressions of recognition of whatever attention he might be able to divert to, or away from, a donor, depending on the circumstances.

The D.A. was almost never pleased to get a call at home, the exception being the congratulatory calls he received in the days following an election, of course. He was particularly indisposed to receive calls late at night, especially from someone who more often than not had only bad news. In that sense he was not disappointed when his wife passed the phone to him, mouthing "Dr. Montgomery." He listened without replying for nearly a minute. When he did finally speak, it was in monosyllables.

"Yes." Pause. "No." Longer pause. "Right. Right. Yes."

His wife was looking at him quizzically, apparent concern on her face—was there something wrong? Why was the doctor calling this late at night? "Are you all right?" she whispered. He waved his hand impatiently, shaking his head. This appeared to confuse her even more, and he had to place his hand over the mouthpiece. "I'm fine, it's nothing like that," he hissed, then motioned with his head towards the bedroom door. She reluctantly slipped out of bed and into a robe and slippers, while he listened to what Montgomery had to say. She left, closing the door quietly behind her.

"Thanks a lot, Monty," the D.A. said, wondering if Montgomery detected the sarcasm in his voice. Probably not. "Yes, of course," he went on. "If she follows through with this, I will handle it." He glanced at the door to make sure he was still alone. "But I'm warning you, Monty, this had better not go any farther. If she persists in this, it will be up to you to deal with it. Understood?"

He hung up, no longer in a good mood. In fact, his mood was perfectly lousy. He may even have to suggest that Montgomery up his "donations" a bit. Even at the risk of alienating him? That was the problem with dealing with Montgomery. He was just not easy to push around. The D.A. had a sudden thought—he hoped this wouldn't affect the medical appointment with Montgomery that he had coming up. He was a hell of doctor, no denying that. If only he weren't such a pain in the ass.

Strange Birds

Maggie was walking down the wrong slip, a row over from where the houseboat was tied up. She was carrying a slim book, checking out every boat like a door-to-door evangelist ready to knock, salvation in hand. LaFleur was not used to visitors; in fact, he didn't actually mind the proselytizers who occasionally made the effort to come all the way down to the boat. He wasn't sure how they knew someone lived there; he assumed that once it was known, there was some sort of network that spread the news. He always told them politely that he appreciated their efforts, but that his semi-lapsed Catholicism was really all he needed.

He belatedly realized that he may have given Maggie vague and misleading directions, and so walked out onto the boat and called out to her. She looked up and waved, then made her way back to the main walkway and down to his boat. She held up the book as she got closer, but he still couldn't quite make out what it was. He guided her up the gangway, each making their hellos. As she stepped onto the boat, taking his arm with her hand to steady herself, he saw that the book was the Oswego High School yearbook, *The Paradox*. He just caught the date on the cover as she stepped up: 1960. He quickly calculated that as the year Angie had graduated.

LaFleur graciously steered Maggie down to the forward salon (the galley and dining area was central, bedroom aft), offered her a drink—which was refused—and responded good-naturedly to Maggie's inevitable first-timer questions about the houseboat as he showed her around: it's so much bigger than I imagined; do you ever take it out? It has a real kitchen! *Should I offer to make her dinner sometime?* he thought. After a few minutes of this they both seemed to tire of it, so he steered her back to the couch and asked to look through the yearbook. Maggie seemed relieved at the unburdening of the obligation to provide Angie's personal details. She remained silent at first, only occasionally responding to LaFleur's questions with a simple yes or no, or an "I don't know" when it came to anything really relevant. LaFleur turned the pages with increasing frustration. As they perused the book LaFleur saw that Angie was very active in sports, as he remembered reading in the article. Captain of the bowling league, Girl's Athletic Association Vice-President, archery club, a recipient of the GAA "Emblem and Letter" award, and a stand-out in that year's Junior-Senior softball game.

He turned to the Senior Class section, looking for her class photo. When he got to the right section, Fs and Gs, he looked over the pictures, but evidently not seeing hers, flipped to the next page—no, already into H—so Maggie reached over, turned the page back and pointed out her picture to him. Angie had posed for her graduation picture in a dark, unrevealing sweater, a modest string of June Cleaver imitation pearls around her neck; all-in-all a not unattractive girl. She had worn her hair fairly short in the style of the late fifties. "*A small kid with a sweet disposition,*" said her yearbook slogan. The picture next to hers was of a suave-looking kid, pompadour hairdo, a sly grin on his face. He had written his own slogan under his picture: "*Man is the Hunter – Woman is the Prey – Good Luck – Joey.*"

After they had looked over the Glee Club group photo for the fourth time, Maggie was eventually forced to fill in some post-high school information. Fresh from nursing school at nearby Crouse-Irving in Syracuse, Angie had come back home to live in Oswego in May of 1964. In order to save money, she had moved back in with her parents and had easily gotten on at Oswego Hospital working as a surgical nurse. Both Maggie and Montgomery knew her from Syracuse—Montgomery had taught a couple of basic courses there the first summer Angie was in school, and Maggie recalled Angie from a couple of classes, though being in different years, there were only a few general courses that they both could have taken at the same time. She remembered Angie as a particularly quiet girl, embarrassed when called on in class even when she gave the right answer.

Maggie asked if the offer of a drink was still good. LaFleur went to the galley and opened a bottle of a local New York state vintage called *Eye of the Dove*, a light red, the name of which enchanted Maggie. He brought back a glass for each of them.

As they returned to idly paging through the book, not seeing anything more directly related to Angie, Maggie's recollections became a little more personal. Even after three years away at Crouse, Maggie said, Angie's outgoing nature and easy smile had put her back in the swing of things in a short time. According to Maggie, it was as if she had never left home. By the time she returned to Oswego, however, she had shed many of her high school inhibitions and was starting to expand her horizons. (Maggie was starting to sound like an old "This is Your Life" narration, LaFleur thought as he repressed a grimace.) As Maggie recalled, she had even updated her old-style glasses with a "mod" look. Not quite Twiggy, but an improvement. She had played softball that summer on the Portside Tavern team as pitcher (no shrinking violet position), and had joined the local bowling league. She did a lot of fishing; on the river, in Oswego Harbor, or up at Sandy Pond, a favorite spot a few miles north of town on Lake Ontario. Being an "avid fisherman" (mentioned twice in the obituary, he recalled) was not anything unusual for a woman, then or now—a brown trout record catch, twenty inches, had been set just that summer by a 13-year old girl from Oswego. In spite of this, Angie's aptitude for sports, her short hair, and her friendship with other girls with similar interests invariably led to the type of rumors that always seem to follow "tom-boys," even in 1964. Maggie insisted that there was never any basis to the rumors, that she had a boyfriend, even. She continued to be a bit coy in her response to LaFleur's continued probing into Angie's love life, so he shifted gears momentarily, waiting for the right moment.

He prompted Maggie for more family background. Did Angie have a good relationship with her parents, had they welcomed her home or was she an imposition? Did she have brothers, sisters? He wanted some sort of baseline he could use to evaluate her standing with her family as well as in the community and at the hospital. The Frascatis were an unusually quiet Italian family, she responded. Most evenings were spent at home watching television, Wednesday was midweek Mass, and sometimes Friday if her work schedule allowed. Sunday was early morning Mass at St. Joseph's (Maggie's church as well) followed by a traditional Italian dinner in the afternoon. Angie's father, Joe, was a reserved, neat man, a foreman at the shipping yard, who spoke softly without a lot of animation and hand-waving. Angie's older brother and older sister had also lived in Oswego. Angie saw them frequently, and they were regulars at her weekly softball games. Her sister Mary Elizabeth occasionally joined her on one of the regular fishing expeditions with their father, and once in awhile a brother tagged along. Angie out-fished them all. Her father and mother would be long dead by now, she said. The brother she knew of had died a few years ago. She didn't think any other family still lived in Oswego or know if any other close relatives were still around.

"And what about boyfriends?" asked LaFleur casually, circling back.

"In high school? Maybe." *Should I mention that she used to go with Tommy? No, she decided.*

"What about in the hospital?" LaFleur asked. "A lot of suicides, at that age, are related to relationship issues; unrequited love—or too intensely 'requited' love, if that is a word—misunderstandings, mistaken feelings, overblown emotions. Was Angie seeing anyone?"

Maggie sighed resignedly. Le Fleur picked up his notebook.

"There was someone. A doctor."

LaFleur had a sudden intuition. "Someone still at the hospital?"

"Yes."

Waves slapped quietly at the side of the boat. LaFleur looked out the window at a cormorant perched on the railing. *Where did that come from?* he wondered idly; this was not their normal range. Looking back at Maggie, the image of a different bird flashed into his mind; the storm-petrel, harbinger of trouble. He poured them each another glass of wine.

*

"Angie was always a little naïve," Maggie continued. "I guess that's what got her into trouble, more than anything else."

"What kind of trouble?"

"Well, first of all, Angie was having an affair with Dr. Mahoney. But there were rumors that she had also been involved with—"

LaFleur interrupted before she could say what else Angie was up to. "Mahoney, you said? Which one?"

"Paul Michael."

"The same one who was called to the lounge by Nurse Gale?"

"Yes. The anesthesiologist." She hesitated. "It went bad. He was married." Maggie shook her head in disgust. "*Doctors*," she said.

LaFleur made a note and asked the logical next question. "Was Angie pregnant?"

"I don't think so."

"But she could have been?"

"Maybe. But I don't think so." Maggie looked away.

A note to follow up on this went into the pad. "So the Billy Joel song has it wrong, huh?" he continued, trying to lighten the mood. Maggie gave him a blank look. "'You Catholic girls start much too late,'" he prompted. She didn't seem to get it, or else she did get it and didn't like it. She scowled. Maybe he was being too casual here; sometimes it paid off if it created a temporary rapport.

"Oh. Right," Maggie finally said. "We didn't all 'start much too late.' Maybe we should have. Started later."

He had a feeling that the Mahoney affair was going to be a key part of this story. He pressed her for more. "I don't think we can dismiss this so easily, especially given what you just told me. Sounds like it was very serious, both for Angie and for Mahoney. There could very well be a connection."

"Oh, I don't know," she temporized. "She was confused and upset, maybe, but not suicidal. She had no trouble talking to me about the affair. She had been conferring with her priest. I still don't believe there was any real concern there. At the time she died, it was completely over, according to her. It ended Dr. Mahoney's marriage, actually; but I believe Angie had already resolved her side of it. At least that's the impression I got from

Angie."

"All right, we'll work under that premise," he conceded for the moment. "Lots of women go through the same thing, and are not necessarily suicidal." He glanced down at the notebook. "Well, then, what else?" he said. "You were about to say earlier that she had been involved with someone else?"

"Well. It was after she died mostly, that the rumors got worse," she said quietly. "There were a lot of things that..." She stopped, obviously reconsidering. "I'm not sure how to say this without giving it too much importance. Once in awhile there would be some slight made against Angie, the kind of petty vindictive thing that people sometimes indulge in, rumors about her being, well, involved with other girls. Other nurses. Older nurses, even. No one *ever* took it seriously. I think it was mostly jealousy, and maybe her being so good at sports and all."

LaFleur pondered this. "True or not, that could have had quite a bad effect on her, don't you think? And how do you know that no one took it seriously? That kind of thing could be devastating, if she took it harder than you seem to believe. Combined with everything else. It sounds like what you're saying is there may have been indications, after all. Especially if she was already troubled by the affair with Mahoney."

Maggie bit her lip, a habit LaFleur had already recognized as a tell; Maggie was not being entirely up front here.

"Let's not go into it now, okay?"

LaFleur wasn't sure how to respond to this. He could not remember ever having had a harder time following the thread of a story. This was turning into a riddle within a puzzle wrapped in an enigma, or however that went. "Tell me more about the thing with Phil," he finally said, changing the subject.

There was the usual hesitation. "How much do you know about it?"

He hesitated himself now, unsure of how much she knew, how to extract the most information from her; he didn't want to lead her. "Ruled an accidental death. And after he died, the burglaries stopped and no more Demerol went missing. The police investigation was dropped soon after. That's one of the things I want to know more about."

"I don't know anything about that, the drugs, I mean. And I don't really know much about the burglaries, either."

"Well, then, just tell me what happened to Phil. How did he die?"

"He was…it was…um, during…routine surgery at the hospital."

Is she holding back? Just when he thought they were getting somewhere, she gets coy again. "Yeah, I know that much. And it doesn't sound all that routine. If you die during 'routine' surgery, I mean."

Maggie shook her head. "No, you're right. It wasn't routine. I mean it *was* just routine surgery—an appendectomy—but it was being done outside of normal procedures. Some deal Montgomery and he had made. Montgomery was doing it for free. I found out all this later, I didn't know anything about it at the time. Before we all heard about it, I mean."

"So Montgomery himself did the surgery?"

"Yes."

"Anyone else involved?"

"Paul Mahoney did the anesthesia."

LaFleur could barely refrain from shaking his head in frustration. He briefly wondered why she hadn't mentioned any of this earlier. At least some consistent threads were starting to appear. "But how did he die?" he repeated patiently.

"That's what I'm trying to get to. Near the end of the surgery, he apparently started showing signs of extreme distress, had some sort of seizure, and just died. We were told that it was something called 'malignant hyperthermia.' It's a pretty rare reaction to anesthesia, no one knew too much about it at the time. It's fairly well understood now—it's actually genetic, so it's possible to be tested if there is any reason to suspect you are 'carrying'—if there were ever any adverse reactions to anesthesia in a family member, say—and there are treatments now. Then, there was no treatment; all you could do was wake them up. Not a good option, obviously. Anyway, that's what we were told at the time. It sounded like a reasonable explanation, unusual, maybe, but we were in no position to question it."

"Who first told you?" he asked, trying a new tack.

"Angie. There was a lot of confusion over what had happened." She picked up the high school annual and starting turning pages, stopping occasionally to hold the book closer, as if trying to identify individuals in fuzzy group photographs. He read along upside down. Chess Club. Latin Club. Spanish Club Fiesta Night. Schools didn't have many clubs anymore, he had heard. Kids were all too busy with their private dance lessons, or bassoon, or some other strange thing he had never heard of before. One of the detectives said his kid was in Feng Shui classes, which LaFleur thought was great until he found out that it wasn't a martial art but some sort of new age home decorating mysticism. *Couch goes here, table over there, how hard is that?* Maggie still hadn't looked up from the book or said any more about Phil's hemorrhagic—no, hyperthermic—reaction. LaFleur chafed at the procrastination but remained silent.

Maggie finally put down the book, laying it carefully on the coffee table. He noticed that it was now open to Angie's class photo. Maggie pointed to the book. "The only other person in the room at the time was Angie. She was the scrub nurse."

He looked at her without betraying the fact that he already knew this. "How soon before Angie's suicide did this happen?"

"About three weeks."

"Was there any connection made at the time between Cathcart's death and Angie's suicide? I still need to find the record of the inquest, by the way. Among other things."

"No, no one at the time had any reason to think there was any connection," Maggie said.

"How did Angie react to Phil's death?" LaFleur asked, wondering if she had intentionally answered the previous question ambiguously.

"Badly. Well, it wasn't Angie who reacted badly as much as it was Paul. Along with everything else that was going wrong, with the affair and all, for some reason Paul was taking the blame. Or there was an attempt to force the blame on him, I should say. Angie got caught in the middle of it." Maggie bit her lip again, then sat back; obviously this was all she was going to say about that. LaFleur took a deep breath, realizing that he had unconsciously dropped into his old interview mode and she hadn't seemed to respond to it all that well. *Maybe I need a new approach. Shouldn't be this hard.* He hoped he hadn't said any of that out loud. He penciled in one last entry in his notebook.

"Let's drop that for now," he said, resignedly. "This is a lot of new information." He went on in yet another different direction. Sooner or later, he thought. "I didn't press you on this earlier, but after what you've just told me, and with everything you already know about what happened, I have to ask: why do you really want me to do this investigation?"

Maggie's gaze didn't waver, but LaFleur heard a slight catch in her breath before she answered.

"You know," she began, "the term 'closure' seems to have gotten a bad rap lately, maybe from all the pop psychology you hear these days. People like Dr. Phil or Dr. Laura are always telling you that you've got to have closure on everything, from a school shooting somewhere in Colorado to, oh, I don't know, the loss of your pet goldfish. Sorry, I don't mean to sound cynical— especially since I know that in spite of the pop psychology, the need for closure can be real. I've seen it, many times, in patients, in families, nurses. Even doctors. And I feel it now." Another slight catch in her throat caught her off guard and she stumbled on her next words. "I'm retiring soon—did you know that?"

"No, that hasn't come up."

"Well, I am, the first of the year. And now this article showing up, well, the timing has to be intentional. Someone has been waiting to bring this all out, and with me leaving…it just seems like it's brought up a lot of feelings for a lot of people around here that I thought had been well and truly buried. For me especially. Feelings of helplessness, or remorse, or whatever that feeling is that wakes you up in the middle of the night sometimes, wondering what you could have done differently. And feelings of guilt. A lot of guilt."

"Guilt over what?"

"A lot of things. Then and now." She self-consciously straightened her shoulders. Looked LaFleur in the eye. Made up her mind. "I can trust you, right?" He nodded agreement. She went on in a voice that would have calmed the waves. "This can't leave this room, as they say. Or should I say 'can't leave this boat.'" She

101

smiled weakly, then went on. "I was, um, having an affair. With Dr. Montgomery."

He was surprised at this, but not shocked. Surprised, and unexpectedly disappointed, until he put it into perspective—young doctors and nurses playing "doctor and nurse"—not so unusual. And it happened a long time ago, he told himself quickly.

She went all quiet again, sipping her wine, maybe waiting for a reaction. LaFleur knew better than to say anything that might interrupt this new confessional mood and waited for her to continue. Just when he thought he had misplayed it, that she wasn't going to say anymore after all, she dropped another shoe—the third, he thought, but he was starting to lose count.

"There was another, um, a different kind of trouble, that I got into. I knew that I was being too smart for my own good, and that made me act stupidly, if that makes sense. We were so young and stupid. Angie was only twenty-two, for God's sake, and I was only a couple of years older. But we should have known better. I should have known better."

Maggie shifted in her chair, discomfort settling around her eyes like an invisible haze. She squinted as if trying to clear it away, while LaFleur was trying to see what the connection to Angie was here. If there was one, it could be a big deal. Bigger than the affair. A long pause followed; LaFleur sat back quietly.

"Illegal abortions," she finally said quietly. "Performed at the hospital, after hours. Under the table, cash-on-the-barrelhead, money straight into the doctor's pocket. I assisted." LaFleur didn't trust himself to comment, only nodded his understanding.

After another unhelpful squint, and a breath of resolve, Maggie continued. "I want you to know, I'm not proud of this. I thought there were good reasons." She corrected herself. "Well, at first I wasn't sure what was going on. But as I came to understand more, I convinced myself—I let him convince me—that there were good reasons. In those days, you know, doctors had a lot of influence, or a different kind of influence. You don't see it as much these days. Thank God. But it was very hard to resist. I still should have known better. About a lot of things."

She looked out the window. "You know, there's another line to that song you mentioned earlier. 'Only the good die young.'"

It was several hours and another bottle of *Eye of the Dove* later that Maggie finally left the boat.

In the Confessional

She sat down in the booth, making the Sign of the Cross automatically. She faltered part way through, however, suddenly recognizing the priest's voice as they concluded, "...and of the Holy Spirit." It was Father Thomas. Tommy. She had somehow (how could she have) forgotten that he was hearing confessions now, he being new to the church, and she not thinking that he would be here, hearing confessions. She always confessed to the old Father. *This was Tommy.*

She closed her eyes in confusion. How could she confess to Tommy? Her thoughts became a jumble of the things she had planned to confess mixed with the bits and pieces of her Catholic training as she tried desperately to figure out what she should do; passages she had learned from the Rites of Penance; lessons and recitations, the Rite of Reconciliation, all ran through her mind at once. These rules, these precepts, these sins. Her fornication, the knowledge of sinful practices at the hospital that she was condoning by her silence, her breach of trust. *But this was Tommy.*

"Bless me, Father, for I have sinned," she managed to gasp.

She sat there a moment in silence, and then realized she hadn't finished properly. "Uh, it has been, uh," she stammered, "four weeks since my last Confession." She sat still again, waiting. The priest (*Tommy!*) began reading a passage of scripture in preparation. She closed her eyes even tighter.

No, this is not Tommy, she told herself in a sudden revelation. *This is not even Father Thomas. This is a vessel of God, God's voice on earth.*

With a sigh of relief that must have surprised the priest behind the screen with its heartfelt vehemence, she began. It would be the first of her many confessions to Father Thomas, God's vessel, her friend.

Med School Confidential

Michael had agreed to meet LaFleur at the hospital to give him a tour and the promised crash course in anesthesiology. LaFleur had been sitting near the reception desk at the hospital for about forty-five minutes. He assumed Michael must have gotten hung up somewhere, and was about to leave when Michael finally showed up, politely apologetic. A surgery had gone long, the patient had an unusual reaction to the anesthetic, other complications he didn't really want to go into, and so on. LaFleur waved it off as Michael led the way back upstairs to change out of his scrubs.

As he followed Michael into the elevator he thought over what he wanted to talk about. He'd been reading up on the Internet about anesthesiology, those sites he could get into without registering, anyway, so thought he had at least a place to start. Fascinating stuff. Some things had surprised him. Some of the common drugs, Pentothal, for example, he was familiar with, but in other contexts; others were either completely unknown or had raised questions he needed answered, particularly as they related to the circumstances of the suicide. He also planned to use the opportunity to get into some of the other aspects of the case he found unsettling that Maggie could not—or would not—discuss, as yet. He'd need to be careful about what he said, and how he said it, but that was something he had always been good at. He wondered how much Michael knew about Maggie's past.

Just as they came out of the elevator and turned toward the physicians' changing room, Dr. Paul Michael Mahoney came around the corner from the opposite direction, and they all nearly collided.

"Oh, hello, Paul. Sorry," Michael said.

"No problem," Mahoney said, as they backed away from one another.

Michael quickly introduced LaFleur and started to explain what he was doing there, but Mahoney already knew all about it. "I know." He turned to LaFleur and said, as if challenging LaFleur to deny it, "Maggie said you were looking into the story about the nurse who died in the sixties."

LaFleur didn't flinch. "Yeah, that's right. Did she mention that I'd like to talk with you?"

"Yes. Yes, she did mention that, as a matter of fact."

"Great. When would it be convenient for us to meet?"

"Well, that's a good question. I'm not sure when I'll be able to find the time, actually."

"Oh? Well, I promise I won't take that much of your time. Just a couple of things I'd like to get straight about what happened when you found her."

"I didn't find her," Mahoney said. "Martha Gale found her." The flatness in his voice was less than encouraging.

LaFleur tried to moderate his own tone of voice so as to not come on too strong. "I just meant what happened when you got called to the scene. I would like to establish some of the details surrounding the scene; who was there, exactly what was done."

"I'm sure Maggie has told you all that."

"She has given me some idea, yeah, but I'd really like to get your description of what happened. She was not even there at first, was she?"

Mahoney looked over at Michael, then back at LaFleur. "I really don't have anything to say about it." He turned and walked away.

Michael called after him, annoyed but not particularly unsurprised by his abruptness. "Hey. Wait a minute, Paul!"

"Nothing to say," Mahoney called over his shoulder, leaving them standing in the hallway.

Michael shrugged, then turned and made his way down the hall to the locker room. LaFleur followed. That didn't go too well. He really needed to talk to Mahoney.

As they approached the changing room, another doctor was coming down the hall, obviously in a hurry. Michael stopped him.

To LaFleur's surprise, it turned out to be Dr. Paul Matthew Mahoney. He thought again about the fact that here were two doctors who had both been at the hospital at the time of Angie's suicide, and who were still here, after forty-some odd years. All of them still here, he thought: Montgomery, Maggie, the Mahoneys. Remarkable, really. Even more remarkable in light of what Maggie had been telling him recently.

After another quick introduction, Michael approached Dr. Mahoney with an observation on their recent meeting with his brother. "We've just had the strangest encounter with Paul Michael, here in the hallway."

"Every encounter with Paul Michael is a strange encounter."

"This was stranger than usual. It was about the suicide of the nurse, back in the sixties."

Paul Matthew raised his eyebrows and closed his eyes in what looked to LaFleur like mock exasperation. "Don't tell me, Maggie has been after you too?"

Michael frowned. "Has she said something to you about it?"

Mahoney opened his eyes. "To me, and to Paul Michael, yes. She practically accused us of planting an old newspaper article in the OR. Yesterday afternoon after the staff meeting. Said you had found this article and were asking a lot of questions about it."

"*I* was asking…wait a minute. *She*'s the one asking the questions. I don't know what's going on. And then just now…"

The changing room door opened and a priest walked out. "Paul, Michael, how are you tonight?" he said brightly, stopping in front of them in the hallway.

"I'm Paul Matthew, Father, and I'm fine," replied Mahoney, apparently not realizing that the priest had been addressing both him and Fuentes. The priest started to protest that of course he knew who Paul Matthew was, but Paul Matthew ignored him and nodded in Michael's direction. "Fuentes, here, though, I'm not sure about him."

"I'm just fine, Father, thanks," Michael said, then quickly turned to LaFleur and started to introduce him to the priest. LaFleur, however, had already reached out to shake the priest's hand. "Father, good to see you again."

"Oh, that's right," Michael said, "of course you two know each other."

Father Thomas Manetti—"Father Tommy," as everyone knew him—shook LaFleur's hand vigorously. Tall, good looking, with sandy hair turning gray, but so subtly that it was scarcely noticeable (he joked that his hair was in a permanent state of grace), the Father was both well known and well liked around town. A local boy made good, Tommy Manetti had been a bit of a hell-raiser in high school, nothing serious, pranks and fast cars, mostly. It had been his mother's dying wish that he go into the priesthood. To everyone's surprise, that's exactly what he did, entering the seminary right out of high school. His mother died a happy woman. Tommy had never left town again after coming back to Oswego to serve at St. Peter's as an assistant. He was still there now, the senior priest, any youthful transgressions long forgiven and forgotten, but he had never lost his youthful spirit. LaFleur had not seen Father Manetti for years; he had known him both from St. Joseph's and through the Father's work in the precinct; Father Tommy spent a lot of time with the prisoners over at the jail.

"Detective LaFleur. Well, a long time, long time."

Dr. Mahoney leaned toward the priest and pointed in Michael's direction. "Say, Father, Michael was just asking me about Angie Frascati's suicide." Father Tommy stood there expectantly.

"Maggie's been concerned about it," said Michael finally, "and someone, I don't know who..."

"That was a sad day, sad day," Father Tommy said, as he clasped his hands behind his back and looked up at the ceiling. To LaFleur, it looked a bit like an affectation, perhaps Tommy's way of claiming the moral high ground, but it was endearing all the same. He had more reason to suspect that the slight Italian lilt to Father Tommy's voice was something of an affectation as well. Had he ever even been to Italy? "But a long time ago, a long time," the Father was saying, "and, sad to say, a long time forgotten. Forgotten by some," he finished gravely, "but not by me." He turned back to Michael. "So, I understand you've received some information about this, Michael? And that our friend Detective LaFleur has agreed to look into it?"

109

"That's right, Father. Although I don't have any idea why it's come up out of the blue like this. All I know is that a copy of the obituary has been left in my OR several times—well, I guess you could call it an obituary, it's a newspaper clipping, about half police report and half obituary…"

The intercom speaker in the wall hissed and popped with an announcement: "*Father Manetti. Father Manetti. Please come to the third floor visitor's lounge. Father Manetti.*"

"Sorry, Michael, you'll have to tell me about it later. I'll be doing rounds again tomorrow, starting at two." He stopped a few steps down the hall, and looked back at them. "Don't forget to come see me, now, Michael, don't forget. Goodnight, Paul Matthew. And good to see you again, Detective." He turned and walked away with a practiced ministerial stride.

As the priest turned the corner, Michael looked over at Paul Matthew, who had been standing there taking this all in. He tried again. "Well, anyway, Paul, this thing with Paul Michael a few minutes ago…"

Paul Matthew slipped on the coat he had been holding at his side. "I've got to run, Michael. And whatever Paul told you, that's probably all he's going to tell you. And I can't say I would really blame him."

"But… he didn't tell us anything. And he was there, wasn't he? How could he not know anything about it?"

"Sorry, I really have to go. Grandkid's in some kind of Halloween play, or Celebrate Fall play, or some damn thing, I don't think they're allowed to do Halloween anymore, anyway I can't miss it, she's been telling me about it for days. Later." Paul Matthew rushed off to see a six-year-old dressed as a pumpkin, or a wood sprite, or whatever politically correct embodiment of the pagan rite the school board had approved this time around.

Michael shook his head in an unspoken apology as LaFleur followed him into the locker room, saying he'd take a shower when he got home. He suddenly stopped in the middle of the room, looked back at LaFleur and motioned to the locker next to him with his head. A piece of paper, a photocopy, was taped to his locker door.

"'*Apparent suicide,' DA says*." Same article, but with one

difference. This time, the word *Apparent* was highlighted in florescent orange, brilliant even in the dim locker room light.

*

Michael scraped a chair around to one side of a dilapidated Formica table in the corner of the room. He sat down heavily. LaFleur slipped off his coat and hung it on a chair across from him with a practiced ease. Reminded him of the interrogation rooms at the old station; same yellow light, cracked and stained floor tiles, off-color walls. Back offices, locker rooms, basement stockrooms; there was a homey comfort about rooms like this that LaFleur had always liked; it was a rational nostalgia, a cultivated idiosyncrasy. Like living on a houseboat.

"Where do we start?" he asked Michael.

"What do you want to know?"

"For starters I need enough to make sense of whatever Mahoney can tell me about what he found at the scene."

"Based on that encounter a few minutes ago it doesn't sound to me like he'll tell you anything."

"Oh, he'll talk to me. Just need to work him around to the idea that it's in his own interest. Trick of the trade."

"If you say so."

"Oh, you'll have to help me get to him. Maggie, too, probably. But in any case, there are things that as an anesthesiologist only he would know; and I need you to tell me what those things are. I don't know enough about it at this point to ask an intelligent question." He reached behind him and pulled his notebook out of his coat; searched around for a minute looking for a pencil. He looked at Michael impatiently. "Don't wait for me." He finally found a pencil in his shirt pocket.

"Well, what general anesthesia does, obviously, is to put someone into a deep enough state of unconsciousness that just about anything can be done to them, both without pain and without the risk of extreme shock. It's a state that is physically pretty close to death, actually. Low rate of respiration, slowed heart beat, low blood pressure. Then you have to bring them out of it safely. That means that respiration has to be maintained at the same time the

111

anesthetic is suppressing the respiratory system, along with the rest of the nervous system. This is done with a combination of oral drugs and injections, like muscle relaxants, and various anesthetic gasses. Oh, and oxygen, all carefully monitored.

"Any major differences in how anesthesia was administered between then and now?" he asked.

Fuentes wasn't sure how to answer that at first. "Well, it's pretty much the same theoretically; some gases we don't use anymore—cyclopropane, methoxyflurane, trichloroethylene. Some of the older gases are still used occasionally, halothane, for example, and of course nitrous oxide. The machines themselves weren't as sophisticated then; no oxygen analyzer, less control over some of the delivery systems."

"What's an 'oxygen analyzer?'" LaFleur asked.

"A fail-safe device. Oxygen sensors alone don't prevent the system from possibly delivering a hypoxic mixture. There are different types of oxygen analyzers, but a good system can monitor the O_2 and nitrous mixture simultaneously. Without it you could theoretically turn on one hundred percent nitrous."

"But there would have been nothing like that failsafe system in 1964? The anesthesiologist was on his own? There would have been no automatic shutoff or anything like that."

"Nope," Michel agreed. "Seat of the pants. Well, not quite that bad, but more difficult in some ways. Simpler in others. From the description we have, it sounds like a very basic system was what was used in the lounge. A couple of cylinders, a regulator, valves, hoses. A mask. Also simple because it was portable."

LaFleur looked up from his notebook. "What gases would have been set up in that machine?"

"Typically? Nitrous. Maybe cyclopropane or halothane. A question for Mahoney."

LaFleur nodded. "If she was looking for kicks, what would she have used? As opposed to intentionally killing herself."

"Nitrous. Some other drugs act as hallucinogens, but nitrous is the easiest and safest high. And someone who's not an anesthesiologist would probably not know what else would give you a good high. There's a long history of recreational use of anesthetic gases, by the way. People have been playing around with nitrous oxide since the 1700s. And one of the inventors of modern anesthesia, a dentist named Wells, was a chloroform addict. He sort of went off the rails, for a variety of reasons, really, but it ended up with him being arrested in a state of delirium after throwing acid on a prostitute. He killed himself in jail. Anesthetized himself using a bottle of chloroform he had brought in with his personal effects, then slit his own femoral artery with a straight razor."

LaFleur blanched a little at that in spite of himself. "Guess it's a good thing it's hard to smuggle drugs and razors into prison these days. Well, not that hard," he amended, "but apparently harder than it used to be. Can you even still get chloroform?"

"Sure. Any chemical supply house. It's not used anymore in anesthesia, of course. Neither is ether."

"But recreational use isn't out of the question."

"Well, the timing doesn't fit with rec use; 'ether frolics,' we call it," Michael said. LaFleur decided not to ask if this knowledge was based on personal experience. "Sunday morning, nice weather," Michael continued. "She's alone. None of the right conditions. But not out of the question."

"So, she could have set it up herself. Turned on the gas. Maybe by accident, there's no oxygen, she loses track of what's going on, happy as a lark, except this time it's bye, bye, birdie."

"Could be, yeah."

This all went down in the notebook, even the bit on Wells and chloroform. Old habit, never assume anything is unimportant until you know you don't need it. Notebooks were cheap.

He reached back behind him, pulled the Xerox of the article from his coat pocket and spread it out on the table alongside the notebook. "All right. Maybe now we can go over a couple of references in the article, you can tell me what I need to know about them; what I need to know from Mahoney. First reference is here; *'Miss Gale opened the door to the lounge and found the victim sprawled on the couch with a mask from a portable anesthesia machine covering her face.'* What's the difference between a 'portable' and a non-portable machine?"

"Well, like I said before, fewer options in terms of the anesthetics that could be used, limited as far as the type of

113

procedures it would have been used for; simpler procedures, probably. But most machines are portable to some extent."

"Probably not important, then. Alright, next: '*a child's airway tube, generally used to depress the tongue, was protruding from her mouth.*' What's an airway tube?"

"This is something I've wanted to talk to you about. It's bizarre. It makes no sense, for a lot of reasons. One, the article confuses 'airway' with 'tube.' An airway is a sort of fancy tongue depressor—it's a solid piece of plastic with a curved section that fits up against the palate, and a bite wing at the outside to hold it in place. It's used to keep you from swallowing your tongue while you're unconscious. A tube, on the other hand, implies intubation, which is only possible when you are completely unconscious. In fact, it often requires that additional muscle relaxants are administered, typically succinylcholine, to relax the airway—the trachea—in order to intubate the patient. Can't do that if the patient is conscious, the gag reflex is too strong."

"So an airway isn't something you breathe through?"

"Not exactly." Fuentes got up and walked out to the hallway. "Hang on a second, I'll get one and show you what it looks like."

He came back in a few seconds with two small plastic packages. He tore one open and handed LaFleur an odd-looking device made out of translucent white plastic. LaFleur held it up—it was about four inches long and an inch wide, made up of two thin layers about a quarter of an inch apart, separated by a thin bridge. Just as Michael had described, had a "J" shape, with a flat section about an inch long, a flared end, and a smoothly curved main section. LaFleur had never seen anything quite like it.

"No, you're holding it sideways," Michael said. "Here, it goes like this." He took it and held it horizontally, curved side up. "The airway depresses and holds the tongue in place. But you can see how big this is. Same as a tube, you can't insert this into a conscious patient. Gag reflex has to be suppressed first."

"Then how could she have gotten that into her mouth?"

"She probably couldn't have, even if she wanted to—but that's not the issue. The issue is what is says there, that '*a child's* airway was protruding from her mouth.'" He picked up the other package and ripped it open, and held up another airway, identical to the first

114

but about a quarter of the size. "This is a pediatric airway. Too small to be of any possible use in an adult."

He handed both airways to LaFleur, who held them up side by side for a minute.

"Strange looking things. Even the little one would gag me. No reason to have it in her mouth, huh?" He slipped them into his coat pocket. "What will Mahoney have to say about that, d'ya think?" He paused as Michael apparently reflected on whether or not it had been a rhetorical question. "What do *you* think it was doing there?"

"I've been trying to figure that out."

"Would Angie have known what it was? For that matter, how much would she have known about anesthesia?"

"Well, as a surgical scrub nurse, she should have known more than average," Michael said. "Still, she could have known an airway was a standard part of anesthesia, but might not have really understood its real function. Hell, I've worked with surgeons whose total understanding of anesthesia is that the patient isn't screaming for some reason. That's more or less why anesthesia was invented, by the way, more for the doctor's convenience than for the comfort of the patient. But back to the airway—why would she use one at all? Maybe because she knew it did something to aid the delivery of the anesthetic agents, which she was presumably interested in optimizing; or maybe she had tried an adult airway and gagged on it, and so used one she could keep in her mouth."

"So if it *was* a first time deal, and if she wasn't quite sure of the details, then you're saying that she could have been doing whatever she thought was necessary to make it work."

"Maybe."

LaFleur pulled the airways back out of his jacket pocket, and held up the small one. "Without an airway—even this small one—which is what you're saying is effectively the case here since the pediatric airway is too small to be of any real use—would it still work? The anesthesia, I mean, since the airway wasn't there to keep the throat open?"

"With the mask, it probably wouldn't have made a big difference. It would have worked anyway. It would be helpful to know more about the exact configuration of the machine, or how the mask was positioned, things like that. The article isn't all that

115

clear on that. Sort of contradictory, in fact."

LaFleur looked down at his notes. "So, here's what we still need—one, find out if she knew anything about anesthesia; two, find out what gases were turned on."

"Right. And we should try to find out more about her condition, when she was found. Position of the body, other factors—had she vomited, for example. She could have choked."

"Like a rock star who's O.D.'d," LaFleur said.

"Right. Or was it simple asphyxiation, brought on by lack of oxygen? That kind of thing would be essential to know."

"There's something else in the article that doesn't make any sense," said LaFleur. "Why was—here, give me the article for a minute." LaFleur held the article in front of him and read from the middle of the page: "*A hospital official revealed that the anesthesia machine, which had been placed in the hall outside the nurses' lounge, was turned on when the victim was found.*"

Michael frowned as he tried to make out what he was getting at. "Yeah, we knew it was turned on when—" He stopped and sat back in his chair. "Wait a minute. What…"

"…was the anesthesia machine doing outside of the lounge?" LaFleur finished his thought for him. "Not too big to go through the door?"

"Don't think so."

"Let's go look at the room again," LaFleur suggested, as he slipped the article back into his coat pocket.

They walked out into the hallway and made their way down to the small hallway that branched off just ahead of the doors of O.R. #3. They started into the hall, but were stopped by a pile of construction debris. The contractor had already started to strip out the interior walls of some of the rooms in preparation for demolition, and had left a stack of wood trim and a tangle of copper wiring right in front of the door. Michael stood at the doorway turned to LaFleur as he pulled a pen out of his pocket. "Got something to write on?" LaFleur handed him the copy of the article. Michael held it up against the wall and sketched a rough drawing on the back of the photocopy.

"Main hallway, O.R. here and here," marking each, "this hallway, and the door into the lounge," gesturing to his right at the end of the dark hallway, "and based on the descriptions we have, the machine must have been sitting right next to the couch. There is no way it could have been outside the room." He scribbled a box at a spot outside the door on his diagram and handed it to LaFleur. "Doesn't reach."

"And Mahoney—it was Mahoney, right?—had actually passed by the lounge that morning, and he didn't see anything unusual?" LaFleur asked. "Other than that the door was locked?" He tapped at the diagram with the tip of his finger. "And wouldn't it have been a slight bit unusual for an anesthesia machine to be sitting in the way, right by the door?"

"Well, yeah. You'd think so."

"Would the machine have been making any noise, you know, psssht-psssht?" LaFleur asked, feeling a bit silly.

Michael shook his head. "That's what a ventilator sounds like, sort of. No, an anesthesia machine wouldn't have made much noise, just a faint hissing sound, maybe."

LaFleur took the drawing from Michael's hand. "I don't think we know how the machine got outside the lounge; that might be nice to know, but I think we can ignore it as being significant."

He stopped and looked around, then pulled the article out of his coat pocket. "It says that the gases were turned on when she was found," he said, pointing to the passage. "There's something there that I'm still not getting."

Michael agreed. "I've been thinking about that, too," he said slowly. "That is really key. We have to know what was turned on in order to know what might have actually killed her."

"Explain," LaFleur prompted.

"Let's assume the simplest and most likely case, nitrous and oxygen together. Going back to what I said earlier, with no automatic analyzer in place you have to balance the anesthetic with oxygen—O_2 levels have to be kept above 30%. If both tanks were full, and both running wide open, say, the oxygen would have run out first—nitrous is denser—so it could conceivably have been an accident. If only the nitrous was turned on, of course that would have killed her, but in that case it's hard to see how it could have been self-administered, recreationally."

"And oxygen by itself is harmless," LaFleur offered.

"Oxygen by itself would have been fine, no danger—well, pure oxygen can cause some problems long term, or if used under pressure—scuba divers using enriched air have to compensate for oxygen toxicity—but, no, no real problem."

Michael had a sudden thought. "If both tanks were full," he said, considering, "they should have lasted for hours. We need to know how much was left in the tanks when she was found."

"And we need to know who turned them off," LaFleur concluded. "It says here only that it was 'a physician,' so that appears to point to Mahoney. He was supposedly the first person on the scene, right? After Gale, that is." As an afterthought, he added, "But it also says this information was revealed by 'a hospital official.' That's *not* Mahoney. Maybe how that machine got moved is important after all."

They turned to leave. "By the way," LaFleur said without turning around, "I saw something interesting on the Internet today. What can you tell me about curare?"

*

Back home, LaFleur looked again at the rough drawing Michael had made.

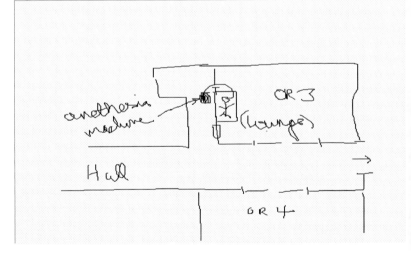

The handwriting was surprisingly legible for a doctor, even

considering the conditions in which it had been done. He had also drawn in the small glass-brick window in the small hallway, the one he had pointed out that was just above eye level. Too high for anyone shorter than LaFleur or Michael to look through easily. And the couch was on the same wall, next to the window. That would explain why no one had seen anything inside the room even if they had passed by, it would have taken a special effort. The couch was out of the line of sight of both the hall window and the window in the door. But to get to the door, you would first have to pass by the anesthesia machine. Unless it wasn't there earlier, and had been moved later. Which was really the only thing that made sense. Who moved it, when?

He pushed the drawing away in frustration and went back through his list of everyone who had been working at the hospital at the time of Angie's death. There were the Mahoneys. LaFleur couldn't help but think that there were some deep-seated animosities there, and so far no one at the hospital, including the Mahoneys themselves, had done anything to contradict that feeling. Apparently around the hospital they barely spoke to one another. Paul Michael Mahoney, the older brother, had been in med school just a couple of years ahead of his brother Paul Matthew. Paul Michael had become an anesthesiologist, which by some reversal of a normal older/younger sibling rivalry had made him the target of scorn of his younger brother, a surgeon. Well, surgeons typically had a pretty high opinion of themselves. LaFleur had repeatedly asked Michael to talk to Paul—Paul Matthew? no, wait—Paul Michael—again, to convince him to talk to LaFleur about the scene at the lounge that day. And then there were the even trickier shoals to cross; bringing up a forty year old love affair was not something he was particularly anxious to do, but there were quite a few things that could only be answered by Paul Michael Mahoney. Had he moved the machine? After turning off the gases? What gases had been set? Who else was there, who would have had access to the machine when she was found? Too many unknowns. But these were the key questions. If they could determine exactly what had happened in the immediate aftermath of the discovery, before the anesthesia machine—and her body— were moved, maybe they could draw some reasonable conclusions

119

about what happened in the hour beforehand. Mahoney had to know something.

Then there was Franklin Montgomery, of course. Montgomery was an odd duck, if he could trust Michael's opinion, and by this time he was pretty sure he could. Michael said he had known from the first day he met Montgomery that he was one of those doctors who were in it for only two things: money and prestige, and woe betide anyone who blocked his way.

Montgomery effectively ran the entire hospital by proxy, even now, as he had for years. Nominally the head surgeon, he was actually more of an emeritus; he rarely took on anything other than the simplest cases these days. He just didn't have the stamina anymore, even if he still had the skill. He was not particularly liked by the staff and was mostly feared by his underlings. Still, he had been respected by his former peers (and still was by those few remaining), even if grudgingly. He had always been given free reign by the various administrators over the years, based not on his personality but on his undeniable competence as a surgeon and diagnostician—and their willingness to let someone else shoulder the heavy issues. Rarely proven wrong about anything, in or out of the O.R., he did not waste the advantage that gave him, and so was able to maintain a nearly uncontested state of authoritarianism for over forty years. Not unimpressive in its own way.

Of course, Michael had said, Montgomery was also very good at keeping the "money river" flowing—look at what he was doing at the hospital—an unheard of expansion for a hospital in a town this size, LaFleur was sure. He wondered just how much of that river Montgomery had dipped into over the years, and was he still dipping into it? Approaching Montgomery about Angie's death was going to be tricky. What was his actual involvement in all this? Michael had promised to arrange a meeting.

And then there was Maggie. What to think of Maggie?

He looked out the porthole. The cormorant was back.

Body Check

Maggie called the next day with the news that Mahoney had agreed, very reluctantly, and only after a tag team assault by both Maggie and Michael, to meet with LaFleur that afternoon. There were conditions. The "interview" was to cover strictly medical issues directly related to the day Angie was found and the actions taken by the staff that day. There were to be no questions concerning any personal relationships, either past or present. LaFleur agreed. He knew how to get the information he wanted, conditions or no conditions. He had been doing this a lot longer than Mahoney.

"You understand that I agreed to speak with you only under duress," Mahoney began, looking across his desk at LaFleur belligerently. "However, there is little or nothing that I can tell you outside of what was very clearly stated in the article you have."

LaFleur barely heard the protestations. He was taking in the body language. Mahoney was signaling with nothing as obvious as crossed arms or body twisted to the side, but even without a baseline, LaFleur could easily sense the attitude: shoulders slightly broadened (or was it just the suit? no, didn't look like a Brooks Brothers); head slightly tilted back; hands down on the desk. *I don't have to do this, but I am anyway, so don't expect me to cooperate.*

LaFleur settled into a more comfortable position and smiled, pulled an earlobe, and tilted his head to one side: *I'm a likeable guy, you don't intimidate me, and you will give me more information than you expect.*

"Since you mention the article, why don't we use that as a starting point? Any idea who has been leaving these lying around the hospital, and why?" He pulled a rather tattered copy of the article from his inside coat pocket.

"Not a clue."

"Okay. Well, then, I'd like to ask you a couple of questions about the article."

"Fine." *Not fine at all.*

"Says here that the head nurse found Miss Frascati, then called you. Is that right?

"Yes."

"What time was that, exactly? The article is a little vague on that point."

"Vague? No, it's not; it has the time right there."

So he had looked at the article recently.

Mahoney gestured for the article, curling two fingers towards LaFleur's chest. "Let me see that." He took the page from LaFleur with an impatient gesture. "Here. It says clearly that she was found at 8:15 a.m., and then goes on to say, right here, that 'the charge nurse, upon finding the body of Miss Frascati, immediately called Dr. Paul Mahoney.' What's so vague about that?" He tossed the article back to LaFleur.

LaFleur turned the article around and looked at it for a moment, as if trying to decide that Mahoney was right, then conceded to him that, yes, that is clear enough, he supposed. Always give a little first.

"So you were called to the scene 'immediately,' and when you got there you turned off the anesthesia machine and pronounced Miss Frascati dead. What gases had been turned on, and at what levels? How full were the tanks?" He had learned something from the session with Michael.

"I don't know."

"You don't know? Weren't you first at the scene?"

"Yes, I was."

"And the machine was hooked up, running, as it says in the article?"

"Yes. But in all the confusion, I guess I didn't notice the exact setup—I remember glancing at it, but it must not have really registered, because later I couldn't say exactly what it was." Mahoney had the sense to look embarrassed at this.

"Then what would have been set up on that type of machine, typically?" LaFleur asked, not willing to drop it yet.

"Nitrous, oxygen. Maybe Halothane."

"You turned them off?"

"I don't remember turning them off."

"But you may have."

"I may have."

This sounded pretty lame to LaFleur, at first. This guy was an anesthesiologist, and he didn't notice what had been set? Didn't even remember if he had turned off the gases or not? Then again, it would have been quite a shock, especially given the circumstances. That could certainly explain it. They had just broken up, after all, a messy situation all around, as he understood it; and now to find her in that state, well, yes, shock and confusion were understandable. Maybe even if they hadn't been involved. *Give him the benefit of the doubt?* The alternative explanation was that he knows something, may even have been the one to shut the gases off, and is lying about it. LaFleur had certainly seen it before. But he wasn't ready to jump to either conclusion just yet. He flipped a page in the notebook; more to come.

"So, what then, some sort of resuscitation was tried?"

Mahoney for the second time looked disconcerted. "Well, no. She was extremely cyanotic, cold. Any attempt at resuscitation would have been pointless."

"So, no CPR, no medical procedures, no, oh, I don't know, no adrenaline, no other medications, nothing?"

"No."

LaFleur pressed this. "Why not?"

"In my judgment there was no reason to attempt resuscitation, as I just explained. There are situations in which it is obvious that there is no hope. It is not as if she had fallen in freezing cold water or that there was some other extenuating circumstance that might have indicated the possibility of resuscitation. I know that those types of seemingly miraculous recoveries get a lot of media attention, but in this case there was just nothing to be done. It was, again, obvious."

"Any vomitus?"

"No."

"What about the airway?"

"I don't recall."

"The article specifically states there was a 'child's airway tube' in her mouth. Any idea why there had been an airway in her mouth? In particular, a child's airway?"

"No."

"Wouldn't that have been quite unusual? I mean, from my understanding, a pediatric airway would have been pointless. And a normal airway would have been very difficult, maybe impossible, for her to use, right?"

"Yes."

"But you don't recall if at the time you made any particular note of that."

"No."

Several notes went into the book, short notes to match the one word answers. *Getting nowhere here, which in itself could mean something.*

"What did you think had happened?"

"At first I didn't know what to think."

"At first? So what did you think later?"

"That she committed suicide. What else was I going to think?"

"You never had any doubts that it was suicide?"

"No. Of course not."

"Not even at first?'"

Mahoney shifted in his chair. "No, not even 'at first.'"

"Do you have any idea why she might have wanted to kill herself?"

"No."

That sounded forced. *How to get anything out of this guy?* "No suspicions that it could have been recreational, and that it had gone bad?"

"Angie wasn't the type." Dismissively, LaFleur noted.

"What was the position of the body when you got there?" LaFleur continued.

"She was lying on the couch."

"How?" LaFleur asked. "Disheveled? Straight? Arms at her sides? Head back? What? I'm trying to get a description of the— scene." He had almost out of pure habit said "crime scene." He continued, "It says here she was 'sprawled' on the couch."

Mahoney sighed in what seemed like exasperation. "As far as I remember, she was lying...I don't know, 'quietly,' I guess I would say, obviously, but maybe...composed." His body language was confusing, here; he was twisting away with his body, but leaning forward at the same time, a cross between denial and pleading, LaFleur thought. He was obviously showing some discomfort. "What I mean is that she was lying normally on the couch. Her arms were crossed over her body. I don't know what 'sprawled' means, it could mean anything. She was just lying on the couch." Mahoney became visibly more agitated as he described Angie's final resting place, almost rambling now, as opposed to the curt answers he had given up to this point. "I don't see what is so difficult to understand. She was lying on the damn couch, okay?"

"Okay, never mind," LaFleur moderated. He made a quick note, and then looked up. He was giving more than he wanted to here. "Where was the machine located?" he asked.

"What do you mean?" Mahoney responded. "It was in the lounge, next to the couch."

LaFleur frowned inadvertently. "Well, this says not. It says, in fact, that, and again I quote, 'the anesthesia machine, which had been placed in the hall outside the nurses' lounge, was turned on when the victim was found.' How is it that when you got there, it was not only turned off, but was back inside the room?"

"That's just wrong. It was in the room when we found her. It got moved out during the course of ...taking care of things. The newspaper just confused the before and after."

This presented an opportunity. "There's something else that concerns me, something not mentioned in the article at all," LaFleur said. "You had passed by the lounge earlier that morning, isn't that right?" he asked, leaning forward.

Mahoney's physical reaction was subtle but revealing, his entire body involuntarily stiffening before he regained control. "How did—?" he started to ask, then reconsidered, apparently realizing LaFleur must have had access to the official report. "Yes, that's right. As I stated during the inquest."

"What time was it, exactly, that you were at the lounge?" LaFleur asked.

"I don't know, *exactly*, sometime before eight."

"And you noticed nothing unusual?"

"I went past the lounge that morning, the door was locked. That's it." Mahoney crossed his arms.

LaFleur decided to bypass this particular issue for the moment, planning to come back to it later. "All right, well, that helps clear up a couple of questions." *It hadn't.* "There are just a couple of other things I'd like to ask, if you don't mind."

"That all depends on what they are."

"Well, one has to do with the death of the pharmacist. That was, let's see," he thumbed back a few pages in the notebook, "just about three weeks before—"

"I thought we were clear on that. I'm not going to discuss it. That matter was investigated at the time, and the matter was closed."

"All right, it's probably not important. I just thought it could have something to do with why Miss Frascati committed suicide. Since it had happened only a few weeks earlier. Had there been any problems between the two of them?"

"How should I know?"

"She was the scrub nurse that night, isn't that right?"

"Yes, that's right. But again—"

"Were any disciplinary actions taken?"

This drew a resentful glare. LaFleur backed off slightly

"All I'm trying to do is establish whether or not this could have had any bearing on Miss Frascati's state of mind at the time." *And yours, for that matter.*

Mahoney appeared to accept this. "Only in the sense that any unexpected death, for any reason, can be upsetting. However, given the fact that this was totally outside of anyone's control—"

LaFleur interrupted again. "So, no blame assigned?"

"No. It was malignant hyperthermia. No one could have foreseen it. No one was blamed."

This did not jibe with what Maggie had said the other night. Mahoney was covering up the conflict with Montgomery. Which was interesting, given the repercussions Maggie had described. *What else was he covering up?*

"You were fairly close to Angie—isn't that right?" he asked, disregarding his prior agreement to leave personal issues aside. This drew a silent and even more ominous glare from Mahoney. "Weren't you in fact having an affair?" LaFleur pressed.

There was no need to interpret the body language Mahoney displayed as he stood and forcibly pulled LaFleur up out of his chair and out of his office, closing the door behind him.

*

LaFleur walked down the hall in a daze. *Goddamn. What went wrong there? What didn't go wrong there?* would be the better question. He had let himself get distracted. Obviously he had already antagonized Mahoney with the question about the pharmacist, before asking about the affair with Angie. He had planned to use a bit more finesse. He was sure as hell not going to be able to rely on Mahoney for any more information. Not soon, anyway. There were maybe about a dozen questions he had left unasked, much less answered. The autopsy. The gases. No, he had asked that one, much good it had done him. The police investigation; what had they asked, who had they talked to, what had Mahoney told them that day? *Damn.* He would just have to try to get another shot at him somehow.

As he turned the corner on his way down the hall to Michael's office, he slowed with the realization that maybe he had learned more than he had first thought. There is always information, just had to reduce the signal-to-noise ratio. Or maybe in this case, there was information in what hadn't actually been said. He needed to look at the inverse, look at it like an Escher drawing, find out what was hidden in the border between the ducks and the sky.

He stopped and leaned up against the wall. He thought about taking out his notebook, but didn't want to look any more conspicuous than he already was. He was going to have to write this all down, but that would have to wait. In the meantime, try to figure out what he could salvage from the interview with Mahoney, and hope there was something that might open up some other avenue with Maggie. As he went over the conversation in his mind, he was able to identify several new pieces of information. Unfortunately as soon as he came up with each point, he

127

immediately came up with a corollary. The boundaries were ragged.

One: Assume Mahoney did not turn off the gas. Corollary: someone else got to the scene before Mahoney, another doctor. Who was it, what did he do there, and who else knew? Two: Mahoney was definitely covering up. Corollary: What and for whom? The relationship with Angie? But that had become common knowledge. Three: Mahoney had passed by the lounge earlier that morning, had seen and heard nothing. Corollary: Oh, hell, maybe there wasn't one. He started back down the hallway muttering to himself, unconsciously counting his steps. No one paid him any attention.

*

Michael waved LaFleur into his office as he was finishing up a phone call, pointing to a chair as he came in. As soon as he had finished, he turned to the detective and asked how it had gone. LaFleur hedged; he would rather not say, not until he had a chance to go over his notes. Maybe, he suggested, they could all get together later—he, Michael, and Maggie—and talk it over?

Michael called Maggie's station. She agreed, and they made a date to meet at the bar at six. LaFleur had another stop to make on the way; one of the ward secretaries was going to take him down to records storage to get the autopsy report.

"You busy? Right now, I mean?" LaFleur suddenly asked.

"No, not at the moment," Michael said. "Why?"

"Oh, just haven't had a chance to talk to you again about where you think the article came from. It's been bothering me. You still believe it's not Maggie?"

"No, I'm pretty sure it's not her," Michael insisted. "She would have tipped her hand by now. She's not that good at subterfuge. And pretty much says what she thinks. If she were the one behind this, I think we'd know it."

"Yeah, that's my impression, too," LaFleur conceded. "But someone must be pushing her, too, then. Who? Who could possibly have anything to gain by opening this up again?"

"You've got me."

128

"And why you?"

"If we knew that…" Michael started to say.

"…we'd know why," LaFleur finished. "Yeah, we've been here before, I know." He glanced out the window, then turned back as if just thinking of something. "How long have you been back here?" he asked. "In Oswego, I mean."

"A little over five years."

"Here the whole time, right? At this hospital?"

"Yeah. Came here straight from the Dominican Republic."

"Oh, yeah, you told me about that. What brought you back here?"

"My father. He was diagnosed with colon cancer, so I came back to see what I could do. Turned out to be inoperable. Don't know for sure if his G.P. ever recommended a colonoscopy, or if my father just ignored him if he did. My father was like that. Old school. I've stopped blaming myself for not thinking of it sooner. There was probably nothing I could have said earlier anyway that would have made a difference."

LaFleur smile grimly. "Sorry to hear it."

"Thanks. I had originally thought about going into oncology, actually. Changed my mind when I got to the D.R. There wasn't really a chance to pursue it there. Not that they don't do oncology—they are not as far behind as a lot of those islands down there—but they do tend to need more general help."

"Why did you go into anesthesiology?" LaFleur asked.

Michael looked thoughtful before replying. "Maybe because it allows you to provide service across the board, no matter what the specific medical problem. I like being able to cross specialties like that, and feel like I'm more useful that way, I guess. Also more opportunities to do charity cases. I get a lot of 'referrals,' I guess you could call them, from the Father."

"Father Manetti?" LaFleur asked. Michael nodded. "You know him well?" LaFleur went on.

"I've known Tommy almost all my life," said Michael, "an old friend of the family." He chuckled. "I'd say he's like a father to me if it wasn't such a bad pun."

"You did say it," LaFleur laughed. "Has he said much to you about what we're doing? Shown any interest in it?

"Oh, no more than I would expect, I guess. Why?"

"Um. Nothing. Just wondering." He abruptly changed the subject. "Why the Dominican Republic?"

"They needed the help."

"Lots of places need help. Why there in particular?"

"Well," Michael hesitated. "Hmm. A personal relationship, if you must know."

"Oh, I must, I must." LaFleur said, hoping Michael got the movie reference, pleased when he saw that he did get and had laughed along. LaFleur paused for what he thought was a polite span before doing some more prying. "Any girlfriends here?"

Michael smiled enigmatically. "Nope. No girlfriends."

"Well, we've got to get you out more often, I can see that right now."

*

There was almost no one in the ward offices when LaFleur finally made it down to look for the postmortem. He searched around a bit before coming across one of the few occupied offices, which fortunately had the name tag "Francine" attached to the door frame. "Francine?" LaFleur asked.

"Yes, that's right." Francine said, looking up. She was twenty-something, attractive in a way that momentarily reminded LaFleur of his daughter; not a girl you would notice the first thing in a crowded bar, but once you had seen her, could not stop looking at. It had gotten his daughter into trouble more than once. He hoped Francine knew how to deal with it.

He introduced himself as the friend of Dr. Fuentes who was "looking into" the incident in the lounge. Francine knew all about it, both the incident and LaFleur's recent involvement. LaFleur hoped she had not formed any preconceptions; she might be a good source of unbiased information. "I want to thank you for taking the time to do this," he said warmly. "You must have better things to do than dragging an old police hack around, looking for forty-year-old records."

"Not really. Today has been pretty slow. This makes for a change, you know? And it's such an interesting case, don't you

130

think?"

"Sure is. Glad it won't be too much trouble."

They made their way to the basement of the old 1910 area of the hospital, the wing shortly to be demolished. There were rows of open cages lining one wall, made out of wooden frames and chain link fence material, each with a framed wire door in the center.

LaFleur stopped suddenly, looking over the other direction. Francine had continued walking a few steps before she noticed.

"Detective LaFleur? Something wrong?"

LaFleur stood looking across the wide hall at a metal door standing half open, red paint flecked and chipped, and a faded sign attached to the center, below a dirty window: AUTOPSY. Through the door he could see part of a long stainless steel table illuminated by a bright overhead light.

"Hang on a second." He walked over to the door and pulled it open; he didn't go in, just stood looking for a minute. The stainless steel table had a gutter around the edges, and took up practically the whole room. There was a spring scale hanging near the table with a large tray attached to it. The walls were typical institutional green, not quite olive, not quite teal. There was a large discolored drain in the center of the room, just below the table. A stainless steel sink stood in the corner, with both faucets and hose connections; a hose was coiled and hanging on a large hook next to the sink. Looked the same as it had years ago. He had been in here only a few times. Had never liked it. Didn't go to autopsies unless he had to, unlike some of the others he knew. He was never sure why they did it if they didn't absolutely have to. Eighty, ninety percent of the time you got everything you needed from the postmortem, and could always follow up with the coroner, or the doctor, with any questions. He never knew exactly what he was looking at during an autopsy anyway; other than a few easily identifiable pieces—heart, lungs—it all looked much the same to him, slippery, odd-colored, rubbery-looking lumps, layers of stringy red muscle, yellowish fat, unidentifiable things poking out everywhere. Thank God for skin.

Based on the newspaper article, he remembered the autopsy had been done the same afternoon. Maybe that was more common

131

in those days; now the bodies sometimes sat for a day or two before the autopsy was done, even in a small town like this. Not that there were that many to do—not like this was New York City or even Syracuse—but it usually took some time to get to them. Maybe he could find out from Montgomery, when he got a chance to talk to him.

He finally turned away and caught up with Francine. "All right. Let's find that report."

In just a few steps they came to a cage with a crude metal sign attached, identifying this cage as the "Archive." Francine sorted through a ring of keys, their jangle echoing into the dark recesses of the basement.

"Okay, here we go." She unlocked the door and swung it open. They stepped in, LaFleur standing back to one side while Francine started shoving boxes around.

"Wait, let me help you with that," he said.

Francine pointed to a stack of document storage boxes, all labeled *Postmortem*. "Stuff from that long ago is probably at the bottom of that stack." He moved them a box at a time while she checked the labels.

After a few minutes of moving things around LaFleur stopped and sat down on a box in the corner of the cage, slightly out of breath.

"Ok, here's something, it's marked 1963-64," Francine said.

"That should be it, all right." La Fleur went over and hoisted the box up onto a short stack and pulled off the lid.

"Yeah, these are from '63 and '64. '64 in the back. March, April...here it is, September." He pulled a green folder out of the box and started flipping through it. After a minute he stopped and turned to Francine. "Are you sure this is all of it?"

"Yes. This is the only place it could be. Why?"

"Well, there is nothing in here for that week of September. There's something from the first, then the tenth, nothing in between." He paused. "Ok, what about August?" He was thinking about the pharmacist. They must have done an autopsy. He pulled out his notebook to check the date: August fifteenth. He looked in the box. Nothing there.

"Maybe they're out of order," Francine said helpfully.

"I don't think…," he said as he continued sorting through the box. "Wait, here's something." He pulled out a single pink sheet. "What's this?"

Francine looked over his shoulder as he straightened it out. It was a copy of the autopsy order: *Angelina Frascati, age 22, September 5, 1964.* Signed by the coroner and someone he assumed was a hospital administrator. A small notation at the bottom confirmed one thing, at least: *Dr. F. Montgomery, attending physician.*

"Ok, so this means there should also be a full autopsy report in here, right?" LaFleur asked.

"I guess so."

"Then why isn't it here?" he asked, rhetorically.

"Maybe they're not marked correctly," Francine said, helpfully.

They spent the next thirty minutes looking in boxes marked 1962 and 1965; nothing turned up.

LaFleur called a halt. "These are all for the dates marked on the boxes," he said. "The other records just aren't here." He paused. "Who has access to these storerooms? Just you?"

"Well, it's not as if these records are classified or anything. I keep the keys in my desk, but a lot of people know where to get them if I'm not here and they need something."

"Would there be copies somewhere else?" he asked.

Francine looked pensive—an attractive look for her, he thought absentmindedly—and then said, "I don't think so; everything should be here, unless it was marked for separate archive for some reason. But I really don't think so. We're getting behind schedule; all the stuff down here was supposed to have been gone through a couple of months ago, to see if we needed to keep it. But I don't think anything has been done yet." She sensed LaFleur's disappointment at not finding the report and had another thought. "Maybe someone else *would* have a copy; like the Coroner's office, or the District Attorney's office." Then she frowned. "No, those records are purged every fifteen or twenty years or something like that, so nothing there would be any older than that. Nope, this is everything I know of."

I'm getting too old for this, LaFleur thought. Or maybe he had said it out loud, given the perplexed look Francine just gave him. Not a bad look for her, either.

"Well, thanks, anyway. I won't keep you any longer."

*

LaFleur left Francine back at her desk and headed back towards the rear of the hospital; that would take him out on the side closest to the River walk. On his way he happened to pass by Paul Matthew Mahoney's office. Mahoney was at his desk going over some paperwork; the door was open. LaFleur had a thought about how he might salvage the fiasco with Paul Michael, maybe even get a second shot at it. He stopped and poked his head in.

"Sorry to interrupt."

Mahoney looked up. "No, not all, Detective…la…"

"LaFleur."

"Right. What can I do for you?"

"I'd like to ask you a question about your brother, if I may."

"Sure, come on in. Sit down."

"Thanks. Um, I had a rather, well, let's just say I had a meeting with your brother a little earlier today and it did not go very well. I'm afraid I may have offended him, which was the last thing I intended. I'd just like to ask if you could apologize for me. I left his office in rather a hurry." He did not elaborate.

"I don't see him that often, you know. We have not been close for years. We had a falling out over some personal issues, that was before he left town, and we have never really gotten back on the same footing."

"He left town? When was this?" *And why hadn't anyone mentioned it before?*

"Years ago. He moved down to Syracuse; had a practice there until fairly recently. He left very soon after the incident that you are interested in, as a matter of fact."

LaFleur was still trying to process this as Mahoney continued.

"It hit him extremely hard. First that episode concerning the pharmacist, um, Cathcart. No blame was put on Paul, in the end, in spite of some not so veiled accusations by Dr. Montgomery; but still, it seemed to affect him more than I would have expected. And

134

then the young nurse, committing suicide. There had been rumors before she died that they had been involved, which unfortunately turned out to be true. But even though that had stopped, it caused quite a problem. He soon started having…well, other problems as well, I don't need to go into it in detail. In any case, maybe I tried to manage the situation a little too aggressively, and he left. Fortunately he was able to rebuild his career, if not his marriage, so leaving that way turned out to be for the best in the long run. I was glad to see him finally come back. But like I said, things are still strained between us. He came back for his own reasons, not because of me." He ran his hands through his thinning, grey hair, showing LaFleur some of the exasperation he must feel.

"Has he ever said anything at all about why he thought she committed suicide?" LaFleur couldn't help asking.

This provoked a cross look. "Listen, I'll be honest with you," Mahoney said. "For a long time I thought he was hiding something; I still don't know the whole story. He may still be hiding something, I don't know. Probably is. If he is, I'm sure it is for good reason, and nothing that anyone else needs to know. What would be the point? Actually, I'm surprised he talked to you at all." LaFleur did not comment. He was still trying to put this all together when Mahoney continued.

"I think you need to forget about this whole thing," he said, looking closely at LaFleur. "Just let it go, Detective. Tell Maggie Malone that she has taken it far enough."

LaFleur now felt even worse about the way the encounter with Paul Michael had gone, which he hadn't thought possible. *Damn and damn again.*

"Well, when you do see your brother, tell him I owe him an apology," he finished lamely.

"Let it go, Detective. Just let it go," Mahoney said, going back to his papers.

*

LaFleur continued down the hall. He turned the corner in the back, past the emergency room entrance, and was almost out the door when he felt a hand on his shoulder.

"Detective." It was Father Tommy. "Do you have a moment?"

"Of course, Father." He came back into the hallway, and Father Tommy steered him into an empty family waiting room.

"It's about the young nurse who died. I never got a chance to tell you the day we met in the changing rooms, if there is anything I can do to help, that is. As I must have said that day, it has been too long forgotten, too long. I was friends with the family, good friends. Her father was a wonderful man. It broke him. It broke him badly. So please let me know if I can help. Please." At this, he grabbed LaFleur's hands and pressed them to his chest.

LaFleur was a little surprised at the priest's fervor. He gently removed his hands. "Of course, Father. And thank you. I just might need your help, the way things have been going lately."

"Yes?" Father Tommy waited expectantly for LaFleur to continue.

"Well, …" He sat down, followed by Father Tommy, and gave the Father a brief rehearsal of his afternoon—the missing autopsy report, the encounter with Paul Michael, his hope that Paul Matthew could set it partially to rights. He ended with an expression of his growing frustration. "This has become more difficult than I had first thought," he said, hoping the dejection he felt in his voice wasn't too obvious. "I haven't even come close to finding out who is behind the appearance of the article, much less why, and the more I try to find out the more confused the story gets. I'm not even sure where to take it next."

"I knew her, you know, quite well, in fact," the Father said unexpectedly. "In high school. We dated for awhile." Tommy laughed at LaFleur's surprised expression. "Canteens, football games, fishing, things like that." LaFleur's face gave away the relief he felt, and Tommy laughed again. "I haven't always been a priest, you know," he added mischievously.

"I hear she was very good at sports," LaFleur said self-consciously, trying to hide his embarrassment over what he was sure the Father thought he had thought.

"Yes, she was that. More than that, even for all the enjoyment she got from sports, she was at heart a very serious, very devout girl. And very loved, she had a wonderful family. But I'm repeating myself," he said, clearing the morose look from his face.

"So, how are you and Michael getting along?"

"Well," LaFleur answered, "fine, I guess. Just had a nice talk with him, actually."

"Good. He's a grand boy, isn't he?" LaFleur had never heard "grand" used like that in a sentence before. He had forgotten how much he liked Father Tommy.

"I didn't know you two were so close," LaFleur ventured.

"Oh, yes. Michael often says I'm like a 'father' to him." Tommy waited for either the polite laugh or the protest at the bad joke, but LaFleur just smiled.

"I had a chance to talk to Maggie about Angie, you know, a few weeks ago," Tommy continued. "No, more like a few months, I suppose, last summer, at our high school reunion." The Father sensed LaFleur's confusion. "We hold single reunions for multiple years, now that there are fewer of us."

"I never went to any of my reunions," LaFleur admitted.

"Well, you haven't missed much, honestly. I go for selfish reasons. Attendance at Mass is up for several weeks after every reunion. Catholic guilt can be a powerful motivator, you know."

"Yes, it can indeed," LaFleur agreed, not sure where this was going.

"Maggie seemed to be quite upset when I brought up the topic of Angie's suicide," Tommy said. "So I am especially grateful to you for agreeing to help look into it. Maggie is a fine woman, but tends to let some things go too long. I'm sure she appreciates your efforts tremendously."

"I'm doing what I can, Father."

"And Michael, he is the perfect person to help you with this. He has been a big help, I trust?"

"Oh, yes, definitely. But like I said, I really don't know where to go with it now."

Father Tommy raised his hands to his chin in a prayerful pose.

"Do you mean to tell me you haven't talked to Angie's sister yet?" he asked.

*

LaFleur walked down Bridge Street on his way to the 1850

House to meet Maggie and Michael. He started to cross over the bridge, then stopped and looked around. He still had some time to spare. He turned around and walked back to Second and headed south. He passed by the Oswego movie theatre, the only one in town, where the dilapidated old-style marquee announced the latest feature. He then turned down Utica and crossed the river on the pedestrian bridge.

Crossing the river, the numbered streets had changed from "West" numbered streets to "East" numbered streets. Outsiders complained about it being confusing, but growing up with it, LaFleur had never thought it unusual. After all, with the river as the dividing point, how hard could it be?

He soon found himself in a modest neighborhood of smaller Victorian-style houses in lower downtown Oswego. At the end of the next block he stopped in front of a modest house much like the ones he had been walking past; and sure enough, like nearly every other house on the block, it needed paint. This was where Angie Frascati had grown up.

He stood looking down at the sidewalk, spotted with the death masks of moldering leaves. A chill wind a' blowing, he thought. Something Maggie had said in passing last night on the boat stuck in LaFleur's memory. They had been talking about cars they had owned over the years; LaFleur said he had always wanted another '55 Ford, like the one he had when first on the force, until he found one for sale in Rochester and drove it around the block. Like driving a truck. No seat belts. Brakes like dragging a stick on the ground. Safe enough for a Harborfest parade, maybe, but not something he'd want to drive to Florida. Oh, yeah, no air conditioning. This had reminded Maggie that Angie was driving her dad's old '55 Victoria, but had been thinking about buying one of the new Mustangs that came out in late 1964. She eventually decided against buying the Mustang and opted instead to put new snow tires on the old Ford. This was the week before she died.

LaFleur thought ahead to the upcoming winter. The walk from E. Fifth up the hill to the hospital, the walk he had more or less just made in the opposite direction, the walk Angie would have made regularly, he mused, was pleasant enough in the summer, but upstate winters were brutal. Lake-effect snows are legendary in

Oswego. The streets stay snow-packed from November until the next April. Children grow up hearing stories of the snows of 1888, when three feet fell in twenty-four hours. At the end January the year before last, Oswego had gotten six feet of snow in 48 hours.

It may be a little unusual in other parts of the country to buy new snow tires in September, but not in Oswego. Ask any psychologist to describe the warning signs of suicide, LaFleur thought—buying snow tires will not be on the list. Buying a new car, if she had done that, maybe that could be explained away as irrational behavior. But something as day-to-day mundane and practical as buying snow tires? He turned and made his way back towards the bar.

*

Maggie and Michael were in the bar when he got there. A shot of Grouse was already sitting on the bar for him. He settled onto a bar stool after a quick hello and took a sip. He was still not anxious to report on his meeting with Mahoney. Maggie and Michael sat there quietly for a couple of minutes, then Maggie finally broke the silence.

"Well?"

With every ounce of restraint he had, LaFleur did not answer with, "Well, what?" or even worse, "deep subject." He just said "Yes, well." He took another sip of scotch. "Not one of my better interviews," he continued after a few seconds, "though in spite of asking all the wrong questions and antagonizing one of the few witnesses we have...had...I did learn some pretty interesting things this afternoon. I learned enough to start thinking about this thing as more than just trying to find out what the prank is; who left the article in the O.R. may turn out to be the least interesting thing about the whole deal, in fact." He pulled himself back from the brink of babbling and turned to them.

"I walked past Angie's old house on the way here. Not sure why. Maybe seeing the autopsy room in the basement made me a little morose, or something. Oh, no autopsy in the file, by the way. Francine insists that it should have been there, in fact we even found the original order." He pulled the pink sheet out of his coat packet and handed it to Michael, who glanced at it and immediately saw what LaFleur had seen. "Montgomery," Michael said, as he handed it to Maggie.

"But no autopsy," LaFleur continued. "I wouldn't have been surprised if all the rest of records had also disappeared—forty years is a long time to keep those things around—but all the other years were there. The D.A.'s office purges their records pretty regularly, according to Francine. So no autopsy. Since the police records were so sketchy, I had hoped that—oh, I probably forgot to tell you I found the original police report, a friend on the force found it for me, rather, but even the newspaper article had more details in it. There must have been quite a thorough rug-sweeping." He turned his glass around on the bar, staring into it, a liquid amber crystal ball. Nothing there either.

Michael was the first to respond. "Maybe Mahoney can help. He must remember something; maybe he knows something about the autopsy, or where it is…" His voice trailed off at LaFleur's dark look in his direction.

"Mahoney is done talking. To me, anyway. Well, I did ask 'Paul Two' to apologize for me, so maybe it's not out of the question. But I would be surprised if 'Paul One' will tell us much more, if anything. He did claim not to have planted the article."

Maggie leaned forward to see past Michael. "You said a minute ago that you were starting to think this was 'something more than a prank?' What do you mean?"

There was the same intensity in her question that LaFleur had heard from Maggie since the beginning, but now with more of an edge to it.

"Let's move to a table." He pushed back his stool and walked over to Maggie, helping her down. They exchanged a look. One of those looks that is supposed to speak volumes, but in this case it could have been just one page and still would have told LaFleur all he needed to know. He was sure of it, now. There was more to that newspaper clipping than he originally thought.

LaFleur started by putting off Maggie's question in order to go back over what he had learned that afternoon. He went into the meeting with Mahoney in more detail, laying out again the information he felt was significant. He described Mahoney's confirmation of his early morning visit to the lounge—no machine in the hall, door locked. There was some discussion as to what this really meant; could it have been as coincidental as Mahoney described? Maybe so.

Then there was the complete lack of information about what gases were turned on. Michael, not surprisingly, thought this was particularly bad news. And the implication that Mahoney had not been the first physician on the scene (if true), as had been assumed up to this point.

Both Michael and Maggie were taken aback by LaFleur's admission that he had been thrown out of Mahoney's office. But they agreed, after LaFleur pointed out that what he had heard from Paul Matthew, about Paul Michael's adverse reaction to the incident—by the way, LaFleur asked them, why had he not been told that he had left town right after her death?—that for now, at least, they should take whatever they learned from Paul Michael at face value. More or less.

Then LaFleur told them, fully anticipating the consternation that followed, that he had arranged a meeting with Angie's sister for the next day.

Blow Up

Thoughts of her conversation with Angie and her own pathetic situation were running through Maggie's mind as she worked through her shift. She felt like she was in over her head; rather, in the Mindanao trench dropping like a lead weight. She had arranged for another meeting with Montgomery as soon as she had come in that morning. She wanted to try once more to get this over with without having to resort to something drastic, something public. She had thought about going to the hospital administrator, but he was nothing more than a figurehead. Montgomery was running the show. Going to administration would do nothing but complicate things, and accomplish nothing. She wasn't even sure now what good going to the D.A. would do; looked at in the light of day that ploy was revealed to be as desperate as it really was. The day seemed to drag interminably.

She knocked at Dr. Montgomery's open office door late that afternoon; a quiet time in the surgical ward. Montgomery invited her in and offered a chair across from his desk, and even tried a little small talk. Maggie began by asking if anything had happened related to the burglaries.

"Why, do you know something?" Montgomery asked, turning the question back on her.

The nurse shifted uneasily in her chair, unable to answer. She needed an opening; all of her pre-rehearsed gambits had flown. She made several false starts, continuing to avoid the topic. Montgomery quickly sensed her desperation and turned it to his advantage. As their conversation falteringly continued, his disdain at times threatened to overcome his typical pose of self-righteousness, but he had had plenty of practice at this sort of thing, and managed to reassert his authority every time Maggie began to feel that she was making headway.

Maggie finally, if by now desperately, plunged ahead with a renewed threat. She said she had evidence of the illegal operations, records, times, dates, Angie would back her up on everything, and that unless…

She didn't get the chance to finish her threat before Montgomery cut her off. He flatly refused to acknowledge the after-hours sessions with Maggie were anything more than charity cases and totally discounted her claims of evidence against him. He was adamant in his self-righteousness.

In the face of Montgomery's recrimination and threats, Maggie somehow started to feel even more justified. She suddenly stood up and leaned over Montgomery's desk, fists balled. She didn't even remember most of what she said afterwards. It felt like a nightmare in the confessional, pouring out her soul not to her priest but to her inquisitor. Everything took on a sudden clarity while she was standing there, yelling at Montgomery. It was only after she began to shout that Montgomery finally became agitated. He jumped up from his desk and moved towards her, as if to physically restrain her. The door was closed, but the blinds on the windows were still open; a couple of nurses had already glanced in the direction of the office, not sure what was going on. Montgomery rushed to the windows, yanked the blinds shut and stood there, visibly shaken. Maggie had remained standing in front of his desk, shaking herself now. Montgomery turned back facing her and began ranting, showing a loss of control completely out of character. He went on non-stop for at least three minutes, railing about everything from the general insubordination of nurses to the incompetence of every other doctor in the hospital to the injustice of society in general and the subsequent burdens he carried single-handedly. He then threatened her job, but almost as an afterthought. At that he stopped and stood glaring at her.

At this break in his harangue Maggie blindly struck out again, as if inspired by his outburst. "I've had enough," Maggie nearly screamed. "I'm going to the D.A.'s office, and I don't—"

"You go right ahead," Montgomery yelled back. "You don't have any idea—" Then he suddenly dropped his voice, his shout in mid-sentence becoming a frightening whisper, as he stepped up to Maggie and grabbed her by both shoulders. "You will regret this," he murmured. "You have no idea how much you will regret this."

She pulled back in confusion, trying to break away, when he suddenly released her. She fell back, banging into the desk with her hip and knocking a small reading lamp off on to the floor. It seemed to make a horrific crash. It was followed by the crash of the door being slammed open, and Montgomery, now back in full voice, ordering her out.

It was hardly possible that anyone out at the ward desk could have made sense out of anything they had just heard, or had any real idea of what the blow up was all about. No one in the ward said a word as Maggie left Montgomery's office. No one even looked at her as she made her way to the elevator. The elevator door opened and she stepped in, not daring to look back at Montgomery, still standing in the doorway of his office, steadying his hands against the frame. He finally turned away and closed the door. No one came near his office the rest of the afternoon.

Sister Mary Elizabeth

It was a beautifully kept older house in Pulaski, east of Oswego a few miles and right off of interstate I-81. The narrow lap siding was painted a light blue, the trim and windows done in two slightly darker shades of the same blue. As LaFleur walked up towards the six-column portico at the front entrance, he noticed ladders and paint cans piled up alongside the house. He smiled to himself; so someone does paint houses in Oswego. It looked like they had just finished, and probably just in time; the weather wasn't going to hold much longer. He had a good impression already. He stopped for a moment on the porch before knocking, mentally preparing himself. The meeting with Mahoney had painfully reminded him how out of practice he had become; he didn't want to do anything that might offend Mrs. Guiterrez.

Father Tommy had explained how it was that the town had forgotten Angie's sister was still alive—two name changes and two moves, one to Buffalo, then the move back closer to home, but it had been more than enough to erase her from community consciousness, especially since she left Oswego very soon after Angie's death. He had not volunteered how it was that he knew of her whereabouts, and LaFleur, uncharacteristically, didn't feel like prying. Priests just knew everything; it came with the job.

He rang the bell; after a few moments the door opened, and Mary Elizabeth Frascati Menaggio Guiterrez stood looking out through the screen door at him. She was a small, well-kept woman wearing a black dress; she reminded him of the pictures he had seen of the seemingly ageless older Italian women walking down a cobbled village lane in Tuscany, or Umbria. He had calculated earlier that she would be about his age, maybe a year younger. He began to introduce himself as a friend of the Father's, but she interrupted him.

"Hello, Detective. Father Tommy told me you would be stopping by this morning. Please come in."

She led him into the house and offered him a seat on the couch in the living room—it would have been called the parlor when the house was new—then sat down in a faded wingback across from him. Coffee had been set out on the small table between them. Any thought of an easy interview was immediately abandoned at her first words.

"Angie did not commit suicide," she said. "Coffee?"

She picked up the pot and poured as he nodded. As he dropped in two cubes of sugar, she continued. "Her brothers knew it. My husbands both believed it, God rest their souls." She crossed herself at this statement. "Of course, Father knows it;" she went on matter-of-factly. "That is why she is buried in a Catholic cemetery; that would not have been allowed otherwise, not in those days. You know, that reminds me of something I haven't thought about in years. It was so strange." She paused, collecting her thoughts. "We visited the grave on the one-year anniversary, my parents, my brothers, I think also my aunt and uncle, I don't remember for sure. It was a beautiful day; weather even better than this, as I recall. In any event, when we got to the gravesite, there was a beautiful white floral arrangement placed at the headstone—lilies, carnations, white roses—beautiful. I assumed it had been placed there by my older brother, but when I asked, he said, 'no, it wasn't me.' Well, as it turns out none of us had placed it. We looked, but there was no card attached. We asked other family members after we got home, but none of them knew anything about it either. We never found out who it was." She stopped, picked up her coffee, then continued apologetically, "But I shouldn't be going on like this. Please, ask me anything you'd like."

LaFleur took a sip of his coffee. "Yes, well. That is interesting," he replied. He put the cup down carefully—it was china, not the usual heavy mug he was used to. "First I should say how sorry I am for everything you and your family must have gone through, and sorry for intruding like this." She simply nodded. "I suppose the Father told you how I came to be involved in this?" he said as he pulled his notebook out of his jacket pocket, along with a copy of the article. He showed it to her briefly.

"Oh, yes. The newspaper article. So odd that should suddenly appear again. I don't remember the name of the young doctor who found it."

"Dr. Fuentes. You wouldn't happen to know anything about that? Why someone might be bringing this up again? It has been forty years after all. That's an awfully long time."

"Not that long, really. Don't you often feel like there are things that might have happened just yesterday, until you suddenly realize that it's been ten, twenty, forty years? I don't really feel all that different, mentally, I mean, than I did forty years ago, do you?"

He had to admit that growing old had not been either as traumatic or as dramatic as he had feared. "No, you're right; a lot of the past just sort of slides together, somehow, without you knowing that time is really passing." He realized that she hadn't answered the question, but let it drop. "Well, I hardly know where to start. Maybe you can just tell me a little about what Angie was like. If that's not asking too much."

"Oh, no. I hardly ever have a chance to tell anyone what a lovely girl she was and how much we all loved her. But I suppose that sounds sort of silly."

"Not at all." He was moved by her simplicity of expression.

"Well, she was very quiet and could be quite shy at times," she continued, "but everyone who got to know her liked her a lot. She played at a lot at sports; softball, bowling—but you must already know all that." LaFleur nodded and she continued. "She loved being a nurse, she was very conscientious. And very devout."

"Any sign that she was in any trouble?" he asked. "With her friends, or at the hospital?"

"Oh, no. She could not have been involved in any wrong doing at the hospital. If she had known about anything, I'm sure she would have reported it. And she was hurt terribly by some of the accusations made against her."

"Accusations concerning what, exactly?"

"All sorts of things. There had been some sort of conflict with a doctor there at the hospital, or with some other doctor. I was never sure what it all was about. I believe she was protecting

147

another nurse who was having an affair or something. It was all dreadful, very confusing." She paused. "She wanted nothing more than to work at the hospital—she had some very good friends there—then, well, eventually settle down, marry, have children, keep a Catholic home. She wanted a simple life."

"Did she have a boyfriend?" LaFleur asked carefully.

"No, I don't think so. Afterwards," she added morosely, "there were some terrible rumors being spread about her." She raised her head and looked at LaFleur. "But there was nothing to them."

He could sense the plea in her voice for him to believe her; she must have suspected that he had heard of the rumors from Maggie and others at the hospital. But she gave no indication of having any doubt, herself, of their falsehood. He moved on to the key question.

"During this time," he said, again being careful to modulate his voice, "was there anything to indicate that she was despondent, any sign she would do anything drastic?"

"No, nothing at all," she said immediately.

"How much do you know about the death of the pharmacist," he asked, "and could that have had anything to do with Angie's— death?" Already, he was unwilling to use the word suicide.

"I don't know much about that at all. Except that after Angie got over the shock of actually being there when it happened, she was very relieved that all the police investigations and all that stopped. She was quite shaken by that whole incident. She saw a lot of Father Tommy in those days. He was—a Godsend." She smiled at her little joke.

"Yes, I imagine so." She seemed to have finished, so he decided to move on. "So about the article. There are some details I'd like to ask you about."

"Yes, that's fine."

He started with what he knew of how Angie had been found. He thought he would try to describe his own perception of what had happened, based not only on the article but also on what he had learned from Maggie. He hadn't gotten very far before she interrupted.

"Oh, no, that can't be right," she said. "She would never have had religious music playing on the radio. It's not something we ever listened to at home. I think it's more of a Protestant thing, don't you?"

"Possibly. So that was out of character?"

"Yes, definitely. She even made fun of it at times, you know, not meanly but in a funny way, if we heard one of the old evangelical programs, with all the shouting and carrying on and singing. Nothing like a proper Catholic mass. Though I think that was a little too strict, at times. I don't mind the modern mass. Well, maybe not the guitars. But she would not have had a religious program on the radio. I know that."

They quickly covered the basic details of how she was found. At first, Mrs. Guiterrez—she had not asked him to call her Mary Elizabeth—didn't have much to add, until LaFleur happened to read the passage concerning the lack of a suicide note. He was about to ask again whether or not there had been any indication at all, even the slightest doubt about it being suicide, when she interrupted.

"There was a note." She immediately shook her head at his raised eyebrows and widening eyes. "No, *not* a suicide note. There could not have been a suicide note, obviously. No, this was a note I found later, in the pocket of the uniform jacket she wore that day, sort of stuck in the corner of the lining. Just a minute, I'll get it."

She left the room, and a few moments later he heard muffled scraping and shuffling, as if she were in a closet. Then there were footsteps on a stairway, his curiosity growing as he listened to her walking around upstairs. There was more scraping, then the sounds of her coming back down. She returned holding a small piece of paper, folded in half.

"Here it is. I've had it so long; I forgot where I put it. I forgot I had it, really, until you read that other thing about a note. That reminded me. It's a note to Angie from Maggie Malone."

LaFleur took the note and unfolded it carefully. It was written in block letters. "'COME TO THE OR AS SOON AS YOU GET IN. URGENT. M,'" he read. "Any idea what this is about?"

"No, none at all. I'm not sure why I even kept it."

"Does Maggie know you have this?" *A stupid question.*

"No. I haven't seen Maggie since I moved away. And I really had forgotten all about it. Maybe my memory isn't so good after

149

all."

"And you think this note is from the day she died?" he asked. *A better question.* "How do you know that?"

"Oh, it was a Sunday. Angie was very fastidious regarding her uniforms. On Sunday, it would have been a fresh jacket. Oh, yes, it had to be from that day."

"May I take this? For now, anyway?" She agreed, so he folded the article up into sort of an impromptu envelope, slipped in the note, and slipped that into his pocket. He could hardly wait to hear Maggie's explanation.

He went back to the scene at the hospital as described in the article. She expressed her disgust at over how it had been handled. "Everything had been moved and cleaned up before the police were even called. So even if the police had tried to do a real investigation—which they didn't—there would have been nothing for them to go on." When it came to the question of the autopsy, she was able to confirm that it had been done—she had seen a copy—that the cause of death was listed simply as "asphyxiation," and additionally that Angie had not been pregnant. LaFleur made a note to check the reliability of the pregnancy test with Michael; in his experience, depending on how that determination was made—a blood test as opposed to a physical examination, for example—it may or may not have been conclusive. While making these notes, he realized he had almost missed something she was saying about the autopsy.

"I'm sorry, what was that again?" he asked.

"The autopsy. It was incomplete."

"How do you know? We have not been able to locate it."

"Well, we were very close friends with the funeral director. Enrico Abruzzo," she explained. "Close family friends for years. He came to the house the day before the funeral and told my father something, something none of us ever forgot." She stopped and stood up. "Let me show you something." She walked over to a china cabinet and opened a heavy drawer. After pulling out two or three photo albums and leafing through them for a minute or two, she found what she was looking for and came back over to the table. She laid two photographs down, side by side, facing LaFleur. They were two black-and-white photographic portraits.

"This is my father in 1963," she said, pointing to the photo on his left. It showed a well-groomed, handsome man of about forty-five, posing with an unselfconscious smile and a clear, direct look. She motioned to the photo on the right. "And this is my father in 1966." Barely two years after Angie's death, LaFleur thought as he looked at a face hardly recognizable as the same man: sagging eyelids, cheeks drawn and sallow, facial expression strikingly different; not even somber, it was simply flat. The eyes were vacant.

"What Mr. Abruzzo told him that afternoon destroyed my father," Mrs. Guiterrez continued, her voice lower now. "There were marks on her body, Mr. LaFleur. Marks that were not reported in the official autopsy. The autopsy done by the doctors at the hospital. 'Hematoma,' that's what Mr. Abruzzo said. We didn't understand. Then he told my father that they were actually needle marks."

She stopped for a moment, regaining her composure, which for the first time had started to slip. "My father tried in vain for months to convince the police to reopen the investigation, but they refused. He began drinking heavily. A year after this photo was taken, he was dead."

LaFleur didn't know what to say. She looked up at him, now clear-eyed and unemotional. "I would authorize an order of exhumation. Do you think you could get one?" she asked.

Well, I could tell her there's nothing left, he thought; *that the flesh has long since rotted off the bone; her clothes wasted away to a few ragged, dusty scraps; even hair and fingernails practically gone. Nothing left.*

"Yes, I think I can," he said instead.

The Dance

LaFleur sat at the 1850 House bar waiting for Maggie. He ran his fingers along the bronze skater's cape, now brightly polished by the many nights he had sat there musing over one thing or another: a stubborn case, family matters, life, the universe, and everything. He wondered how many lovers walking across that bridge in Budapest, or Bruges, years ago, had stopped to do the same. He swirled his Grouse in the glass, held it to his nose, remembering a day at St. Andrews in Scotland years ago, walking the greens with his wife, to the beach; he could not afford to play there.

LaFleur imagined that he had just stopped on the bridge next to the statue, Maggie on his arm, snow drifting around them like tiny cobwebs, catching in their eyelashes, when Maggie woke him by touching his arm; the real Maggie touching his real arm. It startled him and he jerked his hand away from the statue.

"Caught me daydreaming."

"Worked out a deal with Joe yet?" Maggie asked in reply. "You really should have it on your boat, you know. It's beautiful."

"Oh, one of these days I'll break down, or Joe will decide he's tired of looking at it and make me an offer I can't refuse."

"Speaking of offers that can't be refused—have you had dinner yet? I've wanted to try the new Irish pub on Water Street. Michael says it's pretty good, for a town this size, anyway. My treat."

"You know I'm too old and set in my ways to ever let a woman buy me dinner. We can go, but I'll buy."

"Oh, come on, A.C., this is the 21st century, remember? I said you can't refuse, anyway."

"Well, I'll compromise at Dutch treat." He set his face in what

152

he hoped was a stern but friendly cast. It seemed to work, and Maggie agreed.

"So you were all out of breath when you left me the message to meet you. Must be something pretty exciting."

"I was out of breath because I had just carried a bunch of boxes up to the storeroom. Getting the boat ready to pull out of the water."

"Oh, that's right. When does that happen, again?"

"Week from Friday. Then it's off to the land of oranges and blue hair."

Maggie laughed in spite of herself. "I thought you said 'orange and blue hair.' Styles haven't gotten that extreme yet, not even in Miami. I hope."

LaFleur took another sip of whiskey, and then realized Maggie didn't have a drink yet. Where was Joe? He was usually there before you could sit down properly. He looked around and saw him out in front. "Hey, Joe! Someone dying of thirst back here."

Joe looked around, laughed and waved. A couple of minutes later Maggie had a glass of *Eye of the Swan* sitting in front of her.

"That's better. Now we can get down to business," LaFleur said, pulling out the increasingly dog-eared notebook. He flipped it open to a page near the back. "Going to need another notebook if this goes on too much longer." He sat staring down at the page.

Maggie put her hand on his elbow. She could tell that he was reluctant to start for some reason. "What is it?"

He reached over and put his hand on top of hers. "You know, when you asked me to do this, at first I just went along because, well, I didn't have much else to do; and to be honest, I was starting to worry about my state of mind. Thought this might be a good mental exercise, even if it turned out to be nothing. Which I thought it would. Even after our last conversation on the houseboat, I wasn't convinced that there was anything to this except a weird coincidence. And someone trying to be cute by stirring it up again. I even suspected you of planting the article. Maybe still do," he smiled at her; fortunately she smiled back. "But now..." He patted her hand lightly, then picked up his drink. She waited for him to go on, giving his elbow a light pat in return.

He went back to the notebook. "Mrs. Guiterrez—Mary

Elizabeth, Angie's sister—is convinced that Angie's death was...something other than suicide." He hesitated for a split second, and then went ahead. "She's convinced—has been convinced since the day it happened—that it was murder. And while I have been resisting it, trying to find alternative explanations for everything that happened, after what she told me—if it's true—I can't help but agree with her."

Maggie felt as if she were going to split in two—there was at once a sense of vindication, the relief of having someone on her side, and at the same time the dread of finally facing up to it. It had been forty years—years that for her had passed slowly, painfully. She thought about leaving the hospital more times than she could count. But she had become comfortable on the path of least resistance. As long as no one pushed her too hard, it was easy, one foot in front of the other, the days come and go, the route never varies, and time passes. No different than anyone else; except for the fact that she was aware of it. And where would she go? What real difference would it make, a hospital was a hospital; an apartment a place to live. She had long ago given up on marriage, family, and had never been all that sure that was what she wanted anyway. The fact that it had never happened simply reinforced the belief that it was not what she wanted. Or so she rationalized, tripping down the path. Then the article appeared in the O.R.

"After she died," Maggie began—not first asking what Angie's sister had said that had convinced him—"I thought I would never forgive myself. I thought I had helped drive her to it. Or at least had not done enough to try to prevent it. There are some things I've left out of what I've told you, as I'm sure you know. I have been trying to be so careful, trying to protect myself, maybe. Or just trying to avoid thinking about it too much." She held up her glass to the light and rolled the wine around, creating little rivulets down the side of the curved glass. "What was it you said to Michael that night we first met here? 'Drink it, don't dance with it?'"

"Something like that."

"I haven't been dancing in a long time."

He wanted to pretend this was a romantic movie, take her in his arms, tell her it was all right, do all the things he thought he was supposed to do. He had never really been good at this sort of thing. He supposed that's why so many people in the end resorted to the movie clichés, at least it was something shared, something easily recognizable. *It should not be this hard. He didn't get this old for nothing*, he told himself; *if I've learned anything, it's that there is no use in holding back.* Easier said than done. He did it anyway. He put his arm around her; she leaned her head lightly on his shoulder, not enough to make him uncomfortable, but just enough to let him know that…well, to let him know. They sat like that for quite awhile, not saying anything.

*

"What did she tell you?" Maggie asked.

LaFleur straightened up. Maggie turned on her stool to face him, arms dropping to her side. He picked up his notebook, ruffled the pages, then put it back down on the bar, answered her question with a question. "Did you know her father?"

"Well, I met him a few times. He was very nice; very 'Old World,' made me feel welcome whenever I visited. Which was not that often, really, not often enough." She sighed. "Why?"

"Did you know he died just two years after Angie?"

"Yes, but—"

"Drank himself to death, according to the sister. After what he was told."

Maggie set her wine down on the edge of the bar, almost spilling it. "Told? Told what?"

"The mortician was a family friend. Came to the house, day before the funeral. Told Mr. Frascati—told the whole family, apparently—that there had been some sort of cover up by the hospital. Maybe even by the police. Like I told you, the police report was very sparse. As if it had been dictated by someone interested in documenting as little as possible. My contact at the department was actually assigned to the case. He says he barely had a chance to interview anyone before the case was closed and he was pulled off. No explanation, hints of 'protecting the family,' stronger hints of 'avoiding a scandal,' that is was all about the hospital wanting it kept quiet." He took a drink, emptying the glass, followed by a sip of spring water. He waved the empty Scotch glass in Joe's direction. After Joe had refilled it and gone back out front, LaFleur continued.

"The funeral director—Abruzzo, did you know him?" She shook her head. "Anyway, he claimed that there were needle marks on her body that were not documented in the autopsy. The autopsy that has less than conveniently disappeared. They believed him. She still believes it." He held his Scotch up to the light, swirled it around. "No legs." Maggie tilted her head, questioning. "So, does this story have 'legs?' I think it does. The question is, now what do we do about it?"

LaFleur looked at his watch. "Hey, it's getting late. Still want to go out to dinner?"

Maggie hesitated. "Oh, I don't know if I still feel like going out. Is that all right?"

"Sure. But two scotches without food is my limit. I've got to have something to eat or you'll be taking me home in a wheelbarrow."

"I meant I didn't feel like going out, not that I didn't want to have something to eat. How about eating in? I've got some leftovers from a couple of days ago; do you do leftovers? My place is an easy walk from here."

LaFleur didn't think twice about accepting the invitation.

*

"That stuff about 'avoiding a scandal,' that is exactly what was happening." Maggie said as they crossed over Bridge Street. "Except at the same time, someone was trying to create a bigger scandal, spreading rumors. There were a lot of bad feelings at that hospital for months afterwards."

They were walking quickly. It had gotten cold after dark, and a little foggy. LaFleur pulled his sport jacket a little tighter around him. Should have worn the London Fog.

"What do you mean, trying to create a bigger scandal? Bigger than what, the suicide?"

"Well, yeah. The administration at the time was really old school, very conservative. But at the same time, Montgomery had somehow gotten into a position of power, without actually being on the board or anything. It seemed like he was able to do whatever he wanted, no questions asked. Just look at everything he was getting away with. Especially after the drug rumors started, and Phil dying suddenly. Then when Angie died, somehow it became open season on her. It was bad enough that she killed herself—that made the hospital look bad in itself—but the way it happened, that was just too much. And Montgomery, well he had plenty of reasons not to want any attention drawn to the hospital. We were told to *never* talk about it, ever. And Martha was almost worse than the administrators; she hounded us about it for weeks. It was horrible." Maggie was getting out of breath and paused for a minute. LaFleur wasn't quite following what she was getting at.

"So what kinds of rumors?" he asked, going back to where she had started. "Something besides a possible affair with Mahoney?"

"Yeah, but those rumors had not circulated that much, and that was before she died. And by then, they weren't actually rumors any longer, it had come out, even if it was not that well known." They started back up the street. They were both gasping a little now, but they were almost at the top of the hill. "Here, down Seventh. Just a few more blocks." Maggie steered them to the right, past a big boarding house on the corner. "My apartment is the top floor of one of these big old mansions."

She stopped under a streetlight and turned to LaFleur, who had just managed to stop beside her. "Maybe there was something else going on," she said. "Something Angie saw or heard, or rather thought she heard. She may have inadvertently brought some of Montgomery's animosity on herself. All somehow tied in to the thing with Phil. There were stories going around about some drug trafficking that had been going on, or maybe was still going on, run out of the pharmacy. And that someone in a position of authority was in on it, made it possible, even. Even after Phil died, after we thought it had all been dropped, the stories kept cropping up once in awhile. And now, you find out there were needle marks. What in hell does that mean?" She ignored his questioning look and went on. "But anyway, like I told you before, after she died, there were rumors of—" She broke off, obviously struggling.

"Of what, exactly?"

157

"Of a relationship. Between Martha Gale and Angie." Maggie took a breath, flustered. "But they were only rumors. No one had ever thought anything like this, until after." She looked at LaFleur, eyes pleading. "It was nothing, really. It can't have been true."

LaFleur sighed. So this is what she had been hinting around at days ago. Finally got it out. "But if Angie had been sleeping with Mahoney, how could anyone believe that she was also in a relationship like that?"

"I know. It doesn't make any sense. It didn't make any sense then. I was never sure, but I always suspected that it actually came from Mahoney, odd as that sounds. And no one, not even Montgomery—especially not Montgomery—did anything to stop it. It was so unfair; but we were all under so much pressure to keep our mouths shut, everyone was tiptoeing around. So she ends up getting slammed, and no one does anything about it—me maybe least of all—and in time it's all nothing more than a creepy hospital legend. 'Her ghost can still be seen at night, roaming the halls, an anesthesia mask on her face.'" Maggie stopped and had to grab LaFleur to steady herself. After a minute, she caught her breath. LaFleur looked at her closely, his face now taking on the same long look as Maggie's.

"Come on," he said quietly. "You promised me dinner."

Neither one spoke the rest of the way to her apartment. Maggie seemed to brighten up as she led LaFleur up the long wooden stairway at the side of a huge Victorian house. Gabled and porticoed like the rest of the houses on the block, it had its own special look, and was in better condition than most of the others.

"Isn't this a great house? Built with cornstarch money, I think." She opened the door into a small entry hall, took his coat and hung it on a hook, did the same with hers, then led him into the apartment, flipping on a light on the way in.

She did the quick tour that women think is obligatory and men never give a second thought to—everything except the bedroom, which she said was a mess, closing the door quickly—but LaFleur was impressed. It was a large apartment, taking up the entire top floor, with great dormers and a large covered balcony off the back of the living room. LaFleur peered out through big French doors and could see harbor lights peering back through the mist. The owners had retained a lot of the character of the older house while providing a lot of nice updates—kitchen, bath, all brand new and stylish without detracting from the Victorian finishes that predominated. Maggie had furnished it in an eclectic style that LaFleur thought he could learn to like. He started warming up. Maggie poured each of them a glass of wine, put the CD player on "shuffle," and settled him onto the couch.

LaFleur stayed settled while Maggie bustled; he knew enough to stay out of the way. They didn't return to their previous topic, rather contented themselves with patter about what she was putting into the salad—did he like radishes? I like them, but they don't like me, he said, regretting it, until she laughed, genuinely, he decided.

"Okay," she said after a few minutes, "dinner." LaFleur came in and sat down in his designated spot. A couple more sips of wine topped off the glow he had started at 1850 House, and he was feeling positively domesticated. It was the best feeling he'd had in years.

It wasn't until after they cleared the dinner table—and after LaFleur had helped with the dishes, to Maggie's surprise—that they went back to their earlier discussion.

"So you obviously believe her sister, about the needle marks," Maggie began. "Did she tell you any more? Where they were, what they could have been from? Maybe we're jumping to conclusions. Couldn't they have come from some sort of injections given to her in an attempt to revive her?"

"Not as far as I've been able to determine. She said she didn't know anything in detail, where the marks were, how many, whatever. But Mahoney confirmed that there was no resuscitation tried, no injections, no IVs, no paddles. Mahoney got there, the anesthesia was shut down, and Angie was lying there on the couch, cold, stiff, and blue." He saw Maggie shudder. "God, I'm sorry. Didn't mean to be so blunt."

"No, it's not that," Maggie assured him. "It's just hard to imagine that it all happened so long ago. It doesn't feel like it."

"Same thing Angie's sister said to me," he replied.

"So, anyway. Now that it's real," she looked at him as if still expecting a rebuttal, "we have to figure out what to do about, right?"

"Well, before we get there, there is one other thing I have to talk to you about." He moved as if to reach into his jacket packet, realized he didn't have it on, and got up. "Hang on."

He came back over to the couch holding the makeshift envelope he had made the day before. He thought about asking her why she hadn't told him about it before, but just handed it to her instead.

"What is this?" she asked, turning it over in her hand.

"Just unfold it and take a look."

She turned back the edges of the sheet where they had been folder over, then opened it all the way. The note fell out into her lap. As she read it, LaFleur watched her for any sign that might give away something; but either impassiveness was a skill at which Maggie excelled, or she was genuinely unmoved by what she saw.

"Where did this come from?" She finally asked.

"From her sister. She found it in the pocket of the uniform Angie had been wearing that day. It had sort of slipped down into the lining through a hole in the pocket." He waited.

"This was found the day she died?"

"She found it later, after they went to the hospital to collect her things. I thought you said you didn't go in that morning."

Maggie looked perplexed. This look was quickly losing favor with LaFleur. He said, more impatiently than he intended, "Well, what about it?"

"What do you mean, 'what about it?'" Maggie said defensively. "I didn't write this note."

"You signed it," he said quickly.

"A.C., I'm telling you, I did not write the note. Not that day, not any day. For one thing, it's written on the back of blank prescription."

God damn it, how could I have not noticed that? I really am losing it, after all.

"And furthermore," Maggie went on, not trying to hide the irritation in her voice, "I would never have signed a note with just a single initial. Anything that does not require a full signature I sign with my initials, 'MM.' With the "M's" sort of overlapping, with a little loopy thing. It's something silly I started doing in high school. I still do it. Ask anyone."

"But—" he took a breath. This was not good. "But then how do you explain it? Her sister certainly thought it was from you. Would Angie have thought the same thing?"

"Probably. She wouldn't have known, necessarily, that I wouldn't sign a note like that; she probably would not have paid any attention."

"Then who wrote the note?" He tried not to sound accusatory this time.

"I have no idea," Maggie said. "Someone whose name starts with 'M,' obviously. Not me."

LaFleur finally had no choice but to believe her. Mahoney? Montgomery? They were both reluctant to say it out loud, but he sensed she was thinking the same thing. He apologized. She admitted she couldn't blame him; how would he know? And so they did do some dancing that night—dancing around the question of what to do now; dancing around the supposition of murder; dancing around the extent of Maggie's guilt; dancing around whether or not LaFleur was staying over. That dance was the longest, and as it turned out, the most interesting.

*

The next morning, LaFleur called Michael at the hospital and arranged a lunch meeting with him and Maggie. They met in the cafeteria. Michael was excited by the news, but not as surprised as LaFleur expected; but then Maggie had already laid out some groundwork for him in a quick hallway conversation, even telling him about the note. None of them had any idea what to make of it at this point. They all agreed that the investigation now had to be put on an entirely new level. Maggie even started talking about taking it to the police. LaFleur had to convince her that there still was nothing to go on other than a lot of speculation, possibly unfounded accusations from a biased source, and some dubious third hand information garnered from a not particularly good small town newspaper article. He had easily come up with plenty of alternative explanations for almost every suspicious circumstance that had been brought up so far. It was only after hearing Angie's sister's story that he was willing to make the leap and call it

161

murder; not because he thought she had anything concrete they could go with, but because he thought he could still recognize the truth when he saw it. That still didn't mean he could prove anything. He was not even willing at this point to name a probable suspect, nor were the others. There were still too many variables.

It was now up to LaFleur to come up with a plan. Unfortunately, given the circumstances, he was at something of a loss as to what to do, almost as much as the other two. But he was a professional, and he had agreed, even if never expecting anything to come of it. And then there was the matter of not letting Maggie down. Not something he had expected to have to factor in to the equation, it was rapidly becoming the most important factor of all.

The only thing he was sure of was that whatever tack he decided on, it had to include talking to Mahoney and Montgomery again.

The Note

It was the start of the Labor Day weekend, and things at the hospital were even quieter than usual. Angie had gotten in a few minutes late, about 7:05. On her way in she stopped at the main floor nurse's station to confirm the regular 8:30 coffee break with LaNette and Judy. They said they'd see her in the lounge at the usual time, and she went upstairs to change.

Maggie was not coming in this morning—Angie had even given up her early morning Mass to cover for her. They had made the schedule switch just the day before, at staff. Maggie had some last minute thing come up, something about an uncle coming to town. Dr. Montgomery and Paul had both been overly annoyed by it, Angie thought. They had both been particularly hard on her lately. And Montgomery was obviously riding Maggie about something.

Angie went up to the second floor changing rooms. As she hurried down the dimly lit hallway to the locker room, she went over her previous conversation with Maggie again, and the mess she had gotten herself into. She had to admit to herself that Maggie had been right about one thing, at least, even if she hadn't come right out and said it: Angie had better get over it. Maybe she could get some time to talk with Maggie later, and let her know that she had helped, some.

The locker room was empty. She walked to her temporary locker, the locker she was now sharing with Maggie. Hers had been jimmied and the latch had not been replaced yet. As she reached to open the locker, she was surprised to see that something had been taped to the locker door: a small piece of paper—from a generic prescription pad, she saw—folded in half. She pulled it off and opened it. It was a note, written in block letters, asking her to meet in the O.R., 'AS SOON AS YOU GET IN,' it said. Signed "M." That was odd. Maggie? But she's not here today, she thought, puzzled. But it must be from her—something must have changed and she came in after all. Or Paul? But he surely would have signed "Paul," wouldn't he? Must be Maggie. Why the O.R.? Oh, well. She finished changing and then stuck the note in her pocket. Closed the locker door, locked it.

She left the changing room and started for the O.R., wondering what was going on.

A Meeting of the Minds

LaFleur had finally managed to get a meeting with Montgomery scheduled, but did not have a particularly good feeling about it. Trepidation was not something he was accustomed to, and he was learning to dislike it.

Montgomery did not disappoint LaFleur's negative expectations. Without even a perfunctory hello, he reminded LaFleur pointedly that he had no authority, no jurisdiction, and no business prying into hospital affairs, forty years old or not. Please sit down.

As soon as LaFleur had settled into the chair across from Montgomery, he had the same vague shock of recognition he remembered from the first time he had seen him, during the groundbreaking ceremony, looking down from Dr. Fuentes' office window. Montgomery's hair wasn't as gray as his—treated, LaFleur was sure—and the frames of his glasses were genuine Yves St. Laurent, not knock-offs. But the general facial features, bone structure, dominant nose, strong chin, generally tight, clear skin—LaFleur saw these features every morning in the mirror. If Montgomery saw any self-resemblance he didn't mention it. LaFleur was slightly distressed to think that he had even a superficial resemblance to the doctor, given Michael's less than flattering appraisal of his personality.

LaFleur liked conciliation even less than trepidation— conciliatory was a word that had never been used in reference to him in all his years on the force, but he figured he had no choice at the moment. He graciously acknowledged that of course he knew he had no "jurisdiction" here; he was retired and simply doing a favor for an old friend, Ms. Malone. Montgomery made no comment regarding how old a friend he believed LaFleur and

Maggie to be—for all he knew it was possible that they were old friends; he had certainly not concerned himself with Maggie's personal life all that much over recent years.

"Just so we understand one another," Montgomery said, as he took on a more cordial manner. It was like he was shedding one skin and slipping into another, LaFleur marveled.

LaFleur had gone over this in his mind several times. He began by complimenting Montgomery on the great job he was doing with the expansion; something the town had needed for a long time, and so on. Montgomery played along, throwing out some small talk of his own. They were like two tennis players feeling out each other's backhands. Montgomery asked LaFleur how long he had been off the force, where he lived, what kind of fishing he liked to do. One thing about this part of the country, no conversation went on very long without some mention of fishing.

LaFleur took advantage of a break in the volley to broach the subject they had each been politely deferring to the other, and tried to put it in the context of them being in this together; the sooner it could be resolved the better. He wanted Montgomery to see some clear advantage to talking to him. From everything he had learned about the guy from Maggie and Michael, Montgomery did nothing if he couldn't see what was in it for himself.

"Can I start with this?" LaFleur asked, pulling out the article.

"Ah, yes," Montgomery said. "The newspaper article. I've seen it."

"Any idea why it's been showing up around here lately?" LaFleur asked. The standard opening.

"No." The standard response. "I have no idea what is going on; another one of Maggie's jokes, I suspect. I can't begin to tell you what her motives would be."

"Yes, I'm sure you've been wondering what she is up to," LaFleur said, agreeably. "I know that I've never stopped wondering what's really going on since the first day I talked to her about it. If I could just nail down a few details about this thing, I think we can put it to rest. I never thought it would go on this long, frankly."

Montgomery had been nodding in assent. "I probably won't be able to tell you very much about it that you haven't already learned. It was an unfortunate incident. She was a very troubled young woman. Someone closer to her than I should have foreseen it."

"Did you notice any signs, indications that she was contemplating suicide?" LaFleur asked.

"Personally, no," Montgomery answered. "But I was told later, as I recall, that she was very impressionable, had become involved in some extremely unfortunate personal relationships, of a, um, of a sexual nature—including an affair with a doctor, and, to be blunt, a possible lesbian relationship, with an older woman—and was possibly complicit in other, well, let's just say, unsavory activities."

"Did you have any proof?" LaFleur asked. "Anything to substantiate any of the rumors?"

"No, at least nothing that you would consider 'proof,' I suspect." Montgomery answered glibly.

"Who was responsible for the rumors?"

"I can't say. It was just common knowledge."

He's lying. He must have known.

"Of course," Montgomery went on, "then and now I have always made sure that the environment here was wholesome, productive; but things do happen that cannot be anticipated, especially when it comes to someone like Miss Frascati. We have a very strong mission statement at this hospital. We encourage socialization among the staff, to a point; it contributes to a healthy work ethic as well as fostering individual growth, important factors in building a strong team. At the same time, we expect all of our doctors and nurses to uphold the highest professional and ethical standards, as the community deserves."

As LaFleur tried to digest this, he decided he had not fully appreciated Fuentes's characterizations of Montgomery. This guy could really sling it. It had taken Montgomery about thirty seconds to deny any personal knowledge of Angie's state of mind, impugn her character, take credit for maintaining the professionalism of the staff while at the same time denying responsibility for what had happened, and change the subject by launching into a marketing spiel. LaFleur was impressed, in a perverse way. It was time to step it up, shift to a more aggressive style. Nothing to be gained by sitting back trying to pick up the antes.

"You said 'someone like Miss Frascati,'" LaFleur countered. "From everything I have been able to learn, she was not only an excellent nurse, but a very popular and likeable young woman. What does 'someone like Miss Frascati' mean, exactly?"

Montgomery didn't hesitate. "You misunderstand me," he said. "I was simply commenting on the fact that she did, obviously, given her suicide, have serious problems, regardless of whether or not I was privy to her state of mind. Which I was not, as I said."

"What about the other nurses, the head nurse, um, Martha Gale? Did she ever mention anything that would have led you to believe that Angie, that Miss Frascati, might be at risk?" LaFleur watched Montgomery closely to see if there had been any reaction to his intentional use of the loaded word. Risk took on many guises, LaFleur had learned over the years.

"We were all completely surprised," Montgomery answered. "Hasn't Maggie made that clear by now?"

"What Maggie says is irrelevant," LaFleur shot back. "She didn't come in until later that morning, anyway, isn't that right? That's why I'm here. To determine what I can believe from Maggie, and what I can't." *Will he buy into this? I'm not going too far out on another limb, am I? Starting up the chainsaw as I go?*

"Of course," Montgomery said, sounding conciliatory.

LaFleur picked up the article, which had been lying on the desk in front of him. "Like I said, it's not just what Maggie says that interests me. There are some things in this newspaper report—borne out by the police report, by the way—that bother me. If I'm ever going to make any sense of this, and satisfy our...curiosity, I would at least like to be able to clarify what appear to be inconsistencies in the various reports. That, along with some additional information I have from some of the other staff, should take care of it. I have to admit," he continued, trying not to overplay the hand, "that some of my questions stem from my own idle curiosity, and probably have nothing to do with anything."

"What in particular bothers you?" Montgomery asked.

LaFleur held it out at arms length, trying to get it into focus. *Need new bifocals.* "There are two or three things I'm troubled about. Probably simple explanations for them. First, this reference to the anesthesia machine: 'A hospital official revealed to the Syracuse Times that the anesthesia machine, which had been placed in the hall outside the nurses' lounge, was turned on when the victim was found'. How is that possible? The door had been locked. The machine must have been inside?"

"Let me see that," Montgomery said, reaching across the desk. He read for a few seconds. "Yes, I see. That is just poorly written. All it means is that the machine was moved out of the lounge after she was found. The wording in the article is confusing, I agree." He laid the article on the desk in front of him.

"So, where it says earlier that she was found with an anesthesia mask on her face, that means the machine was in the room, and moved later."

"Yes, exactly."

"Who moved it, do you think?" Montgomery didn't reply right away, so LaFleur added, "Dr. Mahoney is reported as being the first one at the scene."

"Well, then, it must have been Mahoney," Montgomery said.

He turned to a new page in the notebook. "When were you notified, do you recall?"

"Very soon after she was found; I don't know the exact time."

"You were called at home?"

"No, I was in my office at the hospital."

This was new. "Were you normally there on weekends? And this was a holiday weekend, I believe."

"No, I went in to the hospital for some reason that morning, I don't remember why."

"All right." LaFleur paused, skimming his notes, then continued: "How about the fact that no vomitus was reported, and that there was a pediatric airway in her mouth? Is that consistent, medically, with death by anesthesia?"

"That is not in the article," Montgomery said, pointing at the page in front of him.

"Sure it is," LaFleur said, "right there in the same sentence," he half stood up and leaned over to see the article, and read, upside down: "'a child's airway tube, generally used to depress the tongue, was protruding from her mouth.'"

"No," said Montgomery, annoyed. "I mean there is nothing

there about vomitus."

"No, that's right. But the fact that her mouth was clear, other than for the airway, has been confirmed. Can you explain that? Wouldn't that have been expected in a case like this?"

"Not necessarily, no."

"What about the airway? What would be the explanation for that?"

Montgomery grabbed the article off of the desk. "You can't go by anything this report says. It's incomplete, spurious, second hand information."

"There was no airway in her mouth?"

"That's not what I said. There could have been. I don't know."

LaFleur changed the subject again. "I want to go back to something I'm not clear on; when did you actually get to the scene? Was it before Dr. Mahoney arrived and pronounced her dead?"

"No, of course not. I arrived later, when he and the others were already there. It says right there that Dr. Mahoney was called to the scene 'immediately.'" Montgomery threw the article back onto the desk.

"I thought you just said that nothing in the article was to be trusted?" LaFleur enjoyed getting that one off.

Montgomery made a dismissive gesture. "That particular item happens to be correct." He seemed to feel that was enough of a response, so LaFleur moved on.

"So all the inconsistencies in the article—all irrelevant? All mistaken?" LaFleur let that hang. Montgomery had not answered any of the last three or four questions.

"I'll repeat what I just said," Montgomery eventually replied. "You cannot go by anything in that article."

Push once more. "Who provided this information to the newspaper?" According to Maggie, it had been Montgomery. *See if this raises any hackles.*

"There was a coordinated response by several hospital officials," Montgomery replied carefully.

"Coordinated. Who would that have been, exactly?"

"The administrator. The coroner."

"You weren't involved in that? Didn't talk to any reporters?

The editor?"

"I may have," he equivocated. "But certainly not without the approval of the administrator. We did the best we could, given the short time we had to resolve this incident, to provide all the relevant information. If it was distorted by the newspaper, we had no control over that."

LaFleur decided he might as well let it go for now; maybe there was another angle that could produce something more than evasions. He decided to shift the conversation to something that had been bothering all of them since the article had first appeared. He pointed to the article, still lying on Montgomery's desk. "It says there that the police weren't called until two hours after she was found. Is that also inaccurate? No one else has questioned that particular item, in fact it has been corroborated by a couple of other staff who were involved. What exactly took place during those two hours?"

"I can't tell you exactly."

"In general, then."

"It was necessary to move carefully," Montgomery said deliberately. "We thought it was important to have all the facts before contacting the family. We needed to be prepared. These situations are, as you should well know, very sensitive. In order to protect the family from any adverse publicity, we felt it necessary to very tightly control the way information was...disseminated."

"That doesn't explain why the police weren't called sooner."

"I believe it does. I told you, we had to be prepared to deal with the situation in as controlled a manner as possible, in the best interests of all concerned."

Stalemate. LaFleur leaned back in his chair, made a show of going through his notes. The tension hanging in the air between them was like a wall. He glanced up from his notebook. Montgomery was making his own show, thumbing through a small stack of papers on his desk, as if looking for something more important than the current conversation.

"Who performed the autopsy?" LaFleur asked.

"I can't recall," Montgomery answered, looking up too quickly.

Can't recall? LaFleur thought. "I only ask because the

postmortem report seems to be missing," he said evenly. "Francine took me down to the basement archives yesterday. We couldn't find it."

"I would be more surprised if you *had* found it," Montgomery replied.

"And why is that? There were other records from the same time period."

"I can't answer that. Maybe Francine took you to the wrong storeroom."

"Would you mind if I took another look?" LaFleur asked.

"No, I suppose not, but you're probably wasting your time. There was nothing in the report outside of what you already know. She died of asphyxiation," Montgomery said, as if closing the matter.

LaFleur wasn't going to let this one go. "No other drugs?" he asked pointedly. "No evidence of any injections of any kind?"

LaFleur had never seen anyone actually "bristle" before—he had always thought that was just a literary conceit. But Montgomery was definitely bristling, like a porcupine. "No. Nothing inconsistent with the cause of death," Montgomery bristled, as he sat back in his chair. "I'm afraid I really don't have time to go into this right now," he said. "You'll excuse me?"

*

As LaFleur walked down the hall he reflected on how much alike—and unlike—the interview with Montgomery was compared to his talk with Mahoney. It had ended abruptly, like Mahoney's. Unlike the interview with Mahoney, though, LaFleur counted this one as a complete success. With Mahoney he had pressed too hard, not knowing the parameters. Sure, Mahoney had been hiding something, but after talking to Paul Two, he thought he knew why. Which is not to say he wasn't still hiding something, but LaFleur was less concerned about that than he had been just a half an hour ago. This time, the real difference was that he had intentionally been pushing the envelope. And now he had a pretty good idea of what had to happen next. He just didn't know exactly how to make it happen—yet.

*

"Dr. Fuentes."

Michael turned to see Dr. Montgomery motioning to him from a side hall near the O.R. Michael had just spent two hours in surgery and was in no mood; whatever it was it couldn't be good. He walked over to where Montgomery was glowering.

"I just had an unpleasant conversation with your friend Mr. LaFleur," Montgomery said without preamble. "I don't know what you think you are up to, or what you hope to accomplish with this ruse, this article. But be assured I do not think it is amusing." He stepped back and turned away, leaving Michael speechless, before turning back again. "What exactly is it that you know, Fuentes, or think you know, about what happened that day?" Before Michael could answer, Montgomery quickly turned away again, apparently regretting the question; as he walked away, Michael heard him say, muttering to himself: "Nothing, Fuentes. You know nothing."

A Late Night Fishing Expedition

Thump. There were fish bumping against the bottom of the boat. *Thump.* What the hell was going on?

The thumping got louder and more regular. *Thump. Thump. Thump. Thump.* Damned persistent fish, LaFleur thought. He opened his eyes, took a deep breath, closed his eyes. Go away. *Thump. Thump. Thump. Thump.* Now they were flopping around on the deck outside the door. He opened his eyes again. He used to wake up a lot quicker than this, he thought as he looked over at the door. The thumping continued. Ah, someone at the door.

"All right," he called out. Getting no appreciable decline in the thumping he realized it had been no more than a croak, so cleared his throat and gave it another try. "All *right*." The fish finally stopped flopping—whoever was at the door with them must have heard him that time.

He stood up slowly and stretched, becoming more fully awake as he walked to the door. "On my way," he called out unnecessarily, as he was already at the door. He peered through the blinds and saw Michael standing there, peering back in at him.

"A.C.? Are you up?"

Well. Obviously. One more deep breath and he was finally able to shake off the vision of perch, pike, and walleye ramming themselves against the hull. He opened the door.

"Oh. Were you asleep?" Michael said, still standing outside on the deck. "You look a little glassy-eyed. Too much Grouse?"

"Not enough, more likely," he growled. "Just dozed off for a minute. What time is it?"

"About eleven-thirty. Saw a light on so I figured you were still up."

"What, you been out late with some floozy, I suppose?"

174

"Not exactly, A.C. Anyway, we don't have floozies around here anymore. That was in your day. Or was that flapper?"

"Hey, I'm not old enough to remember flappers, for Chrissake." He was still a little groggy.

"Let me in, damn it, it's cold out here." LaFleur waved him in.

Michael held up what looked like a small package as he came through the door. "I went by the O.R.—the old lounge—this afternoon, not sure why; just curious to see what was happening with the demolition, I guess. Anyway, I was sort of poking around there and one of the contractors called me over. He had found something behind an old built-in cabinet while they were stripping the room. For some reason the cabinet had been left intact, even after the conversion to the O.R., I guess. Anyway, they thought it was pretty unusual and thought someone at the hospital might be interested in it. I thought I should show you as soon as I could."

LaFleur herded Michael into the dining room, flipping on a light while guiding him to a chair at the table. Michael put the package down and shrugged out of his coat, sat down and pushed the package across the table to LaFleur. A small stainless steel box, in a clear plastic bag. He picked it up while watching Michael for some clue as to what was going on.

"It had somehow slipped behind a cabinet shelf in a sort of hole in the wall," Michael said, squirming around in his chair with impatience. "Or something like that. The guy wasn't too clear about it. Anyway, I put it in the plastic bag right away, but it had already been handled quite a bit."

There was an apologetic tone to Michael's voice that caused LaFleur to look up. "What is it? And why would that matter?" he asked.

"I think it might be evidence," Michael said.

"Okay," LaFleur said noncommittally. "We'll treat it like evidence." He motioned to a cabinet in the kitchen behind them. "There's a box of disposable plastic gloves under the sink. Grab them for me, will you?"

Michael went to the cabinet, rummaged around for a bit, then returned with the gloves.

"Handy things. Use them for everything," LaFleur said, pulling out a pair of the flimsy plastic gloves and slipping them on.

"Thumbs on both sides. One size fits all." He slid the steel box out onto the table, picked it up gingerly by the sides, and pried it open. "God, that's a scary looking thing,' he said as he opened the lid. He was looking at what looked like a hypodermic, very sturdily made—a thick glass tube marked "5", "10," "20," and "MM" at the top on one side, "0,5" and "1" and "CC" on the other, with bulky stainless steel attachments at each end. There was a complicated looking plunger laying in the box at one side, and a detachable needle held in place by a small clip, all resting on a steel tray, cut out to fit all the parts. "Some kind of syringe?" he asked.

"Exactly," said Michael. "Old style; probably dates back to the fifties, maybe earlier. But still could have been in use in the early sixties." He pointed out the graduated markings, explaining that this would have typically been used for either anesthesia, or pain management—narcotics, primarily.

LaFleur wasn't sure if it was the late hour, or his age, or both, but he wasn't getting it. "I don't get it," he said.

Michael could barely contain his exasperation. "They found this in the O.R.," he repeated. Le Fleur just raised his eyebrows. "In the old *nurse's lounge*," Michael said suggestively.

"You'll have to lay it out for me," LaFleur grumbled, half guessing what was coming next.

Michael pointed at the syringe. "Could have been used by someone at the hospital who was addicted. Or…" He paused dramatically. "Or…what if this was used the morning Angie was killed, and somehow got left behind? This could even be a murder weapon!"

LaFleur had seen this kind of misguided amateur enthusiasm before; every rookie detective he had ever worked with jumped to outrageous conclusions about every piece of potential evidence for their first two months on the job. He supposed he had done it himself, once. Truly amateur detectives were even worse.

"I see," LaFleur said, "that's pretty good. Hmm. Yeah. Could be important." He suddenly *was* tired—really tired—and not at all in the right frame of mind to deal with this. There might be something to it—maybe not what Michael had proposed, that would be an extraordinary coincidence—but there could be something. He rubbed his eyes and stared back at Michael blearily. "You know," he said, "Maybe I am a little tired after all." He closed the box back up, slipped it back into the plastic bag, and pulled off the gloves. "Let's deal with this tomorrow, shall we?"

*

The next morning broke patchily, even colder than the day before. A languid, damp snow had fallen most of the day, obscuring the harbor. An inversion kept the cooling tower fog low and dense, pushing it into town and adding an even thicker cast to the air. The lake was barely visible, a line of cement gray with a brighter halo of weak light hanging in a thin streak above it, just as it disappeared into the cloud bank. By late afternoon, the snow had given way to a half-hearted drizzle of sleet. If it got as cold overnight as the local yokel weatherman was predicting, there would be ice on the gunwales by morning.

LaFleur stood at the galley sink and washed down an ibuprofen and a Pepcid AC with an Alka-Seltzer. Get a head start on the day. Maybe a little too much Grouse, after Michael had left last night. He had slept badly, dreaming the whole night. LaFleur always remembered his dreams in great detail, and had loved to relate them to his wife—*ad nauseam*, she once said, which was unusual for her; as an accountant she was not prone to such bookish pronouncements. It didn't stop him, and after a while she actually learned to like hearing him go on and on. Some dreams were much better than others, and at times he bored himself telling the more pedestrian of them. Last night's dreams had been vivid and full of strange symbolism—false floors opening up beneath him, doors without handles, pumping gas at an old-style Gas-O-Mat, the tall glass cylinder full of amber liquid, but the gas barely trickling out—this last one had woken him up, luckily. On the way back from the bathroom, he had a half-baked idea of how to use the syringe to their advantage.

LaFleur spent the rest of the day nursing an Irish coffee and putting his notes in order. They had scheduled a dinner meeting for that night. Michael was going to bring spaghetti. LaFleur had told him about a routine his dad had followed, back in the day. The standard routine was to stop by the old DeMent's Bar & Grill on the way to work in the morning—a few railroad workers would always be there, maybe a couple of shade cloth guys—they'd have a quick shot, and leave an empty tin pail. Then on the way home, they'd stop by for another quick shot (or two), and pick up the pail, now full of spaghetti. Michael had called all over the area; no one did a tin pail anymore, but he was able to get a cardboard bucketful from Canale's. Maggie was bringing the salad. LaFleur had defrosted a loaf of garlic bread. There was plenty of *Famous Grouse* and *Eye of the Dove* on hand. Tonight was the first time they were going to have what he would regard as an actual crime analysis.

LaFleur had made a lot of progress as far as sorting things out—he had a solid time line now, and had even gone through an analysis of suicide factors compared to the known facts. He had gone over again what little they had that could be construed in any way as evidence: the note, the interviews with Mahoney and Montgomery, and anything from the article that had been corroborated by more than two parties. He spent a considerable amount of time that afternoon thinking about what gaps in the story remained, identifying bad assumptions, and trying to come up with ways to resolve some of the open questions.

He was withholding final judgment on the syringe. He was willing to discuss it, and was even willing to go along with Michael's suggestion that they get a lab analysis, in case there was any residue remaining—in fact, Amos had picked it up that morning to get the analysis done. He had even agreed to get the hypo and the box dusted for prints, even though he had earlier tried to impress upon Michael how unlikely it was that anything could be lifted.

LaFleur had mixed feelings about how they had gotten to this point. He resented that his hand had been forced, yet again. He had never been one to admit to being compromised in the past. When he was on an investigation, he was in control. Regardless of what his supervisors, partners, or anyone else thought of it. Only over time had he been given the leeway he expected, after it was clear that he was able to consistently produce results, even if no one understood or appreciated how he did it. In a department that saw positive results as a happy accident, LaFleur stood out as an anomaly, the only one of his generation to really give a damn. Most of his former fellow detectives, the ones of his generation still there, anyway, were on the how-many-more-years-to-my-pension plan, keeping up appearances and churning enough through the prosecutor's office to keep the numbers up. LaFleur had always been in it for the pure joy of doing something well, even if underappreciated. He would periodically threaten to quit unless given the credit due him, but in the end he had to admit to himself that he would still rather be playing the only game in town, and playing it his way.

His initial characterization of this case as nothing more than a diversion had slowly become a matter of importance in terms of actually "solving a case," though he had never liked those terms. That reminded him too much of Sherlock Holmes stories—he had read them as a kid, and still enjoyed them occasionally, but only on that level, not as something to be taken as seriously as most people seemed to take them. He preferred to think of solving a case as one way of restoring order in the world. Not that he was naïve or foolish enough to believe the current judicial system actually provided anything approaching true restitution. But at the least, and maybe this was partially a generational thing, he believed that some level of reconciliation was possible. Bad things could not be made good again, but a reckoning could be made. Sometimes that was all you got; whether it was enough or not was something he tried not to dwell on too much.

In this case, Angie's case, it was becoming clear to him that there had been serious mistakes made in the original investigation. But he had heard the "prevent a scandal" defense too often to be taken in by it. In his experience that only confirmed a cover up. Maggie had never come right out and said it—though Angie's sister had—and even though he had not been personally involved at the time, LaFleur was still vaguely embarrassed by it.

Maybe now he could do something to make it...well, not right, but less wrong.

*

Maggie had arrived a few minutes earlier than Michael, and was in the salon with LaFleur by the time Michael arrived. He carried the bucket of spaghetti into the dining area and turned to LaFleur.

"Where should I put this?" he asked, looking around at the piles of books spilling over from the shelves onto the side tables, counters, the dining table, and even one of the lounge chairs. "Does the library give you unlimited check-out privileges or something, A.C.?" he asked. "This could be a branch, a floating Bookmobile."

"Sorry. Just push some books to one side, I'll clear them off in a minute, before we eat," LaFleur said. "No, wait, just take it into the galley," he said, getting up from the couch. "I'll clear this off now." He went to the table and gathered up the books into two stacks, dumping them in a corner. "There."

Some ground rules had been set by LaFleur earlier: until after dinner, no discussion topic allowed that was any more serious than the latest movie seen, book read, or new CD listened to. Michael tried to protest, saying that he had something that couldn't wait, but LaFleur held him off. So dinner conversation was light, exactly the kind of diversion they needed before diving back into the case. Maggie was reading *Les Misérables*, she said, a new translation, and had been listening to the latest Diana Krall CD. LaFleur approved. Michael had just watched *"A Day at the Races"* for about the fourth time. LaFleur couldn't resist reeling off the real first names of all five Marx brothers. Michael was impressed; most people didn't know they had real first names, or even that there were five brothers. LaFleur had recently discovered the mystery novels of Arthur Upfield, especially the ones featuring the Australian aboriginal detective "Bony." He had just finished *Bony and the Kelly Gang*. The spaghetti, even though from a cardboard bucket and not a tin pail, was excellent.

Michael and Maggie washed the dishes (no dishwasher—it was a boat, after all) as LaFleur propped a whiteboard up against the wall behind the table. He laid out three different colored markers, and set his notebook down beside them.

"Hey, in there," he called to the galley. "We agreed we'd let those go for now. Get in here."

"Ten seconds," Maggie called back. A couple of minutes later, she and Michael came in. "They're all done," she said, as they settled in around the table.

"Well, thanks," LaFleur said. "Taking pity on an old man, or are you always this considerate?" He moved to the chair next to the whiteboard, shifting sideways so he could reach it without twisting too much. "Okay, let's get started with this. I want to do...what do you call it, a differential?"

"That's it," said Michael. "Except in this case the diagnosis is already known, right? Like the old movie, *Diagnosis Murder*. An old Christopher Lee thriller."

LaFleur ignored the distraction. "Let's not get ahead of ourselves. As much as we think we know about this, we still don't know an awful goddamn lot," LaFleur cautioned. "I want to approach this as systematically as we can tonight. You might think this is all too obvious, or that we've already covered it all before, but in fact we've been jumping around a lot, and haven't really gone over this at the level of detail I would have liked, as a team, I mean. I have a lot of notes, which I will use as we go through an analysis. And there are things we haven't really nailed down, like our new evidence, or lack of evidence, or whatever it turns out to be. I'm anxious to get some real traction on this."

"Agreed," they answered simultaneously. LaFleur rolled up his sleeves. He loved this part.

"I've always worked on the basis that the simplest explanation is often the best. Actually, that principle has a formal name, it's called 'Occam's Razor.' Either of you familiar with it?"

Maggie shook her head as Michael said, "Some sort of Middle Eastern logic puzzle or something, isn't it?"

"No," LaFleur said. "It's from an English philosopher, William of Occam. It's used a lot to help explain the scientific method, for example, or how to avoid mistakes when trying to come up with a theory on how something works."

Michael nodded with an enlightened expression on his face. "I understand," he said. "I have heard of it."

Maggie was still shaking her head, saying that she wasn't sure she was getting it.

"Maybe I stated it sort of loosely a minute ago," LaFleur said.

"A better description might be that the fewer assumptions you have to make about something, the more likely you are right about it—or to put it another way, the simplest solution satisfying the all known facts is the most likely answer. Does that make more sense?"

"Yes," Maggie said.

"Good. Well, up to now we have been making a lot of assumptions," LaFleur continued, "we haven't had much choice, really, since there is no hard evidence and no eyewitness that we know of. But we still have a set of facts to work with, and can still use Occam's Razor to narrow the possibilities significantly." Maggie and Michael were now both nodding in agreement.

"There is another aspect to this method that I have developed over the years, and that is to use it, well, almost in reverse, when I am getting lost in a case, say. It can be a good way to work out the M.O., the *modus operandi*." This got quizzical looks. "What I mean," he continued, "is that most criminals obey the rule of Occam's Razor, even if unconsciously. They want the most return for the least effort, and that often means taking the simplest, most obvious course. Even something like a crime of passion. There's nothing complicated about it, really. Very simple cause and effect, but triggered by emotion, or an irrational response to an extreme situation."

"How can it be irrational, if it's a logical process?" Maggie asked.

"That's sort of what I meant by it being unconscious on the part of the criminal," LaFleur answered. "But it's more like what we need to do now, use the principle to reverse engineer what happened. You get better results if you narrow the assumptions down to the same level that the criminal used, even if used unconsciously."

"Okay," Maggie said. "That is starting to make sense."

"Michael? You with me?" LaFleur asked.

"I'm there, A.C.," he said.

"Okay. I've made up a couple of charts to get us started," LaFleur said as he gave each of them two printouts. "I've made two tables, one of some standard warning signs, the other of factors specific to this case."

"You weren't kidding when you said you were prepared to look at this systematically tonight," said Michael. Looking over the pages LaFleur had just handed him. "This is excellent."

"Take a look and tell me if you disagree strongly with any of the rankings or with my final 'scores,'" LaFleur asked. "The conclusions will go on the white board under *Angie/Personal*."

While they were reading, he had started drawing out a grid on the whiteboard, referring to his notes from time to time, making four columns, headed left to right: *Angie, Mahoney, Montgomery*, and *Other*. Under each heading except *Other*, he put in subsections for *Personal* and *Medical*. In the columns for Mahoney and Montgomery he added three more categories: *Behavior: Post-Mortem, Opportunity*, and *Motive*. He wasn't all that happy about using the old standbys "opportunity' and 'motive' but hadn't come up with anything better; and the terms had the advantage of being familiar. His entries for *Other* centered around some of the most enigmatic elements of the case: here he had defined categories for *Evidence* and *Events*. Once he was done with the grid, he sat back and let them finish their analysis of his suicide factors.

Common suicide warning signs/risk factors

Warning Sign	Y|N|Unknown
Talking about suicide, death	N
Depression	N
Neglect of appearance	N
Increased substance use	N
Dropping out of activities	N
Isolating oneself from others	N
Feeling that life is meaningless	Unknown N
Restlessness and agitation	Y
Sudden improvement in mood	N
Making final arrangements	N
Ending significant relationships	Y
Giving away possessions	N
Difficulties in job/school	N
Sexual identity conflict	Possible - Y
Accessibility to lethal methods	Y

11/15 No (75% against), only 4/15 Yes (25% for)

NOTES:

Center for Disease Control (CDC) criteria: need evidence of both intent and if self-inflicted.

Evidence of intent: "absence of evidence of intent is not evidence of absence of intent"

Case-related factors: weighted 1-10, 1 being least probable for suicide, 10 most probable; total possible = 220.

Fact	Rating	Notes
No suicide note found	4	Only 33% leave note (Was it taken?)
Age (22)	2	15-20% under 25
Sex: Female	5	More likely to attempt, less likely to succeed. Accidental OD?
Religion: Catholic	1	Prohibited – Angie was devout
Buried in St. Peter's (Catholic) cemetery	3	Canonical prohibition on funerals for suicide in effect until 1983 – but still was discretionary by priest
Family situation	1	lived with parents; large local family
Meeting plans	1	Coffee with friends
Known prior intent	2	Most have given definite warnings of their suicidal intentions
Personal plans outside of work	2	Just bought snow tires
Personality/behavior	1	Described as a "pleasant girl"
Locked door	7	Suicide-did not want to be disturbed. (Murder-delay discovery.)
Child's airway tube	2	gag reflex; no vomitus; has to be done after patient is unconscious.
Romantic involvements	7	Rumors/relationships: lesbian and/or with a male Dr. - Framed? Pregnant? Autopsy says no)

Social/Community Activities	1	very active - Bowling, sports, fishing; softball, local role model; Natl. Council of Catholic Nurses; Alumni Assoc.
Time of day: 8:00AM	6	If done in a hospital, most common time between 5-7AM; overall between 7AM-4PM – peak at 8am
Sunday	6	Most tend to happen on weekends
Time of year: September	3	peak months: late spring and early summer;
Accessibility to means	10	Easy access
Method	2	Anesthesia (rare); not a usual form of suicide; even when it is done "recreationally" it's done late in day or at night
Region	3	Lower than average rate in eastern states
Christian music	3	Set up as a suicide setting? In place of a note? Or turned up loud to cover up sounds of murder?
Location: Found on a couch in lounge, not in OR	2	As a nurse would have been more likely to have done it in OR; lounge too public

Score assigned =74 -- about a 33% probability of suicide.

Maggie was the first to comment, saying that she would probably have set two or three of the specific factors slightly differently, but that her changes would cancel out, so the overall score was about the same.

"How did you come up with this?" Michael wanted to know.

"It's based on CDC guidelines and an old police department sourcebook," LaFleur answered. "I admit some of it is sort of arbitrary. But it's a way to quantify things."

"Well, it's not what would normally be considered a valid psychological analysis," replied Michael. "But it is an interesting approach. Actually, a lot of psychologists don't do this well," he amended.

"The tricky part," LaFleur elaborated, "is what I've quoted there from the CDC, that 'absence of evidence of intent is not evidence of absence of intent.' Some things about Angie's state of mind we will never know. All we can do is go on what Maggie has been able to tell us. Which is," he added, "probably pretty accurate, in my opinion."

"I don't have any problems with the way you've defined it, A.C.," said Maggie. "If anything, I think that some of the high scores you've given to specifics are outweighed by what we know about what Angie was going through at the time. Yes, she was 'agitated,' and there were some unpleasant job and personal things going on at the time, but I never believed that any of those things could have driven her to kill herself. She would have worked it out. So the combined chance, based on both the standard and the specific factors, might even be less than the 33% you have here."

"I agree," said Michael. "I don't see real evidence of intent."

"So our first differential is the statistical evaluation *Suicide: < 30% chance*," said LaFleur, as he wrote that up on the whiteboard. "But remember that affects our thinking on everything else, so let's keep that in mind as we go through the rest of this. We can go back and adjust it if we have reason to." He turned and reached out towards the whiteboard, marker hovering under the *Medical* heading for Angie. "Michael, you're the doctor; give us the medical factors. Then once we have a good list started, we'll go over them one by one and see what the cat drags in."

Michael leaned his chair back on two legs and looked at the

ceiling, then starting listing as LaFleur wrote it on the board. "One: child's airway. Two: no sign of choking."

"That's no vomit?" LaFleur asked.

"Right," Michael answered, keeping his eyes on the ceiling. "Three: resuscitation. That is, was it attempted, if not, why not? Four: unknown anesthetic gases, and settings on the machine." He looked back down. "That's all I can think of off the top of my head."

"Five," Maggie said. "Position of the body."

"Yeah, great, Mahoney mentioned something about that, too," commented LaFleur as he added that to the list.

"Six," Maggie continued. "Suspicious needle marks. Not in the autopsy, according to her sister."

LaFleur wrote *needle marks*, then switched markers and drew a red star next to it. "Anything else?" he asked.

Neither one had anything more to add.

"Next is Mahoney. I'll do this one," said LaFleur, "since I talked to him." He took up the black marker again, and recited as he wrote. "Under Personal: *affair with Angie*. Maggie, you never really finished telling me what you know, or think you might know, about that; we'll come back to it. Okay, Medical." He added three bullets:

- *turned off deliberately (cover up?)*
- *turned off accidentally (negligence)*
- *already off*

"Next, post-mortem behavior. I wasn't thinking along these lines until recently, even after my talk with the Pauls. I know of two from my interview: *left town*" he wrote, "and *won't talk*. Maggie, what can you add to that, anything?"

"I remember Paul being very upset, several days afterwards, and even back then, even after a few weeks, he still wouldn't talk about it. There seemed to be a lot of animosity between him and Montgomery that had not been there before. So maybe, 'Montgomery conflict.' I hadn't thought about it in exactly these terms before, but it was like they were each keeping something from the other, arguing a lot, that kind of thing."

"Good," LaFleur said, adding that to the list. "So, moving on. The next two categories I might not have put in here two weeks ago; now they seem particularly relevant. First, *Opportunity*. No question about that: *Yes*," he said, adding a red star. "He's admitted he went past the lounge early that morning, but has never explained why. And then, *Motive*. I don't know. *Unknown*," he wrote, adding a red question mark. "For now; once again, something we'll have to come back to."

LaFleur looked around the table. "Excuse me. I can see that we've forgotten something important here."

He stood up and went into the galley, coming back a minute later, three glasses in one hand, a wine glass and a couple of smaller glasses, stemmed but only about the size of a large shot glass. In the other hand, dangling and ringing like a couple of bells, was a bottle of Dove and a bottle of Grouse. "A bird in hand—" he said to them as he walked in, their immediate groans drowning out the rest. He laughed, set the glasses and the bottle of Grouse down on the table, poured Maggie a glass of wine, then switched to the Grouse and poured himself and Michael a shot.

LaFleur settled back into his chair. "Now we can get back to work," he said, raising his glass to the two of them. "Cheers." They returned the toast. "I needed this before we started on Montgomery."

The Montgomery column was similar to Mahoney's— inconclusive concerning a conflict with Angie, at least to the extent that it would be considered as a suicide factor; inconclusive in terms of the anesthesia, given that the autopsy was missing; inconclusive regarding behavior, in that he now seemed extremely reluctant to talk about it; there was agreement that there was an essentially equivalent *Opportunity*; but when it came to *Motive*, Montgomery got a question mark. They would have to come back to this.

"*Other*," LaFleur went on, after finishing with Montgomery. "We have another possibly related event we need to take into consideration: the pharmacist's death." He quickly wrote in *Pharm: Malignant Hyperthermia?* under the *Events* header. "And we also have some physical evidence," he went on. "At least some of which I consider significant," he could not help saying, for

Michael's benefit, as he added *Note* and *Syringe* under the *Evidence* category.

"There's also the appearance of the article in the O.R.," Michael added. "That's what started all this in the first place."

LaFleur added *Article* to the *Events* list, with *[current]* in brackets to differentiate it.

"What about the call to the police, the delay?" Michael asked. "I have been wondering about that all along. The timing, I mean, aren't there still questions about that?"

"Timing," LaFleur repeated, adding it under the *Events* list. "There are still some unanswered questions there, I agree. Anything else?" he asked, turning to each of them. They didn't have any more items. The outline complete, he then turned back to the board and said, "All right. Let's go left to right and try to make some sense out of this. Starting with *Medical*: we have a very loose description of what went on at the time she was found, and who did what; Mahoney claims to know nothing, except that she was dead when he got there. Montgomery claims to know nothing, except that she was dead when he got there. Maggie, you and Michael have done a good job at delineating several specific medical factors here, factors that related to the state she was in when she was found. But our big problem is how to confirm—or refute—Mahoney's story about what he did when Gale called him up there. Can you add to that?"

Maggie read through the list of Medical factors again. She barely concealed a slight shiver. "Not really. We've already gone over this. And remember, I didn't get there until after ten."

"Just go through it once more, to humor me," LaFleur said, trying to keep the impatience out of his voice. "Set a new baseline for tonight's discussion. And we have never talked much about what happened when you did get there, two hours later. Who you talked to, exactly what they told you had happened."

"Okay," Maggie said, still a little reluctantly, LaFleur sensed. "From what I was told, and what was reported, it was Martha who got there first, after she couldn't find Angie. I got the same story from both of the girls. They never said what it was Martha wanted her for, they probably didn't know. Or care. That all happened quite awhile before they were scheduled to meet her—Angie—in the lounge. Just like in the article." She paused, as if unsure about continuing in the manner of testifying in court. "Then Martha came back downstairs, I think." She paused.

"Go on," he said impatiently.

"All right. So, anyway, where was I? Martha came back in a very agitated state, saying she had found Angie in the lounge, and where was Paul, someone has to get up there right away, and things like that. LaNette said she was very upset, not something we saw too often. Well, never, really, so this was unusual. Then she paged Paul over the hospital intercom, and he came down to the office. Then they went up to the lounge together. Like in the article," she finished, lamely.

There was something oddly dissatisfying about all this. Had some aspects of what happened that morning taken on a character of unassailability, simply because they had appeared in the newspaper article? Had they, himself included, missed something here by relying too readily on what the article had to say? That happened all too often, and a small town newspaper reporter would have been very easy to manipulate. It was known that most, if not all, of the information reported there must have come directly from Montgomery. At one point Maggie had even mentioned something about the "steamrolling" done by Montgomery—all contact with police and press had been strictly controlled by him, even to the point of not allowing separate police interviews with some of the staff. And there had certainly been no press interviews outside of police and hospital administration, acting in concert, LaFleur felt sure. Even the tone of the article had become suspect, though he hadn't yet raised that point with the others. Procedure had broken down that day, LaFleur knew; it had been only a matter of hours, after all, that the entire investigation had been called off. But he was afraid he had overlooked something significant in the interactions of the staff that had made the initial discovery. Something was missing.

"What do we think about Martha's part in this? She got there first. Did she ever say anything about either the mask or the airway? Had anything changed since she first saw the body, anything like that?"

"She was never very clear on what she had seen. I guess I've always just put it down to her usual uncooperative attitude. But she was more than just uncooperative that morning, and maybe even less willing to discuss things than usual. She never had a good relationship with any of us, I've told you that; but that morning—and maybe I have also unconsciously put it down to everyone's general state of shock—that morning, she was very evasive. I don't think she ever said right out what she found. Every time one of us would try to talk to her about it, she would either put us off, or answer with a little prepared speech." She paused. "So I guess we don't really know what she saw, if the mask and airway were there or not. Or anything."

LaFleur leaned forward towards Michael with a sudden suggestion. "Is it possible to get in touch with Mahoney?"

"You mean right now?" Michael asked.

"Yeah, this airway thing is really starting to annoy me. Maybe if I press him again on it he'll come up with something new. Not as good as a face-to-face, but we don't really have the luxury of running a standard interrogation."

"Okay," Michael said after a short pause. "He's on call tonight. You could probably get him at the hospital."

"What's the number?" LaFleur asked as he stood up.

Michael called out the number as LaFleur walked into the bedroom to the phone. He came back a few minutes later; all Michael and Maggie had been able to hear were the muffled tones of what had sounded like a strained conversation, with a lot of starts and stops.

"Okay. He wasn't exactly happy about it, but not as unhappy as I expected. He still claims that either there was no airway in her mouth when he got there, pediatric or otherwise, or he took it out and doesn't remember the details. He admits that there could have been one there and he just missed it in the confusion. He did say that any information concerning it must have come from Montgomery. He doubts that Martha would have been aware of any details like that." As he spoke, LaFleur added a red question mark next to "airway," under *Angie/Medical*, added the same under *Montgomery/Medical*, drew a dotted line connecting them, and then turned back to the others.

"And, although I know this may be belaboring the point, since we do not know what gases were turned on, or if they were even turned on at all, really, and will probably never know, we cannot say with any certainty that is what killed her! Though that has been our working assumption. All we still have to go on is the statement in the article that says, let's see, 'A physician called to the scene by the charge nurse turned the machine off.' No confirmation from either Mahoney or Montgomery; however, my money's on Montgomery, since we're sure he was called in, we just can't say at exactly what time. And apparently he was orchestrating things. Michael?"

"Well, we can push them both again on it, but I think you're right. We're not going to get a definitive answer. It could have been either of them."

LaFleur didn't disagree. "The other thing I just asked Mahoney, while I had his attention," he continued, "was about the position of the body. Another topic that we discussed the other day that was not resolved to my satisfaction. According to my notes, Mahoney described her as lying on the couch with 'arms crossed' across her chest. Mahoney just repeated what he said earlier, but was more descriptive this time. He said she was lying straight on the couch, arms crossed over her breast, hands folded under her chin. He even said she looked 'peaceful.'"

"Okay," said Michael. "I think that is significant. I would have expected the body to have been in a more...disheveled...state. Asphyxiation is not pleasant, in my limited experience—I have never asphyxiated someone personally—or been asphyxiated—but this is really suspicious." He appeared to have a sudden thought. "Like a hanging victim. You've seen pictures, a Jim Crow lynching in the south, outlaw hangings in the Old West—not pretty. A lot of kicking and struggling if the neck isn't broken. Which it often wasn't. A.C., maybe you've even seen a hanging victim." LaFleur nodded slightly. Michael paused before voicing another thought. "In fact, that brings up another issue. He didn't say anything else about how she was situated?"

"No, why?" LaFleur asked.

"Well, I was wondering if there was any other evidence that— sorry, this is unpleasant, but you're certainly aware that there may have been other indications of death."

LaFleur looked over at Maggie as if expecting a reaction; when she didn't offer anything, he turned to Michael and asked if he was getting at what he thought he was getting at: "Do you mean evidence that she was moved?"

"Exactly," replied Michael. "Specifically, had there been any evacuation of her bladder or bowel, was there any evidence of that."

"Damn," LaFleur said, getting back up from the table. A few minutes later he returned from the bedroom, after making another call to Mahoney.

"Okay, he was even less happy about that question. Almost hung up on me. But he did answer, after a bit of careful prodding. No obvious stains on her clothing or on the furniture."

"It doesn't happen every time," Michael said, "so it might not mean anything."

"And lack of evidence isn't proof," LaFleur added, "but still, it is a very good point. Had there been something...obvious...that would have ruled out the fact that she had been moved. As it is we simply don't know, and it is still a possibility."

Michael and Maggie looked at one another, as if each weighing the possibility that she had in fact been moved into the lounge; if true, that would put things in a blindingly different light.

*

LaFleur sat back and rubbed his eyes wearily. They had barely gotten started, he mused. He thought better about reaching for the Grouse and picked up a marker instead.

"But what about the airway?" he asked, underlining it on the board, unwilling to give up on the issue, in spite of there being no obvious relevance. "Assume for the moment that we can take the report at face value, even if Mahoney can't or won't confirm it, and that there actually was an airway found. That's got to tell us something, doesn't it?"

Michael nodded. "It has never made any sense to me. A child's airway in an adult only goes back as far as the middle of the tongue. It would do almost nothing in terms of keeping your physical airway open under anesthesia, and nothing to keep you

194

from swallowing your tongue. And as we've said before, an adult airway can't really be put in place, not easily, anyway, when a patient is fully conscious. I suppose if you had a really subdued gag reflex, you could tolerate it for awhile, and it might even work. That's assuming she self-administered the anesthesia," he said, switching pronouns unconsciously, "and knew what she was doing. But to use a child's airway, assuming she knew what she was doing with an airway to begin with, would have been useless."

"Given all that, what can we conclude?" LaFleur asked pointedly. "What does Occam's Razor tell us?"

"Aside from the fact that whoever placed it did not know what they were doing?" Michael asked.

"Exactly. You just said 'whoever placed it,'" LaFleur responded. "Implying that someone other than Angie might have placed it. But does knowing or not knowing how it should be used necessarily leave out Angie? Maggie, what do you think? Would she have known that using a child's airway was useless, and used one anyway? How much did she know about anesthesia?"

"I agree with Michael. Anyone who was consciously using an airway, for its intended purpose, would not use a child's airway."

"So that leaves us with one more indication that she did not anesthetize herself?" LaFleur asked, trying not to lead too much.

"I'd give it about five to one," said Michael. "Maggie?" She nodded her assent.

"Okay, then. So far, so good," La Fleur continued, adding a red star on the board next to *airway*. "And we already have a star on *needle marks*. Any comments on that?"

"You're the source on that one, A.C.," said Michael. "I think there's only one real issue there—how reliable do you think Angie's sister's report is?"

"It's hard to imagine why she would invent something like that. Along with the conviction that it was the knowledge of the needle marks that led to her father's death. No, I think we can count on that. And on top of that we've also got Mahoney's statement," he said, reaching back and pointing out *no resuscitation* on the board, "that no injections were made when she was found. Taken together, fairly suspicious. However," he continued, "we do not know where the marks were located, or how many marks there were. Her sister was not clear on that point. I have no doubt that the mortician reported it to their father exactly as she described, but that doesn't tell us enough. They could have been self-inflicted."

Michael held up his hand. "But what about the fact that they weren't reported in the autopsy?"

"What autopsy?" LaFleur asked.

"Good point," Michael said, dropping his hand.

"Still, the needle marks are real evidence, we just don't know of what."

Michael raised his hand again, this time pointing to the *Evidence* column on the white board. "You're forgetting about the syringe."

"I'm not forgetting it; I'm just discounting it, in advance. That doesn't mean," LaFleur went on, making calming motions towards Michael, who was straining in his seat, "that I think it is an insignificant item. Just be patient a little longer. We'll get back to the syringe." Michael settled uncertainly back into his chair.

Dropping his marker on the table with a gesture of authority, LaFleur this time completed his reach for the bottle of Grouse, saying it was time for a short break. Then changed his mind, about the break, anyway, poured himself and Michael a shot, then poured Maggie another half glass of Dove, and turned back to the whiteboard.

"Let's look at Mahoney vs. Montgomery. Instead of looking at them separately. Maybe that will give us some different perspectives and at the same time speed things up. First, *Personal*. Maggie, you're the expert here. Give us some insights into the personal relationships Angie had with each doctor and what that could mean."

Maggie motioned to the board. "Under '*affair*,' I'd make that 100%."

LaFleur's raised his eyebrows and prompted her to elaborate. "So you believe Angie was capable of having a serious sexual relationship at that time? You have always described her as being pretty naïve, Maggie. Not that Mahoney wasn't trying, I'm sure."

Maggie bit her lip in exasperation, her unconscious "tell" to LaFleur that she was about to hedge her bets. "There is no question there was an affair. It may not have been common knowledge, not at first, but based on everything Angie told me at the time—and what we know from Paul Matthew—it certainly got to the point of disrupting Paul's marriage. Seriously disrupting it. So, I don't know, Angie may have built it into more than it was, but I have no doubt that there had been some level of…intimacy. I just can't say how far she went. Quite possibly all the way."

"So, a factor, either way," LaFleur stated.

"Either way? What…" Michael started to ask, then interrupted himself. "Oh. Suicide or murder." Maggie flinched at the word. LaFleur noticed but did not comment.

"What about her relationship with Montgomery? There was some conflict going on there, right? Phil and all that."

"Yes," Maggie agreed. "Angie really got caught in the middle of that. She said Montgomery was blaming Paul unreasonably. And that it added more strain to whatever relationship she was having with Paul. The fact is that Montgomery was in a position to coerce her to a large degree. And Paul too, for that matter."

Michael raised his hand again, but didn't speak, as if sitting in a classroom waiting to be called on. So LaFleur called on him. "Yes, Michael?"

"I think we need to look more closely at the 'postmortem' behavior for Mahoney. If Montgomery was threatening him professionally, that might give Mahoney a reason to leave town. And the affair with Angie, I'm not sure this fully explains his unwillingness to talk now."

"What do you mean?" LaFleur asked.

"Couldn't this have caused someone to do something drastic?" The question hung there for a moment.

"I don't believe Angie would have been distraught enough to do something as drastic as to commit suicide," Maggie interjected.

"I said 'someone,' not 'Angie,'" Michael said. "What about Mahoney?"

They all settled back in their chairs at this statement, as if to consider a verdict. Then all leaned forward again, as if saying, yes, we are ready to go there. Have been for quite awhile.

"And now that we're there, what about Montgomery?" Michael asked. "Do we have anything that would drive him to do something…well, drastic, for lack of a better word?"

"Now we're getting into motive," said LaFleur. "I suppose that is probably where we need to take it at this point. Maggie, based on what you've been telling me, romance doesn't look like the only factor when it comes to possible motives. What about the illegal activities going on. You've said Angie wasn't actually involved in that, right?"

"What?" Michael sat even further forward in his chair, the exclamation barely out before he said it again. "What?"

"Some of this you haven't heard yet, Michael," said Maggie. "Sorry," she finished, voice dropping.

LaFleur picked up for her. "You've heard about the possible drug dealings out of the hospital, right?" Michael nodded warily. "So. Angie seems to have believed something was going on with drug dealings at the hospital that was, in Angie's mind at least, somehow vaguely related to the death of the pharmacist. Or if not related, there was pressure being put on Mahoney and Angie concerning the death at the same time the affair broke. On top of that, Montgomery was doing illegal abortions at the hospital. Maggie knew about it. Assisted, in fact. There's more to it, of course, but what we need to focus on at the moment is whether or not this was related to Angie's death. According to Maggie," he said as he looked over at her, getting the go ahead to continue, "Angie had come across them in the O.R. more than once. So, the question is, was Angie implicated, either directly or indirectly? Something Maggie might have said. Something Montgomery would see as a threat?" He paused, again checking out of the corner of his eye, and seeing Maggie nodding, went on. "Maggie confronted Montgomery and threatened to expose the operation. She even went so far as to go to the D.A. with it. Which went nowhere."

Michael's expression had been changing from astonishment to bewilderment as LaFleur kept adding complication upon complication. *What the hell had these two been up to in the past few days, and why hadn't they told me?* was practically written on his face.

LaFleur half expected Michael to say exactly that as he finished. "So, could that have been a factor in her death, and if so, how, and more importantly—this question is for you, Maggie—why go after Angie if it was you who was doing the actual threatening?"

Now it was Maggie's turn to look a bit bewildered. She apparently had not anticipated the question, though LaFleur had to wonder why not. Unless he was misreading her. He realized they had all been sitting there in shocked silence for nearly a minute, so he directed a question to Michael, hoping to get Maggie to elaborate as a follow-up.

"So, Michael—first reactions can be very valuable." He left that hanging.

Michael studied Maggie's face for a moment, then gave a low whistle, shook his head slowly, and topped off his Grouse. "You actually went to the D.A., Maggie?"

"Yes, and like A.C. said, nothing came of it. Except that Angie died a few days later."

"Well, it's not at all obvious that's related, not as a first reaction, anyway," Michael said, hesitating.

"And?" LaFleur prompted.

"So, it was a dangerous accusation. Life changing potential, and not in a good way, and in more ways than one. That was serious stuff. Even birth control was illegal in New York State then. Not to mention the alternative. And not to mention the Catholic Church." Maggie held her face stone-still. If Michael was looking for a reaction, he didn't get it. "The fact that the D.A. did not pursue it is very suspicious. Then what, there is the drug dealing, and Angie believed that was connected to the pharmacist's death somehow? What, part of a bigger cover-up? So if Angie knew about both the operations and some sort of drug ring, and if Montgomery had been involved, that might tip the scales and give him enough of a motive to want to get rid of her." LaFleur noticed that Michael had unconsciously shifted all the suspicion onto Montgomery, leaving Mahoney completely out of his discussion, even though he was the one who had practically accused Mahoney a few minutes earlier. Michael went on. "Might. Only might. It is a pretty drastic reaction. And it still doesn't answer your question, A.C. Why go after just Angie?"

Both Michael and LaFleur looked at Maggie, who looked back

with a look of resigned desperation.

"You're right, of course. It doesn't explain it," Maggie said. "That's what I have been struggling with all these years. Why not me? Why the *hell* not me?" She gulped at her wine. Her hands were shaking. "Why do you think I've been so intent on finding out what really happened that day?" She put down her glass and steadied it on the table. "You know, I don't know anymore than either of you why the article appeared again the way it did. I just know that since it did, there should be an answer." She sat back. "Why the hell not me."

*

Michael had gone home; he was exhausted, he said, and had an early morning. Maggie and LaFleur had moved to the salon.

"So, you want to talk about it?" LaFleur asked.

"What?"

"Don't 'what' me. You know what."

"Yeah, I know."

"Want me to tell you what I think?" he asked, after a few minutes had passed with nothing forthcoming.

"Yes, sure."

"Couple of thoughts. You said once before that you had a lot of guilt feelings about this whole affair. Hinted that you felt you may have been responsible in some way, but you never went any farther than that." He waited to see if she had any response. "Something you did, something you said, you think may have gotten Angie in trouble. You also said, practically the first time we met, that you had doubts at the time that you didn't follow through with."

"Yes, that's part of it. Both are part of it."

"And?"

"Well, everything we went over tonight, and for the past several days—we've all come to the conclusion that it wasn't suicide, right? Well, I've known that for forty years. Lived with the knowledge that she had been killed, but could never do anything about it. I've told myself over and over that there was nothing I *could* do; and I know to some extent that is true. What I haven't

200

told you about is the fear I lived with for months, years even, that I would be next."

"You never went to the police?"

"How could I? They had closed the case; the D.A. made it perfectly clear this was one case that would never see the light of day, no matter what was said or done. Angie's father learned that. The hospital administration clamped a lid on so tight that none of us could breath."

"But...." he prompted.

"But I was the one who had threatened Montgomery. Oh, Angie knew what was going on, and even though I had ideas for awhile that she could help me against Montgomery, she never knew any details. I was afraid I had involved her, telling Montgomery I had witnesses, but I don't believe I actually named her, and I didn't think Montgomery really had anything against her. But then when she was killed I—" She broke off for a moment. "Can I get some more wine?" she asked. LaFleur got up to get it as she continued.

"When she was killed I started to think I set her up. I never believed all the sordid explanations, that she had been in a lesbian relationship, with whomever, and like I told you and Michael earlier, even if the affair with Mahoney was a dismal mess, she just would never have killed herself over it. Even so, the rumors were so persistent that for awhile I suppose I bought into some of it, not suicide, but because of the rumors I started suspecting she had been killed, for reasons everyone else believed caused her to kill herself. Is this making sense?"

"Sure," LaFleur said. "I understand."

"The worst part was all the pressure from Montgomery. He made my life a living hell, as they say. I don't know how I got through those months afterwards. I was a complete wreck. My job was threatened constantly by Montgomery. He had found someone else to assist with the abortions, thank God—I literally thank God for that, and Father Tommy. Montgomery even turned the administration against me. It took years for me to get a promotion, finally, after most of the original people involved were gone. But Montgomery wouldn't let me forget it. It ruined my personal life as well. I couldn't maintain a real relationship with any man I cared about. I lost all trust in people, even people who I know cared for me."

"That why you never got married?" LaFleur wasn't sure he should even ask. He didn't want to do anything to jeopardize the relationship they had; both were comfortable with the fact that they could be quite intimate without the complication of unnecessary obligations.

"That's the biggest part of it," Maggie admitted. "Oh, I got close once, but I called it off at the last minute. That made me feel bad for years, too, on top of everything else."

She took a gulp of wine from her glass. "Well, time, you know, it does dull things. Montgomery eventually left me alone, mostly, and everyone sort of forgot about it except as a weird story. Until now, anyway. And I got over my constant fear, fear of what I was never sure of, but it was always there, a kind of dread. Then when the article appeared and Father Tommy encouraged us to try to do something about it, I resolved to go along with it and learn as much as I could. It's been too long, and I'm tired, but I want to know what happened. I really do." A small streak of tears was running down her cheeks by now, even though her voice had stayed perfectly calm.

"I'm sorry," was all LaFleur could think of to say.

"I guess I should go now," she said, starting to get up.

"You don't have to, you know," he said.

"Okay," she said.

The Waiting Room

She should have gotten the note on her locker by now.

The O.R. was dark. The doors were barely open. When she came in, she would have to walk completely around the right side door in order to get to the light switches. Everyone else would be downstairs. Due to the holiday and the low workload, they were short-staffed this weekend. There should be no problem.

If only she had seen reason. Cajoling, threatening, everything but pleading—that was never done, of course—nothing had worked. She simply dug in her heels and resisted even more at every turn.

A portable anesthesia machine sat nearby, ready to go. If interrupted, any questions could be easily explained. *She collapsed suddenly in the lounge, I was trying to get her to the O.R.*; or, *she collapsed suddenly in the lounge, I was trying to get the anesthesia machine over there to get oxygen to her*; or, *I found her in the lounge like this, I don't know what happened.* Or any number of other possibilities, all could be easily dealt with, one way or another.

Where was she?

This was so inconvenient.

Scheming

The day had started out cold and dark, about the way LaFleur felt. A dull mist hung over everything. The squat little lighthouse out at the harbor mouth drifted in and out of view, red roof appearing and disappearing between big chunks of fog drifting up the river from the lake. Snow, as always this time of year, was predicted. The difference today was that they were predicting more than usual; it could even turn out to be one of those record Oswego storms that future grandparents would relate endlessly to their grandchildren.

Maggie and Michael walked up the gangplank, knocked once, and came in. They slipped out of dripping coats, hanging them on the hook by the door.

"How's our comrade today?" Maggie asked brightly, as they walked into the salon/dining room. LaFleur tried to scowl, but was intercepted as Maggie leaned over and gave him a quick peck on his cheek. He returned her kiss a little more enthusiastically than he had planned. She responded just as amorously and sat down at the table next to him. Michael couldn't help but sit there and grin like an idiot, watching them carry on like a couple of kids. They turned and glared at him in a single movement. Michael laughed.

Maggie put the paper bag she had been holding on the table. "Lunch," she said. "Soup from Wade's." LaFleur thanked her with another quick kiss.

Maggie settled back in her chair and faced them both. "So, what now?" she asked, putting a more serious note in her voice.

"I've been thinking about that all morning", LaFleur said. "We need to get more out of Montgomery," LaFleur said. "We need leverage. And Mahoney, too, we know he's hiding something." He hesitated, not quite wanting to admit to himself that he could be contemplating something that could put them all in danger—and that Maggie might already have put them there. She could still be holding something back, even after all that had happened and all that she had already confided in him.

After lunch, LaFleur insisted on picking up where they had left off. They had all abandoned the thought of suicide and were now trying to determine which way to go with the obvious alternatives.

He started by replaying the results of the first interview with Montgomery. "Very evasive. No direct answer on anything, particularly the airway and the machine. No recollection of who did the autopsy. Maybe I should show him the order. Got very defensive when I pushed on the autopsy, and the mention of injections. This brings me back to our biggest problem. Evidence." He walked over to the whiteboard and tapped it with his soup spoon.

"As in, lack of. We have almost no physical evidence; and the only circumstantial evidence we have is third hand, forty years old, or suspect." He shrugged as he put the dirty spoon on the table. "And even the meager physical evidence we have is also suspect— we don't even know that it is related. We're guessing." Michael looked dejected; Maggie's demeanor did not change.

"The note found by Angie's sister in the uniform Angie was wearing that day was assumed by her to be from Maggie," he went on. "Maggie assures us that she did not write the note. That leaves—given our current state of supposition—either Mahoney or Montgomery. We have no hard evidence that it came from either one of them, but based on the content there is at least a fair chance that it did. Someone who's name starts with 'm.'"

"And we are also assuming that she got the note that morning, aren't we, that it was not just left in her pocket from some time earlier?" asked Michael. "And why wasn't it found by the police?"

"It had slipped partially into the lining, her sister said. She didn't find it until later. But she was sure it's from the jacket she was wearing that day, and the family collected her personal things the next day. Why didn't someone else find it first? Don't know. It was all done in a big hurry, everything being swept under the rug. The police may have never really had a chance to look for it. In fact we know that it was reported to them that 'there was no note.'

So they weren't looking for anything. Assuming that it is what it appears to be, we can only guess at a reason for someone asking her to come to the O.R. that morning. That is, if we first make the presumption that she was killed by whoever left her the note, then we can try to work backwards to determine the sender. Or if we presume the reason for sending the note was not to set her up, but had some other, simpler meaning, we might also come to a reasonable conclusion about the sender. In both cases we begin with the conclusion and see how well we can make things fit. Your eyes are glazing over. Is this not making sense?"

"No, it's fine."

"Yes, go on."

"We're trying to narrow possibilities. Reverse Occam's Razor, remember?"

Maggie began to interrupt, but LaFleur held her off. "Let me get this all out before I lose track myself. We also have what we believe to be inconsistencies in the reported events, along with Maggie's long held doubts as to the nature of the incident. Then there is the autopsy order, which while not the postmortem is at least more than we had before. All this," he stressed again, "is more than just circumstantial, it is goddamn nebulous." They both grimaced. "However," he continued, "that doesn't mean we can't make our evidence, flimsy as it is, work for us, rather than against us."

He had been anxiously waiting to spring the results of the lab analysis on Michael and so jumped to that next. "We also have one other piece of what Michael would like to believe is physical evidence; the syringe left in the wall behind the old cabinet. I got the lab results from Amos. There's about a 95% chance that syringe was last used for curare."

"I knew it!" said Michael. "I mean," he stumbled, "I didn't *know* it, I just…." He appeared to realize that he didn't really know anything more than that the syringe had been used for something readily explainable and, not surprisingly, potentially lethal, as are most hypodermic drugs. "What about fingerprints?" he asked, still hoping there was something significant about the syringe.

"Well, it's not impossible to get latent prints from a good surface after a long time, even thirty, forty years, depending on how well the surface has been protected. But nothing in this case showed up. Fingerprints are much more difficult to lift than most people think. Even on a surface like stainless steel or glass, it's often very difficult to get good prints, even when they're fresh. In any case, once you have the prints, you have to have something to match them against. And I don't feel like going around the hospital trying to trick people into leaving their fingerprints on a water glass."

"So it's worthless," Michael said.

"As a piece of solid evidence we can tie to a specific act? Yes. As I expected, and as I guess you expected, even as much as you wanted it to be something more. But there's a way we can use the note and the syringe—both only marginal at best as hard evidence—as leverage. We can represent them as solid evidence to each of our suspects"—no sense pretending that is not how they were all thinking at this point—"and see what we can learn." He then proceeded to lay out his "little scheme," as he called it.

The next day, they agreed, LaFleur would take on Montgomery again; Michael would talk to Paul Michael. They would confront both with the evidence, making much more of it than there really was, and try to force a reaction. LaFleur was going to push as hard as possible at this point, encouraging Michael to do the same; he believed they could really get something significant out of this. He also knew that they were running out of options.

LaFleur had tried and failed to get an appointment with Montgomery through his secretary, so he simply checked Montgomery's schedule and planned to hijack him in his office, after normal hours—his secretary had confirmed that he would be staying late, not realizing she was setting up her boss. Mahoney had agreed to an after-hours meeting with Michael, though noncommittally. The meetings would occur at about the same time. This was almost a necessity—they didn't want there to be any possibility of Montgomery and Mahoney comparing notes, even by chance.

They had a prepared script they were going to follow, making allowances for deviations. Michael had forged a copy of the note that, if not examined too closely, would pass for an original.

LaFleur had both the original note and the syringe. Maggie thought they were both crazy and that it would probably work. And so was a little afraid of what they might find out.

"We haven't got much to go on," LaFleur said, "but that just means we've got to be a little more aggressive. We've really got to push these two guys. And play 'em like you've got 'em, as they say."

And hope for a little luck.

O.R.

The hallway was empty as Angie made her way towards the O.R. Whenever she was in the hospital on days like this, or late at night, when no one was around and the halls were quiet, Angie always had a sense of power, of ownership. The hospital became, briefly, her hospital alone. She would sometimes close her eyes for a second or two during a bad stretch in the O.R., trying for the smallest fraction of a moment to recapture that feeling, in order to calm herself, get back her focus. Just the few steps she had taken into the dark hall as she left the elevator were enough to bring on the feeling now. She would never have described it as serenity, but it was as close as she got to it outside of Mass.

The doors to the O.R. were practically closed, the wire-mesh windows dark. As Angie pushed open the door she could barely make out a glint of stainless steel here and there, reflecting what little light from the hall was filtering into the room. Her eyes had not yet adjusted to the dark. She turned to the left and reached out, feeling for the light switch. As her hand brushed against the wall, sliding along the smooth, cold tile, she sensed something behind her, a slight rush of air. She was abruptly pulled back and away from the wall by an arm across her neck, putting her in a choke hold. She felt a sharp pain in the back of her leg. She began gagging and reached up, instinctively clawing at the hands holding her. She could not think. Nothing about this made any sense. She felt her heart pounding in her chest as adrenaline pumped into her system. She tried to kick backwards at whoever was holding her, but her foot just flopped uselessly in the empty air behind her, then hit the floor and twisted sideways. She was getting dizzy, weak. She slumped to one side, her hands now clutching at the air, now at the arm around her neck, her fists opening and closing as if she were preparing for her piano lesson. Her piano lesson was tomorrow. She felt another sharp prick as a hypodermic needle slid into the soft skin of her inner thigh.

She sagged, but was caught from behind. She felt arms grasping her under the elbows and she was dragged awkwardly to the middle of the room and laid out prone on the floor, face down.

She felt her body turn. As her head twisted back and to the side, she saw a familiar face looking down at her. The attacker saw a flicker of recognition in her glassy eyes.

"Oh, Angie," she heard, as her head fell back against the floor.

Angie's eyes remained riveted on the person bending over her, still focused, still pleading.

She gasped for air.

Presumed Guilty

It was already pitch dark outside, early evening. LaFleur hoped that meant less chance of interruption. It had been snowing hard all day; it had started just after midnight, in fact. There was over a foot on the ground already—enough to be inconvenient, not enough to worry about yet. LaFleur was a bit winded from the walk up the hill from the bridge. He stopped in the lounge next to the E.R. and had a drink of water before going on to Montgomery's office.

"Dr. Montgomery," LaFleur said genially as he walked into the doctor's office unannounced, closing the door behind him. "Got a minute?"

Montgomery looked up in what LaFleur took to be a negative reply, not deigning to speak.

"Promise it will take just a minute, I know you're probably busy. I called your secretary yesterday, couldn't get an appointment, but decided what the hell, this is really nothing that can't be done on the spur of the moment, and will take less of your time than even planning a meeting would take."

The doctor pointedly closed the folder in front of him. "Well, now you're just wasting my time. But since I appear to have no choice, let's get on with it."

*

Paul Michael Mahoney barely glanced up as Michael walked into the visitors' lounge where he had been waiting.

Michael closed the door.

"Thanks for meeting with me again, Paul," he said, pulling up a chair.

"Do I have a choice?"

"Sure. Why do you say that?"

"Well, you are the head of the department."

Michael had not intended any coercion. "Let's not consider this work related," he suggested. Mahoney shrugged. "Get you anything?" Michael asked, motioning to the Coke machine in the corner.

"No, thanks. I don't really have much time."

"Okay. Well, anyway, as I told you yesterday afternoon, there are some loose threads we'd like to tie up regarding the suicide. Well, presumed suicide, that is."

*

Montgomery glared his disapproval at LaFleur's first question.

"We've gone over this before. The last time we met, I told you, repeatedly, that I do not know anything about why she may have committed suicide."

"That's not what I asked," LaFleur countered. "I asked, do you have any reason to doubt the presumption of suicide."

"I believe we have also covered this more than sufficiently. There is no 'presumption,' as you call it. Dr. Paul Mahoney was called to the scene, where he pronounced her dead. Asphyxiated. Self-inflicted. So determined by the Coroner *and* District Attorney, in fact."

"You're right. We have covered all that. So let me tell you what I really want to talk about."

*

Mahoney blinked. "Presumed?"

"Well, yes. Let me explain. And like I said before, tsi is confidential, that's very important."

"Yeah, I understand. What do you mean, presumed?"

"Just what you think it means. We have reason to believe that Angie did not commit suicide."

Deliberate pause. "You think she was murdered."

"Yes."

"I'll have to think about that."

"You haven't before?"

No answer.

"We think we have proof."

"I'll really have to think about that."

Michael waited a minute or so as Mahoney sat quietly staring at the wall.

"Well? Want to hear any more?" he finally asked.

"Proof means a suspect."

"Yes."

"Who?"

"Don't you want to hear the evidence first?"

"You said 'proof' before, not 'evidence.'"

"Is there a difference?"

"Yes."

"Okay, yes. I see what you mean. Let's just say evidence, then."

"Okay."

*

"What was the nature of the conflict between you and the nurses, Dr. Montgomery?" LaFleur asked. "That is, between you, Maggie Malone, and Angie Frascati."

"Why do you think there was a conflict?" Studiously ignoring eye-to-eye contact, LaFleur noted.

"Maggie told me that there was a series of unpleasant encounters, regarding certain, well, unauthorized procedures being performed by someone at the hospital. Given your position there, I hoped you might be able to shed some light on who else at the hospital may have been involved. It could have something to do with Angie's alleged suicide."

"There you go again, Mr. LaFleur," now staring him in the eye. "'Alleged.' What in God's name are you trying to get at?"

LaFleur recognized the misdirection away from the mention of the abortions and used it as a misdirection of his own. "Alright. Sorry if I have been too indirect, the legalese sometimes gets in the way; but what I have to tell you is, well, sensitive. Extremely sensitive."

*

"What kind of evidence?" Mahoney asked.

"Some circumstantial, some physical," said Michael. "To be honest, we were hoping you could shed some light on a couple of things."

"If I can."

"Good. We know that Angie had become involved in a conflict with Dr. Montgomery. Along with Maggie. Maggie has said that there may have been illegal activities going on. We need to know who else was involved. We hoped you might be able to suggest, well, do you have any ideas about who—"

"Ideas."

"Yes. Anything that might help—"

"I wouldn't know anything about that."

Michael looked down at his hands. *Rough start.*

"We have a note," he went on, "asking Angie to the O.R. across from the lounge. You've said you were in that area early that morning. Did you notice anything, do you have any idea who the note might have been from?"

"It wasn't signed?" Mahoney's tone told Michael that he should have expected this question, but still, that was quick.

"It was…initialed." He reached into his pocket and pulled out his copy of the note, which they had slipped into a clear plastic sleeve. He held it out carefully in front of Mahoney, just close enough for him to read, but not so close as to let him take it from him. Mahoney looked at it impassively.

"You think I sent it?"

"Not necessarily, no."

"But you think I might have."

Michael let that hang.

"What else?" Mahoney finally asked, after staring Michael down for almost a minute.

"As an anesthesiologist, you are familiar with the drugs, and the equipment, that Angie allegedly used to kill herself. These are drugs you have used for years, use almost every day. In addition to

214

other drugs, not just general anesthetics, but drugs that—"

"What are you saying?"

"We have reason to believe that she may have been injected with curare prior to being put under anesthesia."

"Fuck."

*

"I'm waiting." Montgomery began drumming his fingers on the desk, looked embarrassed by it, and stopped.

"We have uncovered evidence that leads us to believe that someone at the hospital was involved in the death."

"Preposterous. You can't possibly know that. It was over forty years ago."

"Nevertheless." LaFleur had been waiting thirty years to say that, but had never had the opportunity to interview someone pompous enough to make it work. "Nevertheless. There is really very little question—based on what we have found—that the circumstances of her death were more than unusual; the circumstances alone warrant suspicion, but what we know now goes far beyond suspicion."

"And by 'beyond suspicion' you mean…?"

"We believe we are ready to take this to the authorities."

"Preposterous," Montgomery repeated heatedly.

LaFleur let 'nevertheless' roll around on his tongue for a moment before continuing. "Would you be interested in seeing what we've found?"

Taking Montgomery's silence as a 'yes,' LaFleur reached into his pocket and slowly pulled out the note. "You'll forgive me if I don't let you handle this, I hope. We haven't finished the lab or handwriting analysis." He held the note up so Montgomery could see it clearly, watching for a reaction as the doctor read, his lips unconsciously moving slightly. When he finished he gestured toward the note dismissively.

"So? What does this have to do with anything?"

"It was found in Angie's pocket, the pocket of the uniform she was wearing the morning she died."

"Nonsense. There was no note. I checked."

LaFleur feigned surprise. "You checked? When was that? I thought you said before that everything had been cleared away by the time you got there."

"No, that is not what I said. I believe all I said was that the airway and the mask must have been removed before I arrived. That does not mean I was not involved in the aftermath at all. I assisted Dr. Mahoney with the disposition of the body, and during the course of that disposition we in fact searched for a note. None was found, as was reported to the police. As you pointed out in our last conversation, I believe."

"Well, I don't remember for sure what you said," LaFleur said, taking out his notebook. "I can check...but it really doesn't matter," putting the book away again. "The thing is, we can place the note with Angie that morning. As you can see, it is initialed with a capital "M." Any ideas as to who would have asked Angie to the O.R. that morning?"

"Obviously, Maggie Malone."

"She denies it."

"And you believe that?"

"What reason do I have not to believe her? In fact, I have ample reason to believe that she did not write it."

"There were other people at the hospital whose name began with 'm,' you know, probably several." He paused. "It could have been Mahoney. They were involved, you know. He and Angie."

"Yes, I know that. In fact, Dr. Fuentes is talking with Dr. Mahoney right now."

"So you suspect Mahoney?" *Just how clever does he think he is?*

"Not necessarily. We just feel that there may be information that he has been withholding about certain incidents. Up to now, that is."

"If you believe anything Mahoney tells you, then you are a bigger fool than I took you for."

"No offense taken, thanks," LaFleur answered cheerily; Montgomery glared back. "So, you think it could have been Mahoney." LaFleur sat back in his chair and rested his hands on the arms. As he hoped, Montgomery misinterpreted this as a sign that he was done.

"Yes. So, if that's all you've got, I'll have to thank you for not wasting any more of my time…?"

"I didn't say that was all."

*

Mahoney got up and walked over to the Coke machine, slipped in a dollar, jabbed the button. The clunk when the can dropped made him jump. "Want something?" he turned and asked Michael.

"Sure. Coke is fine."

Mahoney dug into his pocket, appeared not to have another dollar; he started counting out change; put that back into his pocket, pulled out his wallet; still no dollar.

Michael jumped up and pulled a dollar out of his wallet. "Here, I can get it."

Mahoney sat back down and took a sip of Coke.

*

"Remember the problem we had finding the autopsy report?" LaFleur had leaned forward, actually resting his elbows on Montgomery's desk. "Well, something finally did turn up."

"Really."

"Yes. And your name was on it. I seem to recall that the last time we talked you were having problems recalling just who performed that autopsy."

Montgomery didn't skip a beat. "My name commonly appears on many official records as either an authorization or an approval. That doesn't mean I performed the autopsy. It also doesn't mean that records that old are reliable."

You can't have it both ways, thought LaFleur, *even though you seem to be used to getting it that way for a hell of a long time.*

"Well, we believe that in this case we do have a reliable document. We also believe we can prove that she had been injected with curare prior to being anesthetized. Possibly a lethal dose."

Montgomery paled at this, even though showing absolutely no other reaction; LaFleur had seen it a thousand times over the course of his career, and it never failed to impress him, just how little control people have over their autonomous nervous systems. Well, that's why they're called autonomous, he mused as he waited for some sort of response from Montgomery's higher consciousness. When none was forthcoming, he continued.

"Let me show you something else. You might be able to help with this, too." He continued talking as he pulled the syringe box out of his jacket pocket and laid it on the desk in front of him, carefully opening it within its plastic bag to reveal the hypodermic itself. "This was found inside the wall of the O.R. that is being demolished. The O.R. that used to be the nurses' lounge, the one where Angie was found that morning. We've already had a lab analysis done which confirms the syringe was last used for curare. The stainless steel case has also been dusted for prints."

Montgomery cleared his throat nervously. LaFleur went on without slowing down, on a roll and thinking to himself that now was not the time to deviate from the script.

"I believe we have enough evidence to request an exhumation. As you must be aware, hair and fingernails continue to grow after death—" (LaFleur knew this to be untrue, but he was sure enough that even most doctors weren't aware of this to go with it—it had such a ring of truth to it) "—and so even if tissue analysis is no longer possible, recent forensic techniques, using carbon and nitrogen isotope ratios" (glad he had rehearsed this) "allow us to analyze follicle and keratin samples." He ran out of breath.

Montgomery took the opportunity to try to regain control of the situation. "If you think for one minute that I am going to sit here and allow you to continue with this, with this, preposterous…you cannot be serious. What on earth do you expect to—?"

"As I believe I just said," LaFleur interrupted. "We fully expect confirmation that she was poisoned, with curare, with this syringe."

*

"How do you know?" asked Mahoney.
"Know what?"
"That she was injected?"

218

"Um, evidence that was not reported in the autopsy, for one thing."

"What autopsy? I thought that was missing?"

Who told him that?

"No, actually, we, well, LaFleur, found a record, a partial record..."

"A partial record."

"Yes."

The rest of the Coke went down Mahoney's throat like water down a sluice, practically the whole can. *God, how does he do that,* Michael thought, *the carbonation would make me choke.*

"That's it, then, nothing else? No other evidence?" The empty can sailed across the room into the wastebasket in the corner, rattling around the bottom for what seemed like along time.

"Would you agree to be fingerprinted?"

"What?"

"Fingerprinted. You know...ink pad...FBI..."

"What for?"

"We have some fingerprints we want to match."

"Fingerprints on what?"

"A syringe."

"You've got to be kidding."

Sort of.

"Where did you find it?" Mahoney asked, voice breaking for a split second.

"In the lounge, actually," Michael answered evenly. "The O.R., now, well, the one being torn down, but in the same room where she died. Or where she was found, in any case."

Mahoney slumped a little, as if this were too much for words but still required some kind of response.

This was not going quite like Michael had expected. But then again, he had not really known what to expect, so how could it? *What was he going to tell LaFleur? Yeah, I asked him everything. What did he say? Not much. A lot. Time to push more buttons.*

"There are a couple of other things. One is regarding the death of the pharmacist, uh, Phil Cathcart, two weeks before Angie's death? Apparently Angie had serious concerns about what really happened that day, and Maggie thinks it could have a direct bearing on what happened later. Dr. Montgomery has said that there could have been charges of negligence brought—" Mahoney sat up at this, but remained silent. "—and also that there may have been negligence at the scene of Angie's death, improperly managing the handling of the anesthesia machine and other items, no resuscitation, other complaints—but that in consideration of your—"

"Whatever that son of a bitch has to say about it is a goddamn lie," Mahoney suddenly burst out, causing Michael to sit back with a jerk. "Goddamn it! How bloody long does he think he can keep that hanging over my head? That son of a bitch! He's the one who should be charged over that. Should have been charged years ago." He stood up, looked around the room, sat back down, looked at Michael defiantly. Michael stared back, unsure of what to say.

"We've made a request to have the body exhumed." Michael finally said carefully, hoping to hell he sounded believable. "To test for traces of curare."

"How do you do that?"

"Uh, hair, fingernails. There may still be traces. Do you have any objection to that?"

"When?"

"When what?"

"When are you going to exhume the body?" Mahoney asked, leaning forward.

"Um. We don't have a date yet. We, uh, just made the request. We don't have the order yet."

"If you ever get that exhumation order, you let me know." Mahoney sat back in his chair, a little smugly, Michael thought.

Michael hesitated before going on, then decided to risk it. "There is one other thing we should be able to determine in an exhumation," he said. "There is a chance that she was pregnant, and given the fact that you and she were—"

Mahoney stood up and walked out, wordless and glaring.

Michael sat alone in the lounge for quite awhile, wondering what had just happened. He finished his Coke and tossed the can at the wastebasket. It hit the rim and bounced off, hitting the wall, leaving a series of little brown rivulets running down to the baseboard.

220

*

It was like he had flipped a switch. Just like last time. Montgomery settled back in his chair and put on a mask of disdain.

Okay, you s.o.b.

"There's more." LaFleur said.

"No doubt."

"I don't believe you fully grasped the implications of what I said earlier, about Dr. Fuentes's visit with Paul Mahoney? We've been talking with Paul quite a lot, actually. He's being very cooperative."

Montgomery looked like he was about to say something but LaFleur cut him off. He had built up a righteous indignation and was not going to let it fizzle out.

"Let me lay it out for you so clearly that even you can't mistake my meaning. We have the note. We know who wrote it. We have the syringe. We know what was in it, and given where it was found, once we finish our fingerprint analysis we'll know who put it in that wall. We have the postmortem, and corroboration from both medical staff and family that there are—inconsistencies, shall we say—in the medical report. And yes, I know it has been over forty years, as you are so quick to repeatedly point out; and I know that our chances may be slim.

"And the mention of your involvement in illegal activities that you so glibly evaded a few minutes ago? Well, you may be interested to know that Ms. Malone is ready and willing to go to the D.A. with what she knows. Again. We believe it has a direct bearing on Angie Frascati's death. But even if we don't get exactly what we want, what Angie Frascati deserves, I seriously doubt that becoming embroiled in something like this, even after all this time, is what you would have envisioned as the crowning glory of your career. You may want to consider that over the next few days. There may still be a relatively graceful way out for you. Of course, I can't promise anything. I don't have the kind of pull I used to. But either way, you will face this. Publicly."

LaFleur sat back to collect himself. He had gone a little farther than he had planned here; but it felt right. Evidence or no evidence, trumped up or not, bluff or not. If you won the hand, you had the best cards, no matter what they were. He was sure that he had him.

Montgomery just sat there, as if he had just been asked whether he thought it would stop snowing soon.

LaFleur thought he had been prepared for whatever was going to happen in Montgomery's office. He thought he knew malice. He thought he knew hate. He thought he knew himself. What he was not fully prepared for was the extent to which Montgomery was able to intimidate him. He had been threatened many times, in many ways, but what came next was the coldest, most bone-chilling threat he had ever heard. Its effectiveness, LaFleur slowly realized, was in its total lack of emotion.

Montgomery started straight at LaFleur and in a low monotone simply said, "Detective LaFleur, you have just made the biggest mistake of your life.

"And not just you, LaFleur," he went on, voice even more menacing, lower still, his head down like a bull. "Not just you. You think I don't know what you and your girlfriend are up to? This time she is going to pay for it."

*

Recalling Montgomery's words as he walked down the street towards the 1850 House to meet Michael and Maggie made LaFleur's head start aching.

It had started snowing even harder.

Unmasked

Angie's skirt caught on her knees as it was pulled up higher, until it had been forced up almost to her waist, revealing her upper thighs. With one leg twisted to the side, the first injection was matched by a second, a few inches from the other, this time emptying the syringe. It might have been better to do the injection somewhere it would not have been found easily, like in the perineum. Oh, well, it wasn't that obvious. In any case, it could be glossed over in the postmortem, if that were done quickly enough; the hematoma would be delayed.

Her body was harder to move than anticipated. Pushing open the door to the O.R. made every bump and scrape sound like it was echoing all the way down the hall. There was safety in the lounge—best to get there quickly. The body was laid haphazardly on the couch. Next, the anesthesia machine was pushed out of the O.R. into the lounge. Its creaking wheels were even noisier than moving the body. There was a radio sitting on the table next to the coffee machine. The knob made a loud click as the radio was turned on. Nothing happened immediately; it had to warm up. Maybe it was not on a station. After twisting the tuning knob, the blare of religious music filled the room. That should do nicely; it was Sunday, after all. The heavy church organ would muffle everything.

After finally getting the body stretched out on the sofa, the anesthesia machine was moved closer to the couch. Angie's arms kept flopping over the side of the couch, getting in the way of uncoiling the hoses so the mask could be fitted over her nose and mouth. After trying a few positions, folding her arms across her chest with her hands lying flat under her chin kept the hoses in place. Her skirt still needed to be pulled down; this was done quickly, while lightly smoothing it out down the fronts of her legs. One shoe was missing. It must be in the O.R.

Closing the lounge door, it locked with a loud click. There was a short stab of panic while patting pockets for the key, breathing again only after feeling the outline of the key. The missing shoe was lying on the floor just inside the O.R. door, as suspected. It must have twisted off while trying to get the body out of the room, or maybe during the initial struggle.

The sudden sound of the elevator doors opening at the other end surgical wing seemed even louder than the choir in the lounge across the hall.

*

The doctor walked purposefully down the hall. Music was clearly audible, apparently coming from the nurses' lounge. He stopped in the middle of the hallway and listened for a moment, looking behind him. He walked over to the lounge door, turned the knob. It was locked. The window was dark. He thought he heard muffled noises inside the room, but couldn't make out anything recognizable. The music was too loud.

He turned and went back out into the main hall, again looking both ways. The wide doors of the operating room across from the lounge stood propped open. It was fairly dark inside the O.R., but equipment and tables were still visible. Nothing obviously out of place. He moved on.

*

A dark figure hid behind the wide O.R door, clutching the shoe with both hands, waiting until the fire door on the stairwell slammed shut. Then waited a little longer, until it was safe to return to the lounge.

The shoe was almost tenderly placed back on her foot and quickly tied. The anesthesia machine was next. One of the tanks was nitrous, one was oxygen. The mask was positioned over her nose and mouth, the elastic band pulled around behind her head, which kept lolling to one side. One hand wedged under the jaw seemed to hold her head in place. The nitrous valve at first stuck slightly, then turned easily all the way open. The oxygen valve was left barely cracked. A slight hiss was barely audible beneath the music still playing loudly.

The laces on that left shoe looked lopsided. Better tie it straight in the center so it looks normal. The damn shoe. *What was I doing before I got distracted by the shoe?*

The syringe.

The hypo was still lying on the O.R. floor.

The lounge door was closed and locked. The hypo was retrieved, placed back into its stainless steel case, and slipped into a pocket for later disposal. Plenty of time.

The machine was on, the mask was positioned correctly, everything exactly as planned—wait, no airway. That could be a giveaway, couldn't it? The supply room was just down the hall, so, back out again. God, look at this. How do we ever find anything around here? Still not panicked, but definitely getting there. An airway was finally located and the package ripped open. Back to the lounge, yet again, hope to God for the last time. The sound of the elevator opening caused a jerk of the hand as the airway was stuffed into her mouth, barely fitting it in behind the mask.

*

"Have you seen Angie?" Gale called the two nurses over to her.

The nurses looked over at the head nurse from their station without moving. They had hardly seen Gale all morning—who knows where she had been—but they were not surprised to see her in a bad mood already.

"Angie who?" called back LaNette.

"Don't be smart," Gale snapped. "Have you seen her yet this morning? I need to go over next month's schedule with her."

"We haven't seen her," Judy said. We're supposed to meet in the lounge for a coffee break in a little while. Maybe she went up there early."

Gale seemed to mull this over. "I have to go upstairs for awhile. If you don't see Angie soon, try to find her. She has to be around here somewhere."

*

There was still something wrong. Something had been left undone.

The note.

Check the pockets. Nothing there. How could that be? Check again. Nothing. She must have thrown it away, or left it in the locker room. So. Find it later, destroy it. Or even if not, what difference will it make, it can't be connected.

Someone outside was pounding on the glass, trying to be heard above the music. "Angie! Are you there?" No sound other than the music came from inside.

"Angela! Are you in there?"

Yes, she is. The person kneeling next to her, however, was not going to answer for her. Just be patient, another minute. She'll go away soon. While shifting slightly to move farther away from the door, crouching next to the couch, something hard fell onto the floor, clanging like Hell's own bells. The syringe case had fallen out of the coat pocket. The pounding on the door went on. It would not do to be found later with the syringe, a reasonable enough thought forcing its way through the near panic that had started at the sound of the elevator door and had built appreciably during the infernal pounding at the door.

There was a cabinet on the wall next to the table on the other side of the lounge. The murderer duck-walked to that side of the room, stood quickly and jerked open the cabinet with one hand, pulling the hypo case out of an inside pocket with the other. The pounding went on and on. Why would they keep pounding that way? Stretching an arm up, the syringe case was crammed onto the highest shelf. There was an odd scraping sound, and an even odder sounding thunk in the wall near the floor. By craning up as high as possible, a large gap in the back of the cabinet where it met the wall could just barely be seen. The syringe had fallen into the wall.

The pounding on the door finally stopped.

*

226

The head nurse pulled out the master key ring and flipped through about a dozen keys, trying them one at a time, until finding the lounge door key. She opened the door, stepped in and looked around.

*

"Martha. What are you doing here? What's wrong?"

"Oh. Dr. Montgomery. Oh." She motioned toward the couch as he entered the room.

Montgomery turned and pulled her by the arm out into the hallway. "Go find Dr. Mahoney," he said over his shoulder, as he went back into the room.

Lake Effect

The snow had piled up about two inches deep on top of LaFleur's hat by the time he made his way down to the bar. He shook it off as he came in, but there was already enough of a mess in the entry way that it didn't matter much. Michael was already there, waiting for him back at the bar, two shots of Grouse sitting in front of him, little golden reservoirs of liquid peat. LaFleur slid onto a stool.

"Ah, thank you, Michael," he said quietly, raising his glass at the same time. "Cheers."

"Cheers." If Michael noticed the weariness in LaFleur's demeanor, he didn't comment on it.

"So how did it go?" LaFleur asked.

"I'm not really sure how it went, other than this: he knows something. Something big."

An eyebrow rose over a sip of Grouse; LaFleur didn't trust himself to comment.

Michael incorrectly took that as a sign of dubiousness. "I wished you had done it, or at least had been there."

"Sounds like you did more than fine on you own," LaFleur reassured him.

"How'd go with you?" Michael asked.

"Let me hear what Mahoney said first."

"He started out being pretty cagey about it all," Michael began eagerly. "What I imagine your earlier interview with him was like. Wasn't willing to go into detail on anything, answered in monosyllables. He seemed a little out of it. Maybe coming off a hard shift, or week. He was defensive, but in a matter-of-fact way. I didn't get the feeling he was hiding anything other than his personal feelings, or so it seemed at first. Maybe still embarrassed about not helping more, I thought, or not being able to tell us more about what happened, or having feelings of remorse."

"But you were able to stay on message, follow the basic script?" LaFleur asked. "How did he respond to that?"

"Yeah. No real problem there. He was very evasive about the note. But it was the mention of curare that really shook him. I wasn't sure at first how to gauge the reaction, but after a few minutes I was convinced that he was more upset by that than anything else we had talked about so far. He was...shocked."

"Could be read either way."

"I know. So, anyway, I just kept going at him. It was when I started really pushing him on the conflicts with Montgomery that things got interesting."

More eyebrow raising, double-barreled this time.

"I hinted at the possibility of negligence in Cathcart's death, and then questioned his handling of the scene in the lounge—the gases, and so on—and he immediately came unglued. He accused Montgomery of 'holding something over him,' he didn't say what—but it was obviously about the pharmacist—and that Montgomery is the one who should be 'charged.' Then he did a one-eighty, said if we ever got an exhumation order he wanted to know about it. Then he just walked out. He's lying about something, A.C. I'm sure of it."

"Wow," was all LaFleur could muster. Then, "Good job."

"So, how did it go with Montgomery?"

"If I knew the right answer to that, I would have told you as soon as I walked in here," LaFleur answered, rubbing his eyes. "God's bloody truth, Michael? I think I may have screwed the pooch there."

*

While LaFleur and Michael sat warming themselves in the bar, Maggie was still trying to finish up at the hospital, anxious to get away and meet them. She had stayed late that night, covering an extra hour for a colleague who had been called away to a minor family emergency. She was standing at the nurses' station going over charts.

"Maggie, glad I caught you," she heard behind her. It was Montgomery, walking up to the nurses' station. "How are you?" he asked pleasantly.

"Okay." *What does he want?*

"I've been looking for you," he went on. "I was just going over the staff health records and noticed that you still haven't had your flu shot. I can do it for you."

Maggie frowned in confusion. "I haven't had my flu shot?"

"Not according to the list. Fran, hand me that staff vaccination list, will you?" he said, reaching over the counter. "Yes, that's it. Thank you."

"I'm almost sure I had it," Maggie said, "weeks ago."

"Not according to the list," Montgomery repeated. "Maybe you're thinking of something else. Yes, here it is," he said, holding out the list Fran had handed him—the one he had made out earlier and left on the desk. "Not checked off here. Maybe you're thinking of hepatitis. Have you finished the sequence?"

"Well, maybe that's it. I do so many vaccinations myself; these things all run together sometimes."

"Yes, I know the feeling." She guessed he didn't but was simply trying to be agreeable, for a change.

"Okay, then, no problem, I guess," she said.

"Fine, I'll be back to do it later." He turned and walked away quickly before she thought to tell him she didn't really have time tonight.

"I'll be in my office," she said.

"Fine," he called out as he disappeared down the hall.

"He can be so damned annoying," she said to no one in particular.

"I agree," said Fran.

*

"Maggie, there you are," she heard from the doorway. Montgomery was standing outside of her office.

She looked up and forced a smile in greeting. She had learned long ago that it made dealing with Montgomery easier. "Hi, Dr. Montgomery. I was just about to call you. Are these instructions

230

correct, did something change since this afternoon?" She passed over a clipboard with a patient's chart attached.

He took a quick glance at it—good thing she had smiled—and passed it back. "Yes, yes, that's fine. Did Sheryl leave this with you without explaining the problem?" he asked suspiciously.

Oh, crap. "No, not at all. I just wanted to double check, make sure I hadn't missed something."

"No, no, it's fine," he said impatiently. "So, your flu shot. I'll grab the vaccine and be right back. Wait here." He turned and left.

"But Dr. Montgomery, I really don't have time tonight, and anyway, I'm sure that I..." she called out to his back, already knowing it was useless. *Damn him.*

After he left, she remembered she hadn't called LaFleur to let him know she would be late. She speed-dialed his cell, but he didn't answer, as usual. She scrolled down the menu to Michael's number. He answered from the bar.

"Michael, hi. I'll be a little late. Yeah. Had to cover for Janice, but I'm leaving soon." There was a short pause. "No, wait, don't hang up! Montgomery claims I missed getting my flu shot; he's getting it right now. Shouldn't take long. Okay. Yeah, I know. Okay. Bye."

She slipped the phone back into her pocket, and went back to the charts, going over the changes again carefully, now that Montgomery had confirmed there was nothing wrong. Unlike some of the younger nurses—Maggie didn't think she was being too judgmental here—she always went through the charts meticulously. It used to annoy some of the doctors, but she'd caught enough simple mistakes that they all relied on her thoroughness now. She hoped that at some point they could come to expect the same thoroughness from the rest of the staff.

Finally satisfied that she understood the new orders, she thought about taking the charts out to the nurses' station, then decided to just wait for Montgomery and get this over with; she didn't want to be gone when he got back, which would only annoy him and drag this out even longer. She'd drop the charts off on her way out. She was starting to wonder where in the hell Montgomery was when her door opened again.

"Pull up your sleeve. This will only take a second."

He turned away, set a hypo kit and a vial on the counter, and prepared the shot. He seemed to be taking more time than necessary, she thought. "Here we go," he said as he held up the needle.

Maggie reached over with her left hand and grabbed her elbow to steady her arm. "You know, I am sure I've already had this shot. Maybe we'd better double check the file? I don't want to take a chance of—"

"Stop worrying. I'm sure of it," he declared, moving over to the stool she was perched on, taking her arm.

"But—"

As the needle pierced the skin, Maggie felt an unusually strong stinging pain, not like any flu shot she had gotten in the past. She looked down as Montgomery continued to press the plunger. The syringe was much too large, she thought. And the vaccine was the wrong color. It should have been a whitish color, with an opalescent shine to it. This was a completely clear, almost viscous looking fluid going into her arm. And it hurt like hell. *This wasn't the right*—she jerked away, eyes wide, jumped down and pulled away. The hypo came out of her arm.

"What are you—"

"Get back here!" he shouted. He reached out and grabbed at her arm, jabbing in her direction with the syringe. She started to fall, felt the tip of the needle brush against her neck, and then backed away. She flailed out at Montgomery as he continued to approach, and somehow managed to connect, her forearm smashing into his larynx. He fell over a stool and crashed into the exam table at the side of the room, then fell all the way onto the floor, the back of his head glancing off the corner of the table on the way down. He lay breathless, wheezing, struggling for air against the laryngospasm clamping down his throat from Maggie's blow. *If only I were younger*, he thought. He heard her run out of the room, then a thud as she fell. *Ah, that's it, she's done for.* Then he heard her regain her footing, then her footsteps echoing in the empty hallway. *Got to go after her.* He raised himself up on his elbows, then fell to the floor, still unable to get up.

Maggie, back on her feet, ran to the nurses' station, but it was temporarily deserted; the nurses were on their first set of evening rounds. Maggie felt an odd sensation spreading from her shoulder into her torso, and her vision blurred momentarily. She grabbed the edge of the counter to steady herself. *E.R.*, she said to herself. *Got to get to the E.R.* She started running again, unsteadily. She swerved into a wall, then straightened herself out and continued down the hall. She just managed to stumble into the E.R. before collapsing onto the floor, fully conscious, eyes wide open, paralysis seeping through her body in a warm flood.

She gasped for air.

Uphill Slalom

"What do you mean, screwed the pooch?" Michael asked LaFleur, as he closed his phone and slipped it back into his pocket.

"I mean I think I really screwed up." LaFleur said. "Thought I was back in division with some half-assed punk up on minor possession or some shit." Michael had never heard him this down on himself before. "Crap, it's sad to be old and stupid."

"Come on, it can't be that bad."

"No, I think it can. I really got carried away. Laid it on. Had him sweating, perfect for going in later and finishing it right, but then I couldn't hold back. No finesse. I just kept hitting him over the head with it, finally even started using Maggie as ammunition." He leaned over and tried to see out the front of the restaurant. "Where is Maggie, anyway? She was supposed to be here by now."

"Oh. That was Maggie that just called, sorry. She said she would be late, had to cover for someone who left early."

"She's still at the hospital?"

"Yeah. Oh, and she said she had to wait for Montgomery, he was going to give her a flu shot. He made a big deal over it, apparently."

LaFleur looked puzzled. "But she's already had a flu shot, two, three weeks ago. She complained to me about it. Said it gave her the flu, like it always does. She hates it. Montgomery made a big deal over it, you say?" He felt a phantom sweat break out on his forehead. He knew the feeling too well. There was no sweat. Just his autonomous nervous system kicking in, assuring him that, yes, he had really screwed up.

"God damn it!" LaFleur yelled, as he jumped off the stool. "Come on, come on!" he grabbed Michael's arm and pulled him towards the front door.

"What the hell is wrong?" Michael hollered as they ran out the front door. "I don't have my coat!"

"Forget your coat," LaFleur yelled back. "I set her up, Michael. She's up there practically alone with Montgomery, and I set her up! Come on!" LaFleur had started slogging up the sidewalk, snow almost a foot deep. Michael yelled at him to stop.

"Stay there! I'll get my car." Michael ran off down the block.

Hope it's a goddamn four-wheel-drive, LaFleur couldn't help thinking, as he stood there gasping for breath, melting snow trickling down the sides of his nose into the corners of his mouth, down the back of his neck. *Goddamn snow. Damn, better call someone.* 911? No, he'd call dispatch directly. He pulled out his phone and started to dial before he realized the battery was dead. *Damn and damn again.*

Michael pulled up at the curb and waved him over. It was a four-wheel-drive. A Subaru, not an SUV. LaFleur would have trusted an SUV more, but still, at least it was four-wheel-drive. He jerked the door open and jumped in as Michael slid to a stop in the middle of the street.

"What did you mean, set her up?" Michael hollered over the noise of the defroster and the tires spinning in the deepening snow as he pulled away.

"Lost my goddamn head, as usual," LaFleur hollered back, not so much to be heard as out of near panic. "Practically accused him—no, not practically—I *did* accuse him of killing Angie, and with *curare*. Told him we had evidence and that Maggie was going to back us up on it with the D.A. Bloody hell! Look out!" Michael almost grazed a mailbox going around a corner a little too tight, after nearly running into an idiot in an old Oldsmobile spinning his wheels on the hill. He slid to a stop next to a high curb, tires revving in reverse as he tried to back up to get a straight shot around the larger vehicle blocking the road. "Back, back!" shouted LaFleur.

"Yes, I know!" Michael turned around in his seat, looking back over his shoulder as he hit the gas. Snow flew from all four wheels. He backed around the corner into the street he had just been on, and then went straight through the intersection. "We'll go around at the next block."

LaFleur just pounded the dash, nodding vigorously. He suddenly turned and yelled, "Give me your phone!"

Michael twisted in his seat and tried to get his phone from his pocket. "You think he's going to do something?" he asked, trying to steer and get his phone at the same time. "What would he do?" Michael asked incredulously. "You can't have pushed him that far."

"He *threatened* her. And me, too, but what the hell, that doesn't count. He seriously threatened her, Michael! Said that *this time* she was going to pay!" Michael finally succeeded in extracting the phone and started to hand it to LaFleur. "Then when you told me that Montgomery was keeping her there for a flu shot that I *know* she's already had—"

Michael bounced up over the curb onto a front lawn, narrowly avoiding a fender-bender blocking the street two blocks from the hospital. The phone flew out of his hand into the back seat. "Damn!" LaFleur yelled again.

There was a loud crash under the car as Michael drove across the yard. LaFleur glanced back as Michael started to slow down. "I don't know what it was!" he yelled. "Maybe a damn lawn jockey or something. They'll find out in the spring. Go! Go!"

The traffic light at Bridge was red. Michael slammed on the brakes, slid sideways half-way through the intersection to avoid a car just leaving the intersection going downhill in front of them, then pulled it back in line and powered the rest of the way across Bridge. They were in the hospital parking lot less than ten minutes after LaFleur had rushed them out of the 1850 House. They jumped out of the car and ran towards the hospital entrance, the phone still on the back seat.

The Wrong Antidote

Michael was first into the hospital. He stopped and waited for LaFleur to catch up with him.

"Where would she be?"

"God, I don't know."

"Montgomery's office is up on the second floor. Try that first."

They ran down the hall.

Then LaFleur saw her. Lying on the floor of the E.R.

"Michael!" he screamed. Pointed to the E.R. doors.

They found Maggie crawling—trying to crawl on her side, legs dragging, one arm loose at her side, barely holding herself up on the other elbow—towards the door. She must have heard them come in; she looked back over her shoulder.

"Mi—Michael…" Her head made a ripe cantaloupe thump as it hit the floor, eyes wide, still focused, staring up at them in perfect consciousness, feeling her breath fade away.

Michael knelt next to her, tilting her head back, checking her pulse at the side of her neck, kneeling closer to look into her eyes. "Hold on, Maggie, hold on," he said in soft, intense whisper. Maggie's breathing was becoming more and more labored. Michael called to LaFleur to hold her while he rushed to a cabinet and jerked the door open, frantically pulling out boxes. Vials and syringes flew out and scattered across the floor. "Damn it!" He scrambled down on his knees, sorting through the various cartons, tossing unwanted ampoules aside. LaFleur had knelt down next to Maggie, cradling her head in his hands.

"Got it!" Michael yelled. He came back and knelt back down on the opposite side from LaFleur and filled a syringe from two small vials, shook it gently, and turned to Maggie.

"Fuentes." Both of their heads jerked up at the sound of

237

Montgomery's voice. He was standing in the entrance of the ER. Michael looked at him for barely a second, and then turned back to Maggie. LaFleur kept looking back and forth.

The E.R. resident came in from a side office and stood frozen in place a few feet away, staring at them all, mouth open. LaFleur looked over at him and yelled, "You! Call the police!" The resident, quickly deciding that they had whatever it was under control, ran back to his office and grabbed the phone.

Montgomery walked slowly the rest of the way into the E.R. and stood over them at Maggie's feet. "Damn good thing you got here in time, Fuentes," Montgomery said loudly. "Allergic reaction to a flu vaccination. She panicked and ran out of the office before I could do anything. I was on my way here to get a setup myself and go look for her." Montgomery watched as Michael pressed the hypo into Maggie's right arm. "Adrenaline?" he said. "Good job..."

Michael didn't look up. "No, Dr. Montgomery. That is not correct. This is not adrenaline. I just injected Maggie with neostigmine and atropine."

"Not...adrenaline...?" Montgomery stepped back a pace or two. "But surely..."

Michael diverted his attention from Maggie just long enough to give Montgomery a cold stare. "Ah, yes, *doctor*, adrenaline would have been the correct response for an adverse reaction to TIV flu vaccine," he said, using Montgomery's own pompous tone, even though his voice was shaking slightly. "However, reversal of a neuromuscular blockade calls for one milligram atropine mixed with five milligrams neostigmine."

"Well, then, Dr. Fuentes, you've killed her," Montgomery intoned, still trying to brazen it out.

"We'll see, won't we?" said Michael, glancing up at him. "The neuromuscular blockade caused by an attempted overdose of curare, in this case," he added softly.

Michael turned back to Maggie, checking her breathing. "A.C., help me get her up on a table." Maggie was breathing much more easily now, though flushed and still unable to stand.

As they laid Maggie on an exam table, Michael saw Montgomery out of the corner of his eye, leaving the E.R. "Hey,

Montgomery! I'm not done with you!" he called out, as he placed an oxygen mask over Maggie's nose and mouth. They watched Montgomery's back recede into the dim light of the hallway outside the E.R. as Maggie's breathing steadied. Now it was LaFleur who was out of breath.

"Jesus, Joseph, and Mary," gasped LaFleur. "How did you know, Michael?"

"Not the right presentation, A.C. No clinical indication of an allergic reaction," Michael explained. "Occam's Razor, right? It was the simplest explanation for what was happening," he continued, sensing LaFleur's continued astonishment. "Uh, turn that dial there…yeah, that one…see the gauge? Set it at five."

Maggie, still just barely conscious, reached up and weakly pulled the oxygen mask slightly away from her mouth, looking up at them. "Thanks, guys," she said in a rasping voice, nearly inaudible.

Then she closed her eyes and let the mask drop back onto her face.

*

When the police arrived a few minutes later, they didn't make it into the E.R. right away, having first found a man face down in the snow in the parking lot. LaFleur was standing next to him. It took him some time to explain what had been going on inside.

The next day the coroner confirmed that Dr. Franklin Montgomery had died of a massive coronary. No charges against him had been filed, of course.

Cold Justice

It had taken a couple of days for the snow to clear out, and another day after that for the road into the cemetery to become passable. LaFleur had borrowed Michael's Subaru to drive himself and Maggie out there. Michael had a heavy work load to catch up on; he told them to go ahead without him this time, but that he would like to go back with them as soon he was free. Angie's sister told LaFleur she would get to the gravesite as soon as she could, given the weather. She asked LaFleur if they would be at the special Mass for Angie, scheduled for the next Saturday. He assured her they wouldn't miss it for the world.

When they got there, they were surprised to see that someone had been there before them. The snow had been shoveled from the gravesite; the headstone sat at the bottom of an excavation in the snow, like a miniature ruin. They had worried they weren't going to be able to find it. This looked as if someone had known right where to dig.

"Look at this," LaFleur said as they made their way through the snow over to the grave, using the path broken by the previous visitor. Leaning up against the headstone was a large, all-white floral arrangement. "This is exactly what Angie's sister said they found on the grave the year after she died."

Maggie caught up, puffing and red-cheeked, and stood next to LaFleur, taking his hand. "The flowers? What did she say about them?"

"Mary Elizabeth told me the whole family came here on the one-year anniversary of Angie's death, and there were white flowers like this on the grave. No one knew who had left them."

240

Maggie unclasped her hand from LaFleur's to wipe her nose on the back of her glove. She was still a little shaky from the episode at the hospital, but Michael had reassured her that any long term side effects from the curare-induced respiratory failure were not likely. "That's a nice arrangement," she said. "Her sister didn't bring them?"

"No, she said she couldn't get here until the snow cleared."

"Well. Another mystery," she said. "Is she terribly disappointed, at the way things turned out, I mean?"

"Well. She is a bit disappointed, I guess. But also very grateful for what we were able to accomplish. She sends her best to you, by the way; she was extremely relieved to hear you are okay."

"I'll call her soon," she said, then changed the subject. "Do you think Michael will ever stop reminding you that he was actually right about the syringe?" she asked, sniffling.

"Oh, God, I hope so," he laughed. "Especially since we really didn't have a perfect lab result. I just needed everyone to believe that we did. And it ended up saving your life. Amazing." He looked over at her. "There used to be a guy in the division, he was always going around saying 'there are no such things as coincidences.' Well, there are coincidences, plenty of them, everywhere, all the time. But that syringe almost makes me a believer." He paused. "Of course, we would never have gotten anywhere without the information from her sister, either. Talk about coincidences. Some of it we'll never know for sure, I guess."

They stood looking at the headstone without speaking for a few minutes, each letting their thoughts wander.

"You know it was Father Tommy who kept bringing copies of the articles in to the O.R., don't you?" LaFleur said.

"It was? No kidding?"

"Well, who did you—" LaFleur stepped back a foot, hands on his hips. "When did you—"

Maggie didn't let him finish, stepping up and closing his mouth with a kiss, before turning back towards the grave.

They shuffled their feet in the snow, trying to keep warm, but neither one was quite ready to leave yet. Maggie walked over and brushed a little clump of snow off the top of the headstone.

"Did you see Montgomery's obituary?" she asked.

"Yep. Quite a write up."

"I still can't quite believe he did it."

"What, the attack on you? He panicked, pure and simple. In the end he was nothing but an egotistical old man with too many skeletons in the closet, desperately trying to save his reputation. He must have known there was no way he could actually be prosecuted."

"She deserves more. She was cheated out of justice. Especially now that Mahoney has skipped. Again."

"Yeah. He's probably in Canada. He'll never come back here again, that's for sure."

"They'll go after him, won't they?"

"They might consider the case still officially open, I suppose. But no, I doubt that there will be much of a manhunt. If you were the D.A., presented with our evidence, what would you do?"

"It's not fair."

"In a way, he created his own justice," he replied. "Life on the run, at his age...it's going to be a living hell." He looked down at the flowers on the grave. "Sort of fitting, though, don't you think?" Maggie glanced at him quizzically. "Running from the truth, the same way everyone around here has been running from it all these years? Not willing to push it, not willing to face up to the hard questions, saying nothing—all the evasions, the denials. The possibilities." He walked over and straightened the flower arrangement; it had been pushed slightly to one side by a gust of wind. "And we really don't know," he said slowly, "we really don't know what actually happened. Did he kill her? Maybe. Probably?" He looked back at her, questioning.

"I don't care," she responded stubbornly. "It's still not right. There was no justice."

LaFleur looked at her and held up a hand, finger pointing to the sky. "Someone once said," he quoted dramatically, "'neither life nor nature cares whether justice is ever done or not.'"

"That's a depressing thought," Maggie said, shuddering,. "She *deserved* justice," she insisted once again.

"Honey, justice is wherever you can find it."

They made their way slowly to the car and drove back to town, neither one trusting themselves to say a word the entire way.

Requiescat in Pace

The Father sat by the fire in his study trying to warm his hands and knees after his excursion out to the cemetery, his thoughts flickering with the flames. He hoped the flowers he'd left there were going to last for awhile; it had been windy the past couple of days.

He still had not reconciled his actions with his conscience, not completely, and probably never would. Justice was God's, he believed. But that hadn't stopped him from trying to gain whatever earthly justice he could. Even if only a partial justice, a cold justice long delayed, and even if only a select few were ultimately aware of it. That it had taken so long weighed on him. Every year that passed had increased rather than diminished the feeling of guilt over not having done more at the time. With Maggie retiring soon, and with the old lounge—now the O.R.—being razed, he had seen the window of opportunity closing quickly. A chance meeting with Angie's sister, Mary Elizabeth, provided the final inspiration, his call to action.

The last chance to speak for Angie.

He wondered at how long it had taken the team, as he had come to think of the three of them, to work out that he was the one who had initiated the investigation. Or had they known all along, and for their own reasons kept silent? Michael, he thought, had probably known from the start and had stayed quiet out of sense of propriety, or protection. He had known that Michael, once involved, would be a great help to LaFleur. LaFleur staying mute, if indeed he knew, he could understand as a sort of professional courtesy, perhaps. And Maggie? Her motivations in the whole affair were clear in some ways, mysterious in others. She must have known early on that he had put the article in the O.R. She also knew more than anyone else about what had really happened that day. More than she was saying, even now? Well. She had suffered the pangs of conscience over the years at least as much, if not more, than he had himself, he was sure. He hoped that she also finally felt some sense of relief, even forgiveness.

He pulled his chair closer to the hearth. "Oh, Angie," he said, as he unfolded a brittle, yellowed newspaper clipping.

He tossed the clipping into the fire, where it landed on the end of a partially burning log. It smoldered for a few seconds, then burst into bright flame. A sharp gust of wind rattled the rectory, and Father Tommy glanced over at the window. By the time he turned back, it was gone.

Acknowledgements

For the story itself, and many of its embellishments, plot twists, and characterizations, credit goes to Dr. John Fountain. If only he could type. For hours of patient and painstaking review and her fine narrative suggestions, all of which took valuable time away from work on her Ph.D. dissertation, thanks go to Steve's creative nonfiction mentor, Sarah Massey-Warren. For a standard of proofreading and stylistic editing not to be equaled anywhere, we thank Steve's sister, Debbie Abbott.

The members of the Oswego Chapter 1 Book Club gave us a spirited and heartwarming reception and review session in the midst of a typical Oswego lake-effect snowstorm, and provided many excellent suggestions, all of which we attempted to incorporate, along with many typographical corrections, for which we are greatly indebted. Our collaborators from the book club are (in alphabetical order): Sandy Fountain; Pat Grulich; Diane Jones; Pat Jones; Edie Nupuf; Shelley Proano; Kim Schaefer; Arlene Spizman; and Sarah Uva. Also offering a wealth of useful information and corrections were Mary DeMent, Meg Mahon, and Trish Pompei. Additional corrections and suggestions were contributed by Lisa Fountain MacFadden; Mike Nupuf; Father Fran Pompei; Kurt "Chicken" Schmitt; and Larry Spizman. Thank you all.

For their enthusiastic support and superb professional advice, we heartily thank Bill Riley and Mindy Ostrow of the River's End Bookstore, located in downtown Oswego at 19 West Bridge Street (http://www.riversendbookstore.com). Visit them when you are in town.

An esteemed group of early reviewers in Denver and Boulder, Colorado, provided many hours of camaraderie and revelry during John's visits to Colorado, while still managing to provide much needed guidance and encouragement. Many thanks to Karen and

"Hutch" Hutchinson, Casey and Sharon Funk, and Geoff and Claire Chase.

Of course, any remaining errors or misconstructions are ours alone.

And finally, for not hitting him over the head with a 2x4 when shown a segment of the unfinished novel over drinks one night, Steve is grateful to his writing teacher, Professor Peter Michelson.

2118533

Made in the USA